PRAISE FOR
Crazy Heart

"A measure of Thomas Cobb's talent is that he can make Bad Blake's story amusing even as we watch him fall. Bad is entirely sympathetic, and his crazy heart is vivid; the milieu is as resonant as a steel guitar, and the plot moves along without skipping a beat."

—*New York Times Book Review*

"*Crazy Heart* is a beautiful book. . . . The characters are cut cleanly out of America—the roadside West, the dance halls and beer joints, the occasional big concert, Houston, Nashville, Southern California, and the endless, eternal hotel rooms that are as close to home as a country singer ever gets. . . . Bad Blake is a man you will not soon forget."

—*Washington Times*

"[Cobb's] picture of the scraggly underside of Western music is brutally convincing."

—*The New Yorker*

Crazy Heart

CRAZY HEART

Thomas Cobb

Grateful acknowledgment is made to the following for permission to reproduce song lyrics:

Lyrics for "Satisfied" by Martha Carson. Copyright © 1951 by Sony/ATV Music Publishing LLC. All rights administered by Sony/ATV Music Publishing LLC, 8 Music Square West, Nashville, TN 37203. All rights reserved. Used by permission.

Lyrics for "Faded Love" words and music by Bob Wills and Johnnie Lee Wills. Copyright © 1950 (Renewed) WB Music Corp. All rights reserved. Used by permission of Alfred Publishing Co., Inc.

A hardcover edition of this book was published in 1987 by HarperCollins Publishers.

HarperCollins books may be purchased for educational, business, or sales promotional use. For information please e-mail the Special Markets Department at SPsales@harpercollins.com.

FIRST PERENNIAL LIBRARY EDITION PUBLISHED 1988.

REISSUED IN HARPER PERENNIAL 2010.

FIRST HARPER PERENNIAL OLIVE EDITION PUBLISHED 2015.

The Library of Congress has catalogued the Perennial Library edition as follows:

Cobb, Tom.

   Crazy heart.

   "Perennial Library."

   I. Title

PS3553.0194C7   1988   813.'54   87-395

ISBN 978-0-06-091519-3 (pbk.)

ISBN 978-0-06-242101-2 (Olive Edition)

15 16 17 18 19   OV/RRD   10 9 8 7 6 5 4 3 2 1

For my mother and father

Crazy Heart

Chapter One

He's standing in the bowling alley parking lot in front of his 1978 Dodge van with burnt valves. He pulls his shirt away from his skin. Soaked, it sticks to him as fast as he pulls it away. Above him a sign announces: "Winter Leagues Now Forming." Below that it says, "Country Record Star / Bad Blake / Here / Friday, August 12."

He is trying to shake a dream. At a rest stop in New Mexico he dreamed he crouched before a low stone wall. Behind him was a man with a gun. On either side was one of his ex-wives. Bad understood they were to be shot, slaughtered like pigs. He wanted to run, but he could not decide whether to run or try to save one or both of the wives. He could not decide and he could not run. He remained crouched and waiting. He can still feel the pressure on the tendons in the backs of his legs.

He goes for his Pall Malls. The pack is nearly empty, loose and slick with sweat. He gets one lit and looks at the sign. A fucking bowling alley, he thinks. They got you in a fucking bowling alley, right in the fucking middle of fucking nowhere Colorado. You should have known, you're old and fat, and now you are bowling alley material. Oh, Jack, he thinks, Jack, you bastard.

Inside, the bowling alley is full of light and the smell of wax. The air-conditioning hits hard and turns his soaked shirt icy. He is breathing fast, his heart pounding in shuffle time. He reaches for another cigarette, thinks better of it, and goes off to find the manager. A single bowler is working in the middle of thirty lanes. Bad hears the drop, the steady, straight tone of the roll, and waits for the impact. When it comes, it is a hollow thump like a drummer's wood block as the pins drop.

"Bad Blake!" the manager exclaims. "I'm proud to meet you. God, I used to listen to you when I was just a kid." Bad's heart thumps. He manages a wheeze and a smile and pumps the manager's hand.

"Have a good trip?" the manager wants to know.

"Long," Bad says. "Long but good. Played Clovis, New Mexico, last night. Saw some real pretty country. Glad to be here." Momentarily, he has forgotten where the hell he is.

The Spare Room is dark and quiet, though Bad can still hear the faint hiss and thump of the lone bowler. "Down there is the band stand," the manager explains. Bad notes the shadow of a drum kit and microphones on a raised platform. He heads for the bar. Among the bowling trophies and beer company gewgaws behind the bar, enormous fish swim back and forth in a lighted aquarium. Bad slides onto a barstool, careful of his hemorrhoids.

"Darlin'," he calls to the barmaid, "bring me a J.D. up,

beer back." He smiles and points to the fish. "Buy one for the boys in the backroom there, too."

"Three twenty-five," she says when she brings his drinks. She is young and pretty in a sullen way. Bad winks. "On my tab, darlin'."

"No tab."

"I'm Bad Blake, little darlin'. I'm with the band. Hell, I am the band."

She turns and walks away. A minute later the manager is at Bad's side.

"Mr. Blake, we have a real nice room for you over in the Starlight Inn, and of course your meals are taken care of, but we can't let you run a bar tab. It's in the contract. Mr. Greene of Greene and Gold put that in himself."

Bad reaches out. For a second he is ready to grab the gristly knob of the manager's Adam's apple and crush it. Instead, he touches the man's shoulder and squeezes gently. "If you and Jack have an agreement, we'll all have to stick by it. Don't worry yourself about it, old buddy."

Jack, he thinks, you heifer-fucker, someday I will purely kill you. When I'm in your office you're on my leg; when I'm on the road, you're on my back.

"How much?" he asks the barmaid.

"Three twenty-five."

Bad looks hard at the shot. He's sweating. The cigarette between his fingers is wavering. His throat is raw from the Pall Malls. He wants the whiskey, but he has almost no cash left, and he knows he will want the drink even more later on.

Still, right now he wants it more than he ever wanted any of his ex-wives. He digs four dollars from his pocket. When the barmaid brings back the change, he keeps it.

"Mr. Blake." The manager is back at his shoulder. "Let me personally offer you all the free bowling you want."

Bad nearly chokes. He swallows it, but the whiskey still burns in his nose.

"I just want you to know you're real welcome here."

"I can tell that, old buddy, I can tell."

In his room, Bad punches the air conditioner to "max." He hates air-conditioning, but he can't stop sweating. He strips off his soaked shirt and falls across the bed. He runs his hands across his broad belly and groans. Two orders of griddle cakes and sausage he ate in New Mexico have turned to pure, burning sulfur. The bedspread, some sort of cigarette-burned nylon over a thin foam-rubber backing, sticks to his skin. He longs for the old days and chenille bedspreads with zigzag patterns.

On the TV, a man and woman in fluorescent colors embrace. When they part, their lips move but no sound comes out. Bad considers getting up to turn up the sound, but decides it's good enough this way. The couple, he supposes, is talking about what a prick Jack Greene is. He doesn't want to find out any different.

Bad is in the back of his old Silver Eagle touring bus, almost asleep, listening to the bus's wheels on the blacktop, a sound like the softest set of brushes he has ever heard. He loves the sound even more than he loves silence after a night of playing. He calls to Marge and gets no answer. Then he calls Suzi, though he was married to her years after Marge. There is still no answer. He gets out of the bunk and heads for the front of the bus. He wants to know where he is and who he is married to. "Tommy," he calls, but Tommy Sweet doesn't answer. Everyone on the bus is asleep and he cannot wake them. The bus driver is his father, and he can't wake him, either. He returns to the back of the bus.

Bad's heart lurches as though it is coming loose from its moorings. He blinks and groans. Despite the air-conditioning, he is still covered with sweat. The hair on his chest and belly, sweated flat, radiates like a thousand needles from his heart. On the television, a woman throws up her hands in joy as a flock of bluebirds flies from her washing machine. The birds have, he hopes, just crapped all over her clean clothes. He gets up and takes his damp shirt into the bathroom to wash it out in the sink.

"Mr. Greene is still on the other line, Mr. Blake."

"I'll wait, darlin'."

The highlight of this evening looks to be dinner in a restaurant with thin redwood paneling and ferns that drip down to the salad bar.

"Darlin', you ever been in Pueblo, Colorado?"

"I don't believe so, Mr. Blake."

"Well, I wish you were here right now, Sweetness, because you'd sure as hell be the best thing Pueblo ever had to offer."

When she laughs, Bad sees an image of Brenda walking across the plush carpet of Jack's office, bringing him a cup of coffee to take the edge off his embarrassment as Jack makes him wait. He hears the shush of her stockings under her tight skirt.

"Matter of fact, Brenda, I really wish you were here tonight, because I just might be the best thing that Pueblo, Colorado, has to offer."

Her laugh is efficient. "Here's Mr. Greene."

"Bad, how's Arizona?"

"Colorado."

"Right, Colorado. So, how's Colorado?"

"You ever seen Colorado?"

"Yeah, years ago."

"It's still here. Listen, Jack, I got some problems."

"O.K., what can I do?"

"Jack, last night I got a call from Suzi."

"How the hell did she find you?"

"I was going to ask you that, but obviously you don't know where the hell I am."

"Jesus, Bad. I got six acts on the road right now, including a rock group that just trashed a Ramada Inn in Memphis. I get confused, O.K.? Now, which one's Suzi?"

"Four. The little brunette. The one that whines."

"Oh, right. She was a doll, Bad."

"I can't stand whiners."

"Then why the hell did you marry her?"

"I thought she'd stop whining if I did. Jack, she says she hasn't gotten a check in quite a bit. She's whining again."

"Right. Well, receipts are a little slow coming in off this trip. I guess they still use Pony Express out there."

"But there are royalties."

"Yeah, but . . . Oh hell, Bad, I didn't want to tell you until you came in off this swing. J.M.I. cut out *So Sweet, So Bad*."

"Jack, that fucker was still selling."

"It had slowed, slowed a lot, and Tommy's got nine albums right now and a new one next month. That's a lot of product to rack and the chains don't like crowding."

"Fuck the chains. The chains have got less brains than I got ex-wives."

"Them and most of the world, Bad."

"What about Tommy, what about the new album? I'll be off the road in a couple of weeks. I can go straight to L.A. or Nashville. We can get right to work on it."

"Tommy wants to know if you've got new material."

Bad is looking at a cardboard painting above the television set, sailboats on a stormy sea. The colors are streaked and blotchy—red, blue and white against black and gray. He can't figure why anyone would want to look at such a mess, much less paint it.

"You know I don't have new material," he says. "Hell, I'm not new material. There's nothing wrong with the old stuff. We did real well with it the last time out. A hell of a lot better than he did with his goddamned gunfighter albums."

"Tommy thinks he's leaning too hard on the old stuff. He doesn't want people to think he's riding the gravy train."

"That son-of-a-bitch has a lifetime pass on the gravy train."

"Come on, Bad. Remember who's asking who to do a record here."

"Jack, you jerk-off. You get out here in, in, Clovis, god-damned, New Mexico, or Pueblo, kiss-my-ass, Colorado, and you play in a piano bar or a bowling alley, backed by a bunch of old bastards with brush cuts and string ties. You look out on a bar full of blue-hairs who've checked their teeth at the door. You smile and sweat and sing 'Slow Boat' three times a night. You get up the next fucking morning at five o'clock and drive three hundred miles with piles so bad it feels like you've got a nest of fire ants up your ass, and then you tell me about riding the goddamned gravy train. You and Tommy Sweet both try it sometime."

"Bad, Bad. Calm down. Tommy says he wants new material. I'll keep talking, but he's holding the cards. You know that, I know it, and Tommy Sweet sure as hell knows it."

"You keep talking, Jack. And you tell Tommy for me that he wouldn't know country music if it came up and kicked him in his world-famous ass. And tell him that one of these days, it sure as hell is going to."

Jack keeps talking, and Bad puts the phone against his belly and looks back at the painting above the television.

"Jack, is it true they've taught monkeys how to paint?"

"What? What the hell are you talking about? Monkeys?"

"Jack, I'm broke. I need money."

"I sent you money when you were still in Texas. I sent you plenty."

"Wasn't enough, old buddy, I need more."

"Bad, if I send you money, you'll go on one of your famous benders and wind up back here, who knows when, sick, broke and married."

"I ain't going to marry anybody."

"Look, you're going to build a nice piece of change out there on the road. Even when your exes get their cut, you'll have a little left over for once. I'm going to make sure you keep it for a little while."

"I'm down to my last ten bucks."

"That will get you to Santa Fe. You've got cards for gas, and you've got expenses all the way. You'll be there soon. I'll have some cash waiting in Santa Fe."

"Jack, I'm fifty-six years old and I only have ten bucks."

"Spend it wisely, Bad."

"Jack, did I ever tell you that your mother used to bite when she gave head?"

"I love you, too. Bye-bye."

Bad hangs up the phone and rolls over onto his back. Why the hell would someone want to paint a streaky, piddling-ass little picture like that that didn't mean jack-shit to anyone?

In the liquor store, Bad lusts for the short, square bottle of Jack Daniel's. He stoops to the pint bottle of Heaven Hill and something drops down his back. He wears an old shirt that

Nudie himself designed. It is full of beadwork, but the thread is rotting and beads drip down his back into his pants.

"Mr. Blake?"

When he stands, beads fall through his pants and into his boots. His heart stutters.

"Goddamn. It is you. It really is Bad Blake right here in my store." A short, balding man reaches out his hand. "I'm Bill Wilson. I'm a big fan, and just real pleased to meet you."

Bad smiles and looks back to the cheap bourbon.

"Here. Here, Mr. Blake. Here's the Jack Daniel's." Bill Wilson pulls a full liter of J.D. from the shelf. "Being in the business and a big fan and all, I kind of keep track of what the stars drink. It's kind of a hobby, you know. Willie Nelson and his Lone Star Beer, Haggard and his George Dickel, Tommy Sweet and his Southern Comfort, and Bad Blake and his Jack Daniel's. Of course, I never thought I'd actually have a star right here in my store."

Bad eyes the bottle in Bill Wilson's hand and wheezes with desire.

"My wife Barbara is one of your biggest fans. She'll flat die when she finds out you were here in the store. She's out getting her hair done right this minute. We're going to your show tonight. I think she's having it done just for you. Of course"—he winks—"I expect to get the real benefit of it. But if you could sing 'Slow Boat' for her tonight, it would sure mean the world to her. It might"—he winks again—"mean a lot to me, too."

"You got it, old buddy. You sure got it." Bad can't take his eyes off that bottle of Jack Daniel's. "'Slow Boat' for Barbara. You got it."

"She'll be thrilled. She really will," Bill Wilson says. "And here, take this. I want to be able to tell everyone that I bought Bad Blake a drink."

Out in the sunlight, Bad looks at the bottle and then up to the sky. Sweet Baby Jesus, thank you.

A fighter plane trails white across a turquoise sky. Bad is already a quarter finished with the bottle when someone pounds on his door. He gets up, puts on the Nudie shirt. More beads drip down his back.

At the door is a young man with long hair and a wispy beard. "Hi. I'm Tony." Bad blinks in incomprehension.

"Tony," the young man insists. "Tony and the Renegades. Your band."

Of course. Bad nods. The backup band. His backup bands on the road are always of two types: young rock-and-rollers or old men who have been playing his songs for years without getting them right. He supposes that if he got to choose, he would take the kids.

"Me and the boys, we're over at the alley, setting up. We were wondering what time to start rehearsing."

"Soon as you can. Start rehearsing as soon as you can and do it often as you can. That's the secret. You can't rehearse enough."

"What I mean is, what time are you coming to rehearsal?"

Bad sighs and takes Tony by the arm and leads him out

to the van. "I got lead sheets if you all can read music, chord charts if you can't. I got cassettes and a play list. You go on. I'll be by later. I already done my rehearsing."

Bad turns back to the room and the bottle. Tony follows. "Mr. Blake, it would mean a lot to us if you would come on over early. I mean, we need to get the leads down and all that."

"Leads?" Bad asks. "Leads? Son," he asks seriously, "are they paying you more than they're paying me?"

"But," Tony goes on, "I thought you could show us some things, teach us some of that old stuff Bad's Boys used to do. Is it true you taught Tommy Sweet how to play guitar?"

Bad ignores the remark about Tommy. "All right," he says. "You all go listen to the cassettes. Listen carefully. Study the lead sheets. Give me an hour to get some dinner and then I'll be over." Bad doesn't know what he can teach them. He has learned only two things as a musician he could ever put into words: keep your wrist steady, and don't ever marry nobody.

Bad pokes at the chicken-fried steak. Pale gravy oozes from it. Next to the chicken-fried steak is a scoop of mashed potatoes and a spoonful of corn. Road food. Road food is always neutral in color and taste. It only turns exciting a couple of hours later. He has learned to eat early and not make rude noises onstage.

The hostess-cashier slides into the booth across the table from him. She exhales a long stream of cigarette smoke over his food. "Everything O.K.?"

"Fine." Bad nods. "Just fine."

She wears her black hair pinned in curls on top of her head, and her makeup thick. When she winks at him, a small knot of mascara sticks to her lower lash. She wears a red nylon blouse and a plastic name tag that says, "Howdy, I'm Jo Ann." "Mind if I smoke?" she asks. Bad waves his hand.

"This is the time of day I hate," she says. "Waiting for the rush to start. It's O.K. once it does, and after it's over, but thinking about it, my God, I hate that. You must like to eat early and avoid the crowds. Be able to eat in peace without a bunch of people asking for autographs and stuff. Mind if I ask you a question?"

"Shoot."

She reaches over and taps his knuckle with a long red fingernail. "I always wondered if you had a good time singing those songs. Because, God, I hope to tell you, I had me a couple of real good times listening to them." Her laugh is deep and a little raspy from the cigarette smoke. "Of course, I've had a couple of rotten ones, too, come to think of it."

"So have I, darlin', so have I. Anything you want to hear tonight?"

She bites her tongue as she thinks. Her teeth are stained red from the lipstick. "You do anything from that album you do with Tommy Sweet?"

"A few. The standards. 'Faded Love,' 'Please Release Me,' 'Crazy Arms.'"

"Any of those. God, I just love that album. *Memories: So Sweet, So Bad*. Of course, I love Tommy Sweet, too."

"So does Tommy, darlin'."

When she laughs the raspy laugh, she reminds him of his ex-wife, Marge. He likes her.

"You two don't get along anymore?"

Bad shrugs. "What the wives didn't get off that album, Tommy did."

Jo Ann gets embarrassed, then flirty. She runs her finger up his forearm. "Why don't you tell me your real name?"

"You want to know that, you got to marry me, darlin'. That's why so many have. Otherwise, it's just Bad. I was Bad long 'fore any niggers thought to be."

Bad pushes through the door and into The Spare Room. Rock music swells up and staggers him. He moves toward the bandstand, carrying his guitar and amp. Tony and the Renegades stop as they see him approach, though the drummer continues to pound for a few more beats.

"I hope to God that wasn't one of my songs you were playing."

Tony steps down from the bandstand. "Mr. Blake, these are the Renegades." He runs through a list of names that Bad doesn't attempt to catch. The best thing about backup bands is that they are so easy to forget.

"That's it?" someone asks. "That's your equipment?"

"This," Bad says, unsnapping the case, "is a Gretsch Country Gentleman. A Country Gentleman with gold plate from the head to the tailpiece and an action that would put a twenty-year-old whore to shame." He looks at their stacked Marshall amps. "You fellows must go on the road a lot with those. Fun to tote. If you are playing loud enough to drown out this Roland Cube, you are playing way, fucking, too loud."

They take the play list in order. Bad relaxes into an easy set, just chording through the songs, playing simple verse-form leads at the breaks. Twice, he misses notes and wishes he had left just a little more of the Jack Daniel's in the bottle.

"Do some of that Tommy Sweet stuff for us," Tony insists.

There is no Tommy Sweet stuff. There is only Bad Blake stuff that Tommy Sweet has taken for his own. But he doesn't feel any need or use in explaining this right now. In "Slow Boat" he obliges them, running through a break full of hammers and pulls, the style he taught Tommy and that has become Tommy's signature.

"I don't know," Tony says. "I think Tommy plays it more like this." He begins the song again, throwing in double and triple pulls, trilling the high notes. "I think," he says, "that's more the sort of thing he does now. That's the way we like to play it."

"Keep working on that," Bad advises. "Someday Tommy will be playing this very same bowling alley. You all will still be here. You can show him. He'll like it. You can buy each other drinks. You can get drunk and be a couple of guitar-picking wonders together."

There are two hours before the show. Bad is watching television, still without sound. He is trying to get his heart to stop pounding. On the television, men in work clothes are yelling at a man in a suit. Bad takes a long pull at his bottle of Jack Daniel's. The man in the suit is unflappable and continues to smile. A young man in a mustache and a Beech-Nut cap is yelling so hard Bad can see spit fly from his mouth. The man in the suit smiles and nods patiently, pretending he understands rage. The young man seems to be strangling on his. Bad likes the young man. Kill the fucker, he thinks. He takes another long pull on the bottle.

Bad is ready to get off the bus. He is wearing his red suit with the white lightning stripe up the pants leg. They are in the new town, and Bad is ready to do the new song. This is very important. But the young man in the Beech-Nut cap won't let him off the bus. He is screaming but there is no sound. The young man does not want Bad here. He doesn't like Bad's suit. He wants to know where Bad was fifteen years ago. Fifteen years ago, Bad wants to explain, he had to give concerts and make records, get married, divorced and married again. But right now, he has this new song, and if he can just sing it once, everything will be all right. The young man hates Bad's song and his suit. He is screaming so hard he showers Bad with spit. My God, Bad thinks, his spit will hit the lightning stripes on this yellow suit, and I will die.

Bad struggles across the parking lot of the bowling alley, carrying his guitar in one hand and the Roland Cube in the other. He is luminous in orange and white. He tries not to think of himself, an old fat man dressed in an orange suit with a white lightning stripe up each leg, white hat and white boots, and a heart doing the bump and grind.

At the back door, Tony and the Renegades are lounging, cooling off between sets. They watch Bad lurch across the parking lot. No one offers help.

"Hey," Tony calls at last, "it's showtime."

Bad pulls up even with Tony. He is wheezing hard and can feel the sweat dripping from under the band of his hat. The air is sharp with marijuana and Bad watches a joint go from hand to hand.

"We were afraid you weren't going to show."

The band members look at each other, smiling.

"Son, I have played sick, hurt, drunk, married, divorced, on the run, and run to the ground. Bad Blake has never pulled a no-show in his whole goddamned life. Not even in a fucking bowling alley, backed by a band of hippies." He takes the joint as it moves near him and pulls a long drag. He lets the smoke out and takes another deep drag.

"Better watch that stuff," Tony says. "Maui Wowie."

Bad looks at the joint and takes one more drag. "You sure they're not paying you more than they're paying me?"

The bar and bandstand are dark, and Bad stumbles on the riser. He unpacks the guitar, plugs in, adjusts the volume and waits for a note from Tony. He gets an A flat.

"Bring it up a half step."

"I'm in tune," Tony says. "I got an electronic tuning meter. I'm on."

"I got a fifty-six-year-old ear says you're off. Bring it up a half step."

When the band has retuned, Tony steps on the light switch and a single light brings up the microphone. The band moves into "Wildwood Flower," uptempo, but rushed just a little. Back behind the amps, Bad tries to turn up loud enough to slow them down. He can't and speeds to catch up to them.

At the end of the first chorus, Tony moves up to the microphone and says, "Ladies and gentlemen, The Spare Room is proud to present country recording star 'The Wrangler of Love,' Mr. Bad Blake."

Bad steps forward to where the light is supposed to be turned on, but misjudges, and only his guitar neck and left hand are in the spot. He takes a sidestep into the light and swings into his jazzy instrumental, a simple melody, but quick and light, full of triplets that sound harder to play than they really are. Applause from the bar covers a couple of clinkers.

They move through the set as they have rehearsed, but still a little fast. Between "Love Came and Got Me" and "Faded Love," he tells the drummer to slow it down. It does no good. His throat feels full and tight, despite the Jack Daniel's he has been drinking all night. After "Faded Love" he ducks behind the amps and takes a pull from the bottle.

Back at the microphone, he tunes his slipping E string while he talks to the audience. "Thank you all, so much. I can't tell you how good it is to be here in Pueblo, Colorado. I've been all over the country, and I've found it's filled with good people. I want to tell you, a lot of them are right here in Pueblo." While the bar applauds, he turns and gives Tony the

A. Tony returns it, in tune. "You know, one thing I've learned over the years is that if you don't give the folks what they want, they won't want anything from you again. I believe a few of you want to hear this next song. I had a hit on it about twenty years ago, when I was, let me see, just seven years old." He starts "Slow Boat" with the signature shift from A to D-flat minor to D and back to A.

The applause starts again. "This song is for all of you who have been so good to me for a long, long time now, but I also want to send it out special to a couple of my dear friends, Bill and Barbara. God, I think the world of them."

The band comes in behind him and forms a pocket for Bad to fit the melody into. Bill Wilson and Barbara, in matching shirts, jeans and boots, move out onto the floor. Barbara is a handsome woman, young and strong-looking. She is a full head taller than Bill. Bill, Bad figures, must be one capable son-of-a-bitch. Barbara leans her head down on Bill's, and they begin to turn across the dance floor. Bill beams. You may not be able to sell out a concert anymore, or cut a hit record, Bad thinks, but by God, you can still jerk them around.

When the song is over, Bad walks back behind the amps and takes another long pull at the bottle. Back at the microphone, the whiskey starts to push back up his throat. Tony starts "Please Release Me," and as Bad comes in behind him, he feels a flush of cold pass through his body. He intends to sing the song the way Lefty always did, bending the notes, taking them up and suddenly dropping them, but the first time he tries that full octave drop on "go," the whiskey comes up again. He fights it down, but loses the next two bars before he is able to open his mouth again. He starts low, and keeps it there, half a key below what the band is playing.

When he finally drags the song to a close, he says, "I'm awful sorry about that, folks. I've got me a frog in my throat that just don't want to behave. I believe I'll take a quick break and see if I can't send him back where he belongs. Tony and the boys here will do a couple of songs and then I'll be right back. We've got a long time and a lot of good songs we want to do for you yet."

As he moves away from the microphone, unplugging his guitar, he stumbles, and lands on one knee on top of his Roland Cube. When he looks up, all he can see is a red amplifier light, pulsing in the dark like the neon red heart of Jesus.

The next sensation he is aware of is a ridge of cold metal in his hand. He is outside the back door of the alley, on his knees, holding the rim of a garbage can. He pulls himself up and looks at the sky, a wash of stars. He is cold and shivering. He wipes his face with a handkerchief, then checks to see if he's kept his suit clean. It is soaked with sweat. He bends down, picks up his hat and brushes at a streak of dirt that smears across the crown. He leans against the building and looks up. Stars spin slowly, but when he looks down he can focus and hold his field of vision. He coughs once and finds his throat clear.

Tony and the Renegades are just finishing some two-step he's heard on the radio when he climbs back up on the riser and begins the applause for the band.

He is shaky for the next two numbers. His voice wavers, and his playing is mechanical. He concentrates on staying on tempo with the band. They are still playing too fast, but it is easier to accept the tempo than to fight it. The band is getting edgy, bored with the steady progression of chords in the simplified play list. On "Cold, Cold Heart" Tony cuts in on him in the break and takes over the lead himself. Bad falls back into the rhythm pattern behind him.

By the time they are to the end of the play list, Tony has established a pattern of taking the leads. He plays verse form, full of the trills and pulls that he played in rehearsal. Bad's voice has steadied, but his hands are still cold and sweaty. He moves up to the microphone. "I've had a special request for this next song. Old Ray Price did it first, but I did it a couple years ago with a friend of mine." The bar starts to applaud. "Now, Tommy can't be with me tonight, but I want to do our version of this song, and send it out to Jo Ann, bless her pretty little heart."

He begins "Crazy Arms" chording the rhythm part, but determined to do his own lead. Between chorus and verse he plays a bridge of pedal-steel licks, playing three notes, bending the third while playing the other two straight. Dancers swing across the floor, including, he notices, Jo Ann on the arm of a tall, angular man with a high-crowned hat.

At the second chorus, he starts the pedal-steel licks again, intending to build a break based on them, connected by hammered runs. By now, Tony has caught on to the structure of the break and begins to play the melody line an octave higher. The result is a fine break, but it is Tony's lead, though Bad has created it. At the end of the song, Bad invites Tony to introduce the band. Tony finishes by introducing himself as lead guitar.

The last song is "It's Strange." The last couples take the dance floor. Bad has the lead, but he feels Tony crowding behind him, waiting for a chance to move in. The band's attention has revived, and they are playing tight and purposefully for the first time all night. At the break, Bad takes a simple lead, adding in the hammers and pulls he used at rehearsal. When he reaches the end of the verse, Tony picks up the lead and plays it back, adding a blues riff at the end.

Bad accepts the riff and expands on it, remembering nights spent on Maxwell Street in Chicago, listening to the blues in the tight, packed clubs, the smell of smoke and sweat, and deep into the night, the nearly manic playing of bluesmen, entranced and glistening with sweat, picking up each other's leads, expanding and elaborating on them as he sat as close to the little bandstands as he could get, studying the technique, the intensity of some of the best players he had ever heard. He bends strings, first one note and then two. He runs a scale up the neck and then slides back down, making the guitar cry. He creates a shell of sound and climbs in and finds room to breathe. The dancing couples stop, stand and watch.

Tony starts to pick up the blues lead, falters on one note, then two. He swings uptempo, moving across the line between blues and rock, into his own territory. Bad catches the direction of the riff, finds the tempo and moves in on Tony.

He takes the rock riff for a couple of bars and then adjusts his pickup controls and jerks hard on the tremolo bar. The big guitar shrieks. Bad rips through scales and lets the guitar feed back. Sweat pours from his head and splashes on the guitar. His heart pounds. He does not know what he is playing, but he keeps going, sure he will find his way through this. The guitar understands rage. Bad alternates chords and single-string leads. Tony stops and backs up a step. Bad finds an opening and begins a run, moving easily up the neck, keeping the tempo, but working his way back, winding down the furious tone of the song until he finds the spot he is looking for and moves into a quick, delicate reprise of the melody, playing triplets like a mandolin player.

He looks over to Tony and arches an eyebrow. Tony shakes his head and Bad accepts. "Ladies and gentlemen, it's been wonderful with you tonight. You all drive safely now, and the Lord willing, we'll get together again real soon. Good night."

As they settle into one last chorus, Bad shifts the key down a half step so he can end up in basso profundo. Tony steps to the microphone. "Ladies and gentlemen, the star of the show. Let's hear it for the great Bad Blake." He lets go of his guitar and leads the applause. Bad plays a quick riff and steps back as Tony cuts the stage lights.

Light is just starting to come through the window next to the bed. He has slept for a couple of hours without dreams. He is not sure what this means, but his heart has stopped pounding and his head is clear.

Jo Ann is still asleep. Her makeup has worn off, and her hair is tangled around her hand. She looks older, a little drawn, but Bad has always loved them, all of them, best this way. He dresses quietly and carries the white boots and hat in his hand. He waits until he is outside and pisses behind the open door of the van. He figures he has a couple of hours before the sweating starts again.

Chapter Two

By the time the sun is full in the sky, he is starting to climb the hills. He is, he figures, another hour away from New Mexico. Along the side of the road the scrub brush has begun to turn to trees, and Colorado looks more like what he remembers from years earlier. He thinks about last night. He has played drunk before, drunk, sick drunk and stoned. But he has never let go that far in front of a bunch of kids. There is a certain pleasure in taking the boy to school, in showing him just how much he doesn't know about the instrument, but that sort of thing shouldn't be necessary. He shouldn't have to prove himself to a twenty-year-old.

Still, it has been a long time since he has played like that, and it feels good to get in and cut. There is a quick progression he played last night, just the smallest snatch of a melody, no more than four bars, that he still hears this morning. He hums it to himself, seeing if there is anything he can connect it to.

He is getting hungry. He still has only ten dollars and two hundred miles to Las Vegas, New Mexico. The melodic phrase keeps coming back to him, but he doesn't find the note that will carry it anywhere that seems to interest him. How much of his life has he spent just this way, tinkering with a few notes, looking for the next one in the series, looking for the one that will lead him to find the whole from the piece?

God bless credit cards.

A skinny boy with snaggled teeth takes Bad's card and runs it through the machine that stamps his Texaco number on the receipt. It is one hell of a thing when fifty-six-year-old men are sent out on the road with only ten dollars.

"Just the gas?" the boy asks.

"Can I put anything else on the card?"

"Hell, anything I got in here, except beer." He gestures around the inside of the station, which looks more like a damned grocery store than a gas station.

Bad walks down the aisles. Nothing here looks like breakfast. Still, breakfast costs cash. He takes two ham sandwiches, three hard-boiled eggs, a bag of potato chips, three fried peach pies, a handful of Milky Ways, a six-pack of Coke, a carton of Pall Malls, a *Playboy* magazine, and a red-and-yellow plastic lighter that says "Land of Enchantment."

"I got tires and batteries outside," the boy says.

"I believe this is all the hungry I got."

"I mean for your car."

"It ain't hungry at all."

The boy rings it up. Forty-seven eighty-three with the gas. Bad signs the receipt "B. Blake / Greene and Gold Productions."

"You must be on your way to the races," the boy says as he hands Bad the receipt.

"Races?"

"Yeah. You look like a horseman and all. I figured you was on your way to the races."

"Where?"

"Raton. About ten miles south. People have been coming through all week for the races. They run every day, all month long."

"Ten miles. And how far is, what the hell, Las Vegas?"

"Which one?"

"The one on this road—New Mexico."

"Well, the other one is on this road, too, if you're starting on this road. Of course, you'd have to get off it to get there."

"Las Vegas, New Mexico?"

"About a hundred and fifty miles, straight south."

Life has a way of dropping itself into your lap. He is down to his last ten bucks, but he has five and a half hours to make one hundred and fifty miles, and ten miles away there is a racetrack.

He leans on the rail, squinting at the racing form. He has bet two races, and he is two dollars and thirty cents to the good after expenses. He has paid two dollars to park, one dollar to get in, and fifty cents for a racing form. He is making old-lady bets and they are bringing him back. He bets two dollars on the favorite to show. One horse pays two thirty, and the other, which really does run third, pays four fifty.

"Don't believe that thing," an old guy in a straw hat and blue jeans tells him. "Those damn things don't tell the whole story. If they did, you can damn well bet you they wouldn't be selling them for no damn fifty cents."

"It's what I got."

"And you ain't got much there, let me tell you. Damn things don't tell the whole story."

"I don't ever expect the whole story. Except in dirty books."

"And you don't get it there, either. When's the last time some old gal farted in one of them books? You want the whole story, you got to find someone that knows it. Then you got to make sure he knows it. Then you got to convince him to tell you."

"You got someone who knows?"

"Hell, I ain't got nobody. I had me an old woman a while back, but she didn't want me sniffin' after nothing but her." The old guy hacks up a wad of phlegm and puts it over the rail and into the grass. "I sent her packing. I can't be roped down like that."

"Yeah. Well, there's that." Bad goes back to the racing form.

"What I got is myself. Myself is what I trust. And I know a couple things about ponies."

"I'm only betting this race. I got to get back on the road."

"I could use one of those cigarettes you got."

Bad shakes one out of the pack and lights it for him. The old guy doubles over with a fit of coughing. "Shit," he says.

"I ain't got no lungs no more. What is this?" He looks at the cigarette. "Hell. Used to be, I thought only little girls smoked these things. I rolled my own out of Mexican tobacco. Now I ain't got no lungs. Ain't got no knees and I ain't got no lungs. I still got a brain, though. And"—he pokes Bad in the ribs—"I still got me a pecker if you got some old gal who's got the hungries." He wheezes and hacks more phlegm. "I can tell you a goddamned thing or two about these nags here, too. Which one you figuring on?"

"Six."

"Old Judy's Pride. He can run. That form there will tell you that. Of course, that ain't the whole story."

"I kind of figured it might not be."

"Shit. You figure I'm jerking you. Hell, you ask anybody around here if old Shorty jerks people. Shit, no. Son-of-a-bitch. I know these goddamned horses. I help folks out. You're figuring on betting on Judy's Pride. You need helping out. That's all I'm trying to do. Let me explain one damned thing to you. Judy's Pride is skittish as hell. If he gets pushed into the rail, he's going to back off. There's an old boy riding this race that'll push him right through the fucking rail if he gets half a chance. That horse is going to finish out of the money, and your money is going to be about three steps behind him."

"What do you recommend?"

"Well, I was you, I'd get me a bottle of good whiskey and just set here and watch 'em run while the jackasses with the racing forms throw their money at 'em. That'd be a hell of a lot cheaper than the way you're going at it."

"I got to hit one more before I leave. And that number six looks good to me."

The old guy coughs again. "Hell. I got time invested in you. I tell you what. I'll give you the damn horse. You win, you slip me a fin. You lose, it don't cost you a dime other than the money you was all set to lose anyway."

Jesus. Bad wonders if everyone in Judah, Indiana, raises the kind of fools his mother did. "O.K. What do you have?"

"Stick Shift," the old boy says. "Stick Shift to win."

Bad goes back to the form. "Stick Shift hasn't run better than third in a single start."

"That's right. Twenty to one right now. Let me tell you something. That horse started the season with a bad knee. I watched him run this morning. He's ready, and he's got Jesse Castenada on top. That old boy will bring him in. He'll go after the six horse on the rail, and he'll take the rail the rest of the way in. He's healthy. Six is the only one that can flat out-run him, and old Jesse Castenada will make sure he doesn't. That boy is as smart as he is mean. And he's meaner than day-old coffee."

What the hell, Bad figures. He's only got twelve dollars. If he loses five, what the damn difference does it make? The old guy has him too confused to figure anything out for himself anyway. "Let's go to the window," he says. The old guy gimps along behind him.

When Bad has his five dollars down, they head back around the grandstand for the race. "Why don't you bet if you know so much?"

The old guy looks at him. "I suspect you done some drinking in your time."

"Yeah. A bit."

"A bit, my ass. You know what I'm talking about. Betting's gambling. Drinking's too damn serious for gambling. I pick a few horses, I make a few bucks. I never worry about a damn dry streak. I get me a bottle and a place to drink it, what the hell do I need money for?"

When the horses leave the gate, number six takes the early lead, and Stick Shift hangs well back in the pack. Around the far turn, Stick Shift moves up, and they run neck and neck until the last turn, when Stick Shift moves up by a neck and crowds toward the rail. It is just as the old guy has said it would be. Coming out of the final turn, it is Stick Shift on the rail. Judy's Pride has fallen back a full length, and Stick Shift has the rail and only space to the finish line.

Stick Shift has come off at seventeen to one. At the window, Bad collects eighty-five dollars. He gives the old guy a twenty.

"Thanks. I'm obliged. I only need five."

"Buy yourself a good bottle. Have a good time."

"Hell, I'll damn well do that. Someday, someone will do you a favor. Hell, I'll probably be dead by then, but someone will do you one. And I'm going to goddamn hope you don't need it too bad."

He has started the first set feeling good. Things have turned around. He can sense that things are going to go his way for a while. Now, deep into the set, he is getting weary, trying to sing half a beat slower to find the band's pace. When he slows, they slow further. He's afraid the whole set is going to wind down like a four-dollar watch. He has taken to giving the drummer the beat before each song. He counts it, the drummer taps it. When Bad turns his back, the drummer slips right back to the slower tempo.

"That was 'Cold, Cold Heart,'" he says. "Hank Williams did that. He's dead now. Next we're going to do Lefty Frizzell's 'Please Release Me.' Lefty's dead, too. All this done by a singer who's nearly dead. Backed by the band that probably killed them all." And damned if the band doesn't take a bow.

He lets the band take the tempo and tries to adjust to it. Instead of singing the song in the lower register, letting it rumble, he decides to try it Lefty's way, bending the notes. That way, he figures, he can get a little ahead of the band, and bend the notes until they come strangling up behind him. It works better than anything else he has tried. He's not Lefty, but then neither are all the singers who are trying to imitate him, and the people in the audience who don't remember Lefty know the imitators and appreciate the sound.

At the break, he stays at the bar. He has two quick whiskeys, then switches to Coca-Cola. The memory of last night is still fresh, and if he is going to do one more set dragging this band behind him, he's going to have to stay sober.

He shakes hands and smiles. "Of course," he says. "How the hell are you doing?" "Des Moines, sixty-two—hell yes, I remember. We had a fine time." "It's good to see you again." "It's real nice to meet you." "You take care of yourself now." "Sure I'll play 'Slow Boat' again for you." "Tommy's in Nashville, working on a new album. Next time I see him, I'll say 'hey' for you." People are pressing notes written on cocktail napkins into his hands while he talks. He pockets them. Most of them are requests for dedications of "Slow Boat."

While he shakes hands and talks, he looks around the bar. It is full of wood paneling and cowboy art. From the wall opposite him, a deer stares at him with black marble eyes. It is a huge buck that must have run and rutted through the mountains for years until some accountant or bricklayer with a pickup truck, a five-hundred-dollar rifle and a case of jolting bad desire slammed him into the rocks. Someone has put a baseball cap on its head, between the magnificent rack. Bad takes out his glasses and looks.

"Let's fuck," it says on the cap. Jesus, isn't that just the way? As if it isn't bad enough that they run you to the ground sooner or later, they insist on making you into a fool.

"Bad?" A tall, thin man in a western shirt reaches a hand to him. "It's good to see you again, Bad."

"Hell, old buddy, it's good to see you again." Then he stops and looks again.

"Bob Glover, Bad."

"I'll be goddamned, Bob Glover. Jesus." He takes off his glasses and pockets them. "It really is good to see you again. What the hell are you doing here, Bob?"

Bob Glover was his bass player in 1959 or 1960, one of Bad's Boys for a couple of tours during the years that Bad was on the road constantly.

"I live here. In Las Vegas. I been here nearly twenty years. I got a construction business here. I'm doing all right for myself."

"Well, hell. That's wonderful. Why the hell aren't you up here with me tonight?"

Bob Glover holds up his left hand, fingers upright and spread. "Smooth as a girl's cheek, Bad. Not a callous left. I don't play anymore. There's no time for it, the business and the kids and all. I brought someone to meet you tonight."

Bad looks down to a boy in a T-shirt, jeans and sneakers. "Howdy," Bad says. "Bad Blake's my name."

"Hello," the boy says. "Todd Glover, sir."

"Well, Todd, I'm real pleased to meet you. Did you know your dad and I used to play together?"

"Yessir."

"Grandpa, Bad. Todd here is my grandson."

"No. The hell you say."

"Sure enough." He laughs. "Tod is Bob junior's oldest."

"The hell. You had a boy. I remember that. But Bob, he wasn't any older than this boy here."

Bob laughs again. "Time has a way of slipping by. You had a boy, too."

"He's in California, with his mother. But he's . . . Hell, Bob, he's twenty-four years old now. I don't see him. I mean, since the divorce. Todd Glover"—he bends down—"how would you like to see your grandpa get up on the stage and play with me tonight? Would you like that?"

The boy nods.

"Oh no, Bad. Not this old boy. I'm a businessman now. I haven't played in years."

"Oh hell. You haven't forgotten anything. It'll come back. You bring any equipment?"

"No. Bad, I don't play."

"No problem, old buddy. We'll just kick one of these clowns out for a while. You can play guitar. You can play my guitar. I'll take the bass for a while. We can get these yahoos playing in the right tempo. Come on up. Just for a couple of songs. Hell, just for 'Slow Boat.'"

Bob laughs. "Bad, no. I can't. I won't. I appreciate the offer, but that's not my life anymore. I just came by to listen and say 'hi' and let Todd here meet you. I wanted him to see you, to know what I used to do."

"Used to do, hell. Once a musician, always a musician. You know that. It's in your blood, Bob."

"No, Bad, it's in yours. I believe that, but it's not in mine. I'm happy with my life the way it is now. I wouldn't trade it."

"Come on, Bob Glover, don't tell me you didn't have yourself a good old time when you were one of Bad's Boys."

Bob laughs. "Oh no, I'd never try to tell anyone that. I did have some real good times, but that's what they were, Bad, some good times. And it got to me. The road, you know. It wore me down. I loved it for a while, but I got tired. Remember nineteen sixty? We were on the road more than we were

off. God, we'd get home and I'd see Martha and Bobby for
a couple of days, start to settle in for a little bit. I mean, the
dog would start to recognize me again, and then you'd call
and off we'd go again. I got so I knew that bus better than
my wife."

"Jesus, I loved that bus, that old Silver Eagle."

"Yeah, you did. You really did. And I really didn't. I'd
have a great time the first couple of days out, then I just got
tired of the road, the booze, the bars, the dope and the women.
I just wanted to go home. I never understood how you did it."

"Well, hell, Bob, that's the business. When it's your business you just do it."

"Yeah, that's it. It wasn't my business. I'm a born house
builder. I leave at six in the morning, and I come home at five.
And twice a year I get in my Winnebago with Martha, and
sometimes Todd here, and then I go on the road. Only we go
fishing."

"Well, we had us some good times."

"We sure did. And I'm still proud I was one of Bad's Boys.
It's a fine thing to look back on. And I'm real glad to see you're
still at it. You still love it like you did?"

"I've slowed down some. I guess we all have. Mostly I stay
in Houston. I've got a good little band there and steady work,
but I go out every summer for a month or so. I'm the whole
show now. I'm the band, the road crew and the bus driver, but
yeah, I still like it."

"I hope you're easier on yourself than you were on us. You
remember? Work hard, play hard? You expected everyone to

work, and then, when we were done with that, you demanded everyone go play. You were like one of those slave drivers, only instead of a horse and a whip you had a guitar and a whiskey bottle."

Bad laughs and takes Bob by the shoulder. "Like I said, old buddy, I've slowed down a bit. Play one song with me and I promise I'll let you go, and get you home before sunup."

"That would be a change, but thanks just the same, I think Todd and me will just sit and listen tonight."

Bad bends back down to the boy. "Todd Glover, your grandpa here was a real good musician. I want you to know that. Him and me had some real fine times in the old days. And he could still play better than any of these guys up here with me tonight. And I'd like to buy you both a drink." He stands back up. "Coca-Cola?"

Todd nods.

"And?"

"Coca-Cola. A lot of things have changed, Bad. I don't do a lot of the things I used to do. I got a problem or two with my heart."

Bad nods. His own heart jitter-steps.

He hands them their Cokes. The band is already on the bandstand. "You sure you won't change your mind?"

Bob shakes his head and holds out his hand. "It's been great to see you again, Bad. You're still going strong. I'm real happy to see that."

"Yeah. Well, the same here. You were probably smart to get out when you did. The business has gone to the dogs. You take care of yourself. And Todd Glover, you take good care of your grandpa here. Remember, he was one of Bad's Boys. Ain't a lot of them left anymore." They shake hands.

Sweet Jesus, he thinks on the way back to the bandstand. Bob Glover a grandfather. There is another idea connected to that. He jumps up onto the bandstand and grabs his guitar. "Welcome back," he says. "Glad you stuck around. There's a lot of great music, and hell, we might never quit."

Chapter Three

He has three days in Santa Fe. He has never seen such a flat place. Buildings are built low and nestle into the hills. Even signs hug the tops of buildings. He feels he is the only vertical thing in the town.

Jack has sent two hundred dollars, waiting at the desk of the motel when he checks in. It is still morning, and he is doing errands. He has not been able to do errands in three weeks. He stops at the liquor store, and then he finds a laundry.

Back in the motel room, he unpacks, bringing most of the gear in from the van. Sitting on the bed with the television on, he brushes his white hat, working out the stains, then patting it with a cheese-cloth sack filled with chalk dust. He works on his white boots with liquid polish. The heels are getting worn, and there is a small tear near the right toe. He takes a little bottle of white glue and works it into the split with the end of a match. The boots cost him three hundred and fifty dollars two years ago. How many pairs of boots has he bought and worn out in his career?

He is eighteen years old. It is Louisville, Kentucky, one of the first days of spring. He has his first job, playing guitar for

Eldon Morton, who has his own radio show out of Louisville and travels with his band every Friday, Saturday and Sunday to Jeffersontown and Okalona, Radcliff, Eminence, La Grange, Bardstown and Campbellville, and sometimes north into Illinois and Indiana, to Salem and Madison, Crothersville and Versailles. Bad has missed World War II, but he has a job playing for those who did not.

He is looking at his toes. They are in the first pair of pointed-toe cowboy boots he has ever worn. The boots are inside the fluoroscope machine in the middle of the shoe store. He doesn't believe those green bones are his. He is being tricked. His father warned him that people in Louisville would try to trick any boy from a place like Judah, Indiana.

He moves his toes, and inside the pointed shadows of the boots, luminous green sausages move. That makes the trick more remarkable. He moves his toes again, then, alternately, his feet. The green bones move, then the outlines of the boots. It seems that this has some connection to him. He fakes a movement with his right foot, then moves his left. In the machine, the right foot starts to move, hesitates, then the left one goes. He is trying to think of another, trickier move to confuse the machine when the salesman pulls him back and looks in the machine himself.

"They look a little tight," the salesman says. "How do they feel?"

"Fine, they feel fine."

"I guess they'll loosen with time." The salesman steps back from the machine with a smile.

Bad leans forward to look at the screen again. The green bones are pointed at the ends, but his toes are round. He has discovered proof of the trick. He realizes that people are laughing at him.

"What are you looking at in there, boy?"

"Maybe they got one of those strip-tease films running in that thing."

He looks up. Ed and Wade, who have brought him here to buy his band boots, are watching him with amusement.

"If that's it, I reckon I better have me a look," Ed says. "Eldon wants us to take care of this boy. We don't want him to get his head turned before he plays his first job." He walks over to the machine and takes a look.

"Nope. Ain't nothing in there but a whole mess of toes. But holy crimminy, Wade, this boy's feet are bigger on the inside than they are on the outside."

Out in the sunlight, he walks between the two men, who talk about weather and women in towns he has never heard of. He is still walking awkwardly, feeling the pull of the muscle across his shin as he walks with his toes pinched together. Walking is harder because he imagines the green bones inside his toes, glowing and scrunching as he walks. He is aware of his feet, and their movement, and in them, the bones that seem to have a separate movement of their own.

He considers calling Suzi, to tell her why her check is late. He unpacks his guitar instead and begins unstringing it. When the strings are off, he takes a bottle of polish and a cloth and rubs until he brings the luster up. Then he takes a pad of steel wool and gently works over the pickups, taking off stray spots of rust. With this done, he begins to put on new Dean Markley strings, winding each up with a plastic winder until the string nears pitch. Then he begins tightening by hand.

He brings each string up to pitch, checking it by ear. One by one, he bends the strings up, then down, to take the stiffness out, to stretch them as far as they will go. Then he retunes. When the guitar is back in tune, he moves quickly through a song he heard on the radio on the way in. It has a nice tight hook built on two note bends, and a bottom that most of the bands he gets saddled with could handle. It is a straight one, five, four, with only a couple of quick shifts to catch someone up. He doesn't remember the name of the song or the artist, but maybe he could do it as an instrumental. He can rebuild the melody.

From the outside of the bar he hears it. He stops and listens. Someone is playing piano, delicate triplet runs with the right hand over a steady rolling bass. The drummer is working behind the piano with brushes. He thinks of Smiley Robbins, who left him in—what, '63, '64? He pushes on the door and walks in, expecting to see old Smiley just sitting behind the piano, tinkering.

"Boys. Boys. He's here." The music stops and a man almost as tall as Bad walks forward. "Mr. Blake. Welcome. I'm Rocky Parker, and this is Sureshot." The big man runs through the introductions. Bad nods to each name until he gets to the last. "This here's Wesley Barnes, our piano player."

"I was listening outside." Bad shakes hands with each of the band members, coming to the piano player last. "It sounds real good. Real good." Jesus. It has been years since he has had a good piano player to work with.

Rehearsal goes slowly. Bad keeps stopping to ask if they know songs that aren't on the play list. Songs he played years before keep tumbling back to mind. Often enough the band knows them. The ones they don't, they fake pretty well. The bass is a little weak, but the drums and guitars are solid, and the piano player is a New Mexico miracle.

The band is the house band from a bar across town, which has been brought in to back him for the three nights he is in Santa Fe. Rocky Parker is an electrician. The drummer works at Montgomery Ward, and the piano player has his own tax service.

It is best to stick with the play list for tonight, Bad decides, but tomorrow afternoon they can work on some of the other stuff they have played today. Getting away from the play list will be like a vacation.

It can't be done, Rocky Parker tells him. They all have jobs. They have taken the afternoon off today, but they won't be able to do that again. After the show, Bad suggests. They can get together after the show for a few hours and work out some other numbers. That can't be done, either. The bar doesn't close until two. Rocky has to get up at six. The others work early, too. They can fake the songs they know, but they can't work out anything after this afternoon.

Bad wants to go back to the motel room and get some sleep before showtime, but he wants away from the play list, too. He is tired and hot, but he strips off his shirt and they run through five numbers three times each, until Bad figures that they are close enough for New Mexico. The band is solid, but much of the slack is being taken up by the piano player, who senses exactly what is going on and stays right with Bad. By six o'clock they have an emended play list that doesn't overjoy Bad but is the most interesting work he has done in months.

After rehearsal, he seeks out the piano player. "You're pretty good. You work before?"

Wesley Barnes is a little fat man, balding and sweating almost as much as Bad. "When I was a kid. A little. I just do this for fun. I've been playing with these guys for a couple of years now. Just weekends. Just for fun and a couple of extra dollars."

"You're good. It's real nice to run into someone on the road who really is good. It's going to be a pleasure."

"Thanks. Mr. Blake, can I ask you a favor?"

"Bad, buddy, Bad. What can I do for you?"

"You see, I have this niece. And, well, she's a writer. She's trying to be a writer. She writes for this newspaper here. I mean, it's not *The New York Times* or anything. Anyway, she'd like to do an interview with you. You know, write an article about you for the paper."

Holy Hannah, an interview. Bad has not done one for

years. The ones he has done he has hated when he saw them. But damn, he has a piano player who really knows how to play.

"Well, hell yes. You send your little niece around. I'll be glad to help her out."

He is fresh from the shower, wrapped in a towel. He cracks the door to vent the shower steam and sits down to a room-service steak.

"Mr. Blake?"

He looks up. In the doorway is a woman with streaked brown hair and glasses. She is wearing a denim shirt and jeans. She looks to be in her early thirties. He is almost naked.

"I've come at a bad time."

Instinctively, he starts to stand. Then he sits again. "Who the hell are you?"

"Jean Craddock. *The Sun Scene.* Wesley Barnes's niece. I've come for an interview. This is a bad time."

"No. Yes. Shit. I'm having dinner. I just got out of the shower."

"I'll come back. When's a good time?"

"Hell. I don't know. Just wait outside for a minute. Let me get dressed."

When she leaves, he pushes the steak away and grabs for his clothes. In the bathroom he dresses quickly, trying to put his shirt and pants on at the same time. His hair is wet and combed back. He looks bald. He pushes it forward with his hand and tries to button his shirt at the same time. What the hell is he hurrying for? He is wearing his suit pants, electric blue with the lightning stripe down the leg. He has left his socks and boots in the other room. His feet look white and dead.

In the other room, there are dirty clothes and sheet music strewn all over. He pulls on one sock and hops on one foot to a pile of clothes. He bundles these up and throws them into the bathtub. He sits down to pull on the other sock. He straightens the cover on the bed. There is a wet spot where he was sitting in his towel. He straightens up the sheet music, pulls on his boots and goes to the door.

"I'm sorry," she says, "I should have called. I was working another story not too far from here. I swung by on my way."

"Come in." He looks closely at her. She is older than he first thought, mid-thirties, maybe older. Her brown hair is streaked with gray and drawn into a ponytail. Behind the big glasses there are lines at the corners of her eyes. She is wearing little or no makeup, and her mouth is drawn into a tight smile that may be restrained friendliness or a smirk. She is an attractive woman. She has a tape recorder in her left hand and a camera over her shoulder. "No pictures," he tells her. "You want some steak? A potato?"

"No. How about later?"

"Which?"

"Pictures."

"Roll?"

"On stage?"

"Be all right. Mind if I eat?"

She sits across the room and sets the tape recorder on the dresser. When she crosses her legs, he sees her boots are heavy and well scuffed. His are thick with white polish. He cuts a piece of steak, puts it in his mouth and nods.

She bites her lip. "Let's see. You always dress for dinner?"

The chewed steak catches and lodges in his throat.

"Sorry. I'm sorry. Let me see. Where are you from?"

"When?"

"When?"

"Yeah, when. I'm from Houston, Texas, now. Before that I was from a bunch of other places."

"Originally."

"Judah, Indiana."

"Judy?"

"Judah. J-U-D-A-H. Folks say it Judy. I never knew why. Everyone does. I was born there. 'Bout fifty-six years ago, if that's the next question."

"Not anymore. What did you do there?"

"Grew up. Sort of. I left when I was seventeen. Before that I went to school. I hunted and fished. I ran around. I played some baseball. I played guitar and sang."

"How'd you learn music?"

"Yeah. Well, that. I don't rightly know. I just did. One day my daddy brought home an old Washburn steel-string. Someone had given it to him, or he won it off him. Or probably traded him something for it. Daddy'd trade damned near anything. Man lived to trade stuff. Stuff he'd never use in his whole damned life. That guitar. He couldn't play a lick on it.

I just started fooling with it. We had a wind-up Victrola and a Philco radio, other things he had traded for. I'd just listen and try to play. Every once in a while, I'd do something right. I just sort of learned."

"You taught yourself."

"More or less. There was an old woman in church who played the piano. Miss Verna Taylor. She helped me some. Told me the names of notes, taught me what chords were, got me to read a little music, told me some theory. Later, when I was already playing, Leon Grady taught me a lot. That's when I was in Louisville. He took me to Chicago once, taught me to listen to the blues. That taught me a whole bunch."

"Who'd you listen to?"

"Oh, a bunch of people you've probably never heard of— Lulubelle and Scotty, Bradley Kincaid, Clayton McMitchum and the Georgia Wildcats. You ever hear of any of them? I didn't figure. How about Red Foley? Gene Autry, Roy Acuff? Yeah. I listened to them, too. I listened to everything."

"You learned to sing listening to them."

"Not exactly. I learned to sing in church. Everybody sang. We were Southern Baptists. I learned I could sing church songs all I wanted. If I sang radio songs around the house, my momma would hush me up. But I figured out I could walk around singing church songs all day long, loud as I could, and she'd let me be. I could sing loud enough to drown out my brother and sisters. I was the loudest damn thing in Judah, Indiana, but I was righteous loud, so it was O.K. with Momma."

He fishes the Jack Daniel's out of his pack. "Drink?"

She shakes her head.

"You don't mind if I do?"

"Of course not."

He fills a plastic glass with ice, and then fills in with the whiskey.

"Singing is all you've ever done?"

"I started when I was seventeen, and I've been at it ever since. When I was a kid I had to hoe the garden and haul the washtub for the laundry, feed the chickens, that sort of thing. I figured that was enough of working. I didn't care much for it."

"What about your father?"

"He worked. I never figured he liked it much. Worked in the limestone quarry when there was work. When there wasn't, he did whatever needed doing. He worked hard. It never got him shit. You'll pardon the expression."

"I've heard it before. You never wanted to do anything else?"

"I wanted to play baseball for a while. I was pretty good at it. I thought for a while maybe I could be a musician and a baseball player at the same time. You know, sing on the radio during the winter and at night after the games were over. Then a couple of the kids learned how to throw curve balls. I decided to stick to the guitar. The damned thing stayed where it was supposed to."

"I guess it's lucky for us you never learned to hit curves."

"Lucky for me anyway. Don't get me wrong." He motions around the room. "This ain't no picnic most of the time, but

I'm still doing it. A couple of years ago, my brother called me from Muncie, Indiana. He's got a car lot there. He wanted me to go in partners with him. He had it all worked out. I'd go on the television and tell all the good folks to come on down and buy one of Bad's good used cars. Hell, if I'd played baseball, I'd probably have ended up doing something like that. It's one thing to be a jerk behind a guitar, but God, to be a jerk in front of a beat-up Buick—hard to be a bigger jerk than that. You always want to be a writer?"

"Well, yes, as a matter of fact."

"You good at it?"

"Pretty good."

"You ever done anything else?"

"I was a secretary for a while. Before that I was married."

"Raising babies and all."

"Raising a husband and a construction business. I wasn't any good at it and I gave up."

"The construction business or the husband?"

"The husband. I was damned good at construction. I knew more about it than he did."

"I was never very good at being a husband. I tried it a number of times. I always gave up, too."

"You're sort of famous for that, too, aren't you?"

"There are some stories. They've been written before."

"I'd like to hear them from you."

"Oh hell, darlin', we don't have enough time to do my marriages."

"Five, is that right?"

"Four, actually."

"And one of your wives moved out in the middle of the night?"

"I don't know if it was the middle of the night or the middle of the day, but she moved out. That's the one you want to hear, right?"

"Yeah, I would."

"O.K. That was Marge, my second wife. It was nineteen sixty-five, in Nashville. I was drinking pretty hard in those days." He looks down at his glass. "Not like this. Hard drinking. Benders. Rolling benders. I'd start one night in Nashville and then I'd take off, through Tennessee, into Kentucky, or Missouri, down to Georgia. Once I ended up in Pennsylvania. Anyway, I'd go for about a week, sometimes longer, once or twice three weeks. And I wouldn't come home until I was flat busted. More than once I left town in a Cadillac and rode home in a Greyhound bus that I'd wired home to get the money to buy the ticket for. I'd trade a Cadillac for drinks, or just give it to someone I met.

"This went on for quite a while. She did all the usual things to get me to stop. I went to AA and to shrinks. She cried, she pleaded, she threw stuff, and she threatened to leave. And I'd straighten out for a while, but before too long I'd be drinking again, and then I'd just take off.

"Finally, I came home from one. I'd been gone a couple of weeks, I guess. I drove on home. I'd managed to hang on to the car that time, and I drove into our driveway, and it looked wrong. There was a kid's bike out there. I had a four-year-old, too young for that bike, and there was a strange dog. But none of that bothered me. I didn't think anything of it. And I walked in the front door, ready for whatever was coming, the fit, the crying, the cold shoulder. Anyway, everything was wrong. All the furniture was wrong. Nothing looked the way it was supposed to. And I just stood there, looking, trying to figure what in hell had happened. Had she got all new furniture, did I make a wrong turn and wind up in the wrong house? And the next thing I know, there is some strange woman standing in the hallway screaming. And she kept screaming.

"I got the hell out the door, and I just stood there. It was my house. Hell, I spent a fortune on it, I ought to know my own damned house. And I started to go back in, and I thought about that screaming woman, so I just stood there on the front porch yelling for Marge. Next thing I know, the damned driveway is full of police cars and cops are crawling out of them with shotguns and pistols.

"Anyway, the point of the story is that when I took off that time, she took off, too. She called the moving company, had everything taken out of the house and put in storage, and then she rented out the house on me. And she took off. I never saw her again."

"Never?"

"Well, once. O.K.? That's the story. Now can we talk about something else?"

"I did have some questions about Tommy. Are you going to do another album together?"

"I really don't know. You want to find out, you'll have to talk to Tommy."

"Oh, come on. People want to know about Tommy Sweet."

"Look, there are a couple of things I really don't want to talk about. One is my marriages, the other is Tommy Sweet. I told you a marriage story. If you don't mind, I'd like to skip Tommy Sweet."

"O.K. Fair enough. How did you get started?"

"You sure you don't want a drink?"

"No, really. Go ahead."

"I thought reporters drank."

"Some do, some don't. Some do sometimes."

"That you?"

"Yeah. How did you get started?"

"Well, I'd lay awake at nights, listening to Momma beat on Daddy. Not hit him, but she'd get on him about his drinking and how we were poor as niggers, and why the hell didn't he do something about it besides hunt and drink. And I took a good look at him one morning. And I was just a kid but I knew he was a man who had been beat to hell, and I knew it wasn't going to happen to me. So I left home when I was seventeen. I just up and took off one night. I took some clothes, the Washburn, fourteen dollars and my baseball glove, just in case. I hitched. I got a ride as far as Louisville with a policy salesman. I was supposed to pay a dime a week. When I died, Momma would get a hundred dollars to bury me with. Anyway, the first day I was there I walked into WHM radio and told them I wanted a job singing on the radio. They laughed, of course, but there was this fellow there, Eldon Morton, who had this idea for a group and he needed another picker. I thought he was some kind of hot stuff. Turns out he was hustling just like I was. But he talked himself into a radio show with a hillbilly band that sold batteries, and I was part of it. One day out of Judah, Indiana, not even twenty-four hours, and I was a Kentucky Bluebird. Three weeks after that I was on the road. I played guitar and sang a few of the harmonies. Mostly, I was big and I was young. I could fight the drunks, and there were always drunks who wanted a fight. It was the best damned training anybody could have. And I was too dumb to know it. I figured that was just the sort of thing that was supposed to happen."

"Did you make records?"

"Oh, hell no. This was strictly a radio station band. We sang on the radio in Louisville on Sunday and Tuesday nights. The rest of the week we beat through the little towns around Louisville. We sang and played, but mostly we sold auto batteries. The Kentucky Bluebirds were employed by the Bluebird auto battery company. We would do a set, and then, during the break, Eldon would tell people about Bluebird Storage Batteries, the batteries that keep you flying in blue skies. Then we'd come back and play some more. It was a wonderful time."

"And you sang?"

"Not much. I played guitar. Old Eldon wasn't any great shakes as a singer but he did most of it, what there was of it. Mostly he talked and sold batteries. Bob Wills was still around then, and Eldon had that all figured out. He had himself a bunch of pretty good musicians, and he let us do the work. I guess his major talent was finding folks who could do what he couldn't. He'd call on us to take solos. That was where the real training came in. We'd rehearse songs, solos and all. You were supposed to know you had certain solos in certain songs. But old Eldon drank quite a bit. And he'd get confused. Hell, you never knew when he was going to call on you. If he called on you by name, it was no problem. The guy who was supposed to play the solo would just play it. But if he called for the instrument—you know, guitar, piano, steel guitar—well, you played something whether you'd rehearsed it or not. My God, there you'd be, onstage or on the radio, and all of a sudden Eldon would announce you were going to play someone else's solo. You learned real fast." He takes a long pull on his drink. "I got my name from Eldon."

"Bad?"

He laughs. "Yeah. I'd only been with them for a few weeks. We were doing the radio show. He'd do that Bob Wills stuff—you know, 'Here's a man after my own heart, with a razor.' Anyway, right in the middle of 'Deep Elem Blues' old Eldon says, 'Let's hear some of that guitar from . . .' and he looks at me like he's never seen me before, and he starts over, 'some of that very good guitar from . . . ,' and it's clear he can't remember what the hell my name is, so he just says, 'from a very bad boy.' He was tighter than a pig that's got into the corncrib. Everybody in the band started calling me 'Bad Boy.' Pretty soon it was just 'Bad.' I been Bad ever since."

"What's your real name?"

"That's not for publication. I'm Bad Blake. I wasn't born Bad, and when I die I'll have my real name on my tombstone. Until then, I'm just going to stay Bad."

"That's a long time to wait for people to find out."

"Maybe, maybe not. I fight it, but age sure as hell catches up on you. It is going on the tombstone, though. I think I've got to quit being Bad when I die"—he winks—"but not until then. What time is it?"

"Eight. Ten after."

"You got enough?"

"No. I don't think so. I have more questions."

"Listen. I go on in less than two hours. I want to get ready. Maybe you can come back tomorrow and ask the rest of your questions."

"Can you give me just a half hour?"

"Really, darlin', not now. I got work to do, and I got to get ready. There are people out there who've paid good money to hear me. I always figure when all you got is the deposit slip, you better be real nice to the folks that have the checkbook."

"How about after the show?"

"Maybe; let me see. I know you got your work to do. I appreciate that. Let's see how it goes."

When she goes, he strips off his boots, shirt and pants and heads for the bed. God, he needs a nap.

Moths batter the single light bulb, strung from a wire running across the ceiling slats, held up by clinched nails. He watches the blotchy shadows skitter across the wooden floor. It is mid-June and already hot. It is early evening, still light outside, but in the house the corners where the light from the single bulb don't reach are dark. The moths have been around for a week now, large gray moths that send up clouds of dust when you hit them. They fall to the floor dead, and then minutes or hours later they are resurrected and pounding on the light bulb, trying to break their way into the single coiled white filament.

The Victrola next to him drones the song sad and slow. He picks at the strings of the big guitar. Now the song is too sad and slow, and he gets up and rewinds the Victrola, but only halfway so he can pick out the chords they are playing. He places the needle on the record and sits back down with his guitar. The Carter Family begins "Can the Circle Be Unbroken" one more time. A.P.'s voice holds the melody with a quiver, while underneath the bass notes alternate with the brushed chords. He listens to the steady alternation of the bass and brushed chords. He follows along, C, F, G⁷. When the singing stops, the bass notes walk right through the melody.

He has just come into light from a dark room. He knows, suddenly, how this thing was built, how the bass notes are picked with the thumb and the strings simply brushed with the fingers. He tries it, and he sounds right. He does it again and again, stopping to rewind the Victrola so that the song is at the tempo it is supposed to have. He works at the tempo, and when he has found it, when the alternation is regular and his fingers move to the chords without having to stop and consider what they are doing, he gets up and runs to the backyard, where his mother is picking horn worms from the tomato plants, pinching them between thumb and forefinger until the green juice spurts across her fingers. The guitar bangs against his leg as he runs. He has to play her this wonderful song about the mother who is dead.

Chapter Four

The house is sparse and quiet. Throughout the first set, Jean Craddock keeps edging up to the tiny bandstand to flash a strobe light in his face. What he hears is the piano. It is like being home. It is like being home twenty years ago. Behind him it is like the smell of bread or the green of trees. Unexpectedly, in the middle of "Love Like That," he steps back, nods to Wesley and lets him go. There is no hesitation or uncertainty. The right hand weaves the notes delicately, the sound crisp and sure. When the solo moves to the dominant chord of the progression, Bad steps back again and continues the break, playing the same themes, surprising himself with sharps and flats that simply volunteer. He runs the neck in a quick descending scale finishing with an E chord back at twelfth position and then runs the scale again with variations. When they come back to the chorus, the song takes off, soaring as if it were something he hadn't heard in years.

At the break, a woman in a low-cut blue dress approaches, smiling. He was wonderful, she says. She heard him ten years before in Shreveport, Louisiana. He hasn't lost anything. He may, in fact, be better than he was back then. She motions to the bartender. Up near the bandstand, Jean Craddock is talking to Wesley Barnes. The woman in the blue dress hands him a Jack Daniel's, rocks. Will he play "Crazy Heart"? Of course. Her name is Ann. She works as a legal assistant, and she has loved country music all her life. She begins to recite the titles of his songs, even some B sides. Her blond hair is cut short and falls forward over her right eye. She keeps shaking her head to toss it back. If he is not doing anything after the show, they could have a late dinner, or just a cup of coffee. Jean Craddock has gone back to her table and is writing something on a long, thin pad. He thanks Ann for the drink. After the show he has promised an interview to a reporter. That's all right, Ann says, he will be in town for a couple of nights. Another time would be fine. She puts a business card in his hand and walks back to her table. Some other fans move up for handshakes and autographs. On his way back to the bandstand, Ann raises her glass as he passes.

The last set is an easy swing. They work their way through the play list methodically, no frills, no additions. With a good band behind him, the set slides by like water over stone. It is only when he is ready to move into the final "Slow Boat" that he remembers he has promised "Crazy Heart." He dedicates it to Ann, and he tries to sing it to her, though he keeps looking over at Jean. In appreciation for the drink and the damned nice thought, he plays the break slowly, bending the notes, keeping it sad and delicate. They move through that and into "Slow Boat" and out.

The size of the audience doesn't really suit an encore, so instead, he walks through the bar, between the tables, hand-shaking and small-talking. He gives Ann a kiss on the side of the forehead and in return gets his forearm squeezed so hard her nails dig into the flesh through his shirt.

"Are you busy now?" Jean asks. When he says no, she tilts her head and gives him a smile he can't quite read. "It looked like you were going to be busy," she says.

"No," he says. "I said I would answer some more of your questions, and I will. Help me with my stuff and we'll get started." He packs up efficiently, stopping to chat with the band, to thank and congratulate them, to say "good night, well done, and see you tomorrow." He has only the guitar and the compact amplifier. They will be safe here, the owner has assured him; they can be locked up in the backroom, and he can avoid lugging them back and forth each night. All he has left of the days when he traveled with a bus and a band and road managers to take care of the equipment is his guitar and this little amplifier. He keeps them with him. He starts to hand Jean the amplifier, changes his mind, and hands her the guitar instead.

"I can carry the amplifier, you know," she says. "I'm no fading violet. You can carry the guitar."

"It's O.K. I trust you. Just don't drop it."

As they are carrying the equipment, she says, "You said maybe."

"Maybe?"

"Maybe we'd do the interview after the show. You didn't promise."

"How many of those do you smoke in a day?" she asks as he lights another Pall Mall.

As soon as she asks, he begins to cough, a shallow cough at first, then going deeper until it begins to rattle and finally doubles him over. "Sorry," he says when he is able to catch his breath. She raises an eyebrow and then looks apologetic.

"Drink?" he asks again, fishing cubes out of the ice bucket.

This time she surprises him. "A short one. It's getting late."

"What do you want to know?" he asks as he hands her her drink.

He moves over to the bed, pulls off his boots, unbuttons his shirt and leans back against the headboard.

She looks quizzical, as if she hadn't expected the question, or didn't know what she wanted to know. "Records," she says suddenly. "What's your favorite?"

"'Slow Boat,'" he admits. "It made me a hell of a lot of money. You can't turn your back on something that turns your whole life around like that song did. I admit I get tired of singing it twice, sometimes three times a night, but God, I'd sure hate not to have it to sing. If I didn't have it, I might not, hell, I probably wouldn't be singing anymore. I'd be in Muncie, Indiana, selling Bad's Good Used Cars for my brother. And then I'd be dead, and happy to be."

"Was it your first?"

"Oh, hell no, I had a couple dozen before that. I put 'Cheating Night Tonight' in the top ten before I did 'Slow Boat.' My first record? Let me tell you about my first record. It was a rock-and-roll song. It was back in nineteen fifty-six. Elvis had made it. And then all those other guys from Sun—Jerry Lee, Perkins, Cash. I was in Houston then, playing with another swing band, Bill Barnard's Bayou Boys. Word was out that this old boy who had a recording studio wanted to cut some rockabilly. I'd been listening to it, and I liked it. So I wrote this song, the first real song I had ever done, and I took it to him. He cut it—Bad Blake singing 'Daddy Gone.' And there I was all of a sudden, a rockabilly. I had a big pink coat with wide shoulders and lapels, and black slacks and white shoes. We never did real well with the song, sold maybe a few hundred, but I started getting out on my own, playing dances and such with my own band on the nights I wasn't with the Bayou Boys."

He runs his hand across his belly. "I didn't have all this then, but I wasn't a little Slim Jim like Elvis was, either. I went about two-ten, around there. But there I was at all these high school and college dances, swiveling my hips and toe-stepping all over the stage, swinging that guitar like it was an ax. My God, I wish you could have seen me. No, I'm glad you didn't. Thank the sweet Lord that I didn't see me."

"You liked rock-and-roll?"

"Hell yes. I liked it then and I still like it. Some of it anyway. I liked the hell out of being a rock-and-roll star. Even if I was only a rock-and-roll star in Houston."

"But you didn't stay with it."

"No. No, I didn't. Maybe I'm just country at heart. I grew up listening to country, and I started country. Even when I was doing the rock-and-roll, I was doing country, too. I mean, hell, they aren't that far apart, at least they weren't then. They get awful damned close now, too. And maybe I wasn't a real good rocker, I don't know. I know I liked it. I liked the way I did it. Maybe I didn't look rock-and-roll enough for the other folks. I never had that look. I wasn't skinny and swivelly like they were looking for. How many fat rock-and-rollers do you know?"

"You like country music today?"

"Not much, to be honest. There are some I like. I like some of these new kids around. John Anderson, hell, he's swiping Lefty's style, but so did Haggard, right? I like George Strait, Ricky Skaggs. They play country. Not that many do anymore. You know, the damnedest thing, Chet Atkins, who is country, real country, damned near cut the heart out of the music with his 'countrypolitan' crap. O.K. He got a wider audience for the music. He made it what it is, but hell, he sure lost a lot of what it was, what it's supposed to be."

"And what's that?"

"Well, mostly it's supposed to be about people, what they are and what they feel. It's not just some cute saying laid over a nice, tight hook. Music today, you listen to it, say 'that's clever,' and you forget it. I get the feeling it doesn't have anything to do with anyone. At least no one I know, or would want to know."

"Who's real country?"

"Hank Williams was real country. Lefty Frizzell was real country. Roy Acuff is real country. Hank Thompson and Kitty Wells are real country. Hell, there are lots of real country people around. A lot of them are dead, but there are a whole bunch who are still around."

"Is Tommy Sweet real country?"

"More than he'll admit to. When he started, he was as country as you could get. He was so damned country, traffic lights confused him. He started playing country with me. I taught him country. He tries to cover it up a lot, but yes, Tommy is country. When I was growing up, I ate a lot of rabbit. Sometimes it was the only meat we got for weeks, for months—rabbit, possum, squirrel. When I left home, I swore I would never eat another rabbit or squirrel as long as I lived. Now I eat steak. I dream about rabbit, but I won't eat it. No matter how it's fixed. That's sort of the way Tommy is about country music. Maybe someday he'll come around. He did it with me on *Memories*. I'll tell you this, enough of these kids doing country make some money, Tommy'll be back in overalls and bare feet before long."

"How did you meet Tommy?"

"Look, darlin', I don't want to be cantankerous, but like I said, I really don't want to talk about Tommy, O.K?"

"O.K. What do you want to talk about?"

"Where are you from?"

"Originally?"

"Yeah, where are you from?"

"Enid, Oklahoma. Why?"

"That's what I want to talk about."

"Enid, Oklahoma?"

"No. You. I been to Enid, by the way."

"Depressing, isn't it?"

"I'm playing in Benson, Arizona, in a couple of nights. Nothing depresses me anymore. Why'd you leave?"

"It depressed me. And I was young and in love."

"You can be in love anywhere. I've done it in all kinds of places."

"I guess so, but when the one you're in love with is hell-bent to get out of Enid, Oklahoma, and you're not real crazy about it, either, it doesn't take much to get you out."

"That your husband?"

"Yeah. He was going to build the West."

"Did he?"

"Some of it. A lot of houses here. A couple of shopping centers."

"Why'd you leave him?"

"Hold on just a minute. I'm supposed to be the one asking the questions here, and if I can't ask you personal questions, you sure as hell can't ask me any."

"If I let you ask me some, can I ask you some?"

"Why?"

"You're nice. I don't get to talk to that many nice people. Another drink?"

"One more. Short and quick. You haven't told me the

story about how dear old what's-his-name stepped aside one night and let you be the front man for a while."

"What the hell story is that?" He hands her her drink.

"The story I get from everybody I've ever interviewed in this business. They always start as a sideman, then the star gives them their big break and they become stars."

"And I forgot to tell you that one? My lord, the Brotherhood of Nashville Nose and Guitar Pickers will have my behind for missing that one."

"You mean it never happened?"

"Not exactly. When I was cutting those rockabilly records in Houston, we were sending them out around the country. I cut a couple of straight country numbers, too, and Wilson Cruthers from Federation heard one and offered to let me cut a demo for Federation. They liked it and signed me. The third one I cut for them was 'Cheatin' Night Tonight.' Things kind of went from there. I was a sideman and all, but not for anyone famous, and those I played with wouldn't have stepped aside when the Red Sea parted."

"What ever happened to Federation?"

"J.M.I. bought them out in nineteen sixty-two. I recorded for them for another five years, then they cut me loose."

"And now?"

He looks around the room. "And now, this. I've cut a couple for a little independent in Houston, but mostly I've given up on that. The independents can't compete with the conglomerates. It's a whole bunch of people who bust their asses to put out a quality product that can't get airplay. That's controlled by a bunch of yahoos with gold jewelry and Mercedes cars who only care about Jacuzzis and each other's secretaries and how much money they can stick up their noses. Music is just a diversion for them. Hell, I ain't going to sweat for them. Except for the duet with Tommy, I don't really record anymore. What else?"

"What time is it?"

"I don't know, still early."

"It wasn't early when we started this. It must be three or four by now."

Bad digs his watch from the drawer beside the bed. "No, it ain't that late."

"How late?"

"It ain't four yet. It's hardly three."

"It's late enough. I better go."

"I thought reporters stayed with a story until they got it."

"I've got an awful lot now."

"There's a lot more. Hell, I'll tell you stories that will make your readers laugh, cry, shiver, scream and lock up their daughters. I'd keep digging until I cave in and confess, if I was you."

"Really, I better go. You've been awfully nice. I've enjoyed this."

"Me, too. Honestly."

"You know, it's odd finally meeting you and talking with you."

"Odd?"

"Odd. I've heard you for years. Wesley is a real fan of yours. I listened to him talk about you and play your songs. I sort of felt like I knew you."

"Now you do. And I know you, and that's my pleasure."

"Well, thanks. You've been kind. Maybe I'll see you again before you leave?"

"Can I ask you one more of those personal questions?"

"I guess."

"Will you stay? Here? With me?"

"I'm sorry. No. I can't. You're very nice, but no. Really. Thank you."

"I'd like you to."

"I know. I mean, I believe that. But I just can't."

"Boyfriend?"

"No. Boy, four. He's with a babysitter. I've got to go rescue both of them. You turned that woman in the bar down. I'm sorry. I really am. I didn't mean to spoil anything."

"Don't be, it's O.K. I get offers in bars most nights. I don't get nice reporters from Enid, Oklahoma. This was better. I mean that. You go on home to your boy. It's O.K."

He pours himself a drink while she packs up her recorder and notes. "I hope that comes out well." He nods to the recorder.

"I put in new batteries."

"See, not only nice and pretty, but smart, too. Make sure I get a copy when you get it done. Here, let me give you my address." She hands him a pad and her pencil. He writes his Houston address. Then he hands it back to her. When he leans, she leans. When he kisses her she moves in tight. He runs his hand along the twin ridges by her spine. She holds the kiss, then breaks.

"Oops. Sorry, cowboy. I guess I got carried away. I have a babysitter to rescue."

When she is gone, he begins to straighten up. He takes his coat from the back of the chair and puts it in the closet. He reaches into the side pocket and pulls out the business card. Ann Ralston, Legal Assistant. Above her work number, she has inked in another number. He looks at the card and then at his watch. It is a quarter to four. He puts the card back in his pocket. Oddly, he doesn't feel any regret.

It is mid-June, sticky hot in the white clapboard church. He has come in late, squeezed onto the wooden pew next to his sister. Around him he hears the drone of flies, lazy in the heat, describing wide sloping arcs above their heads. Around him, pasteboard fans on thin sticks are snapped by the fat wrists of sweating women, breaking small breezes against thick night air.

"The Old Rugged Cross" is winding down, the last notes descending into the lower register, rumbling in the throats of men whose faces, red from neck to forehead, white from forehead to hairline, are glistening with sweat. He gets in the last note, and with the rest, sits down.

While the others look to the front of the church where Brother Randall is slowly easing his bulk up to the podium, he looks down, checking his fingers for yellow tobacco stains. He keeps his head down, avoiding breathing in his sister's direction, where she might smell the corn whiskey.

"The time has come," Brother Randall says, "for us to make a choice. This is the time. Not tomorrow or the day after or the week after or the year after." He drops his voice to barely a whisper, but a whisper that rushes out and covers the whole church. "This is the time. And it is a simple choice. You don't have to mull it over. You don't have to think on it, sleep on it, or discuss it with your neighbor or the banker. The choice is clear. It is the choice, brothers and sisters, of spending all eternity wrapped in the arms of those you love, those who love you, especially in the arms of Jesus Christ our Lord, whose love is greater than anything you and I can even begin to imagine. A choice to move into the light of that promise, the greatest promise ever made, the promise that will be kept now and for all time."

Around him, the air has grown denser and wetter. It sinks into his lungs and he has to push it out. When he has pushed it out, more wells over him and sinks into him and he pushes. Sweat gathers and drips in his ears and from the tip of his nose, and the smell of his sweat gathers and combines with the smell of other sweat and the smell of his sister's lilac toilet water. It stings his eyes and clogs his nose. And beneath it all, the other smell that comes welling up from him. He is getting sick with it; he folds his arms across his stomach and bends forward.

"Such a simple choice. To rest yourself forever and all

time in the greatest love, or to fall naked into the everlasting flames that burn and blacken but never consume. The flames that keep biting and burning. And there is no way out. There is no water that will drown the flame, no blanket to smother it.

"When I was just a boy I watched a barn burn. And in that barn, there was a horse trapped. And there was no way to get through that fire to save that poor animal. And I still think of the horse, caught in the burning barn, screaming and terrified. And I think of the sound and the smell, the terror and the pain of that horse. But then I think, those flames, brothers and sisters, consume. And after the minutes of that animal's terror and suffering, he was released, and it was over, and it will never return. And then I think once more. I think of the flames that do not consume, that burn and burn, and the smell and the terror and the agony that is never over. The burning from which there is no release."

The whiskey is moving now. It begins to churn in his stomach and crawl up his throat. And from his crotch the smell of sex keeps rising, overpowering the sweat and the lilac toilet water and coming up in great waves that roll over him. He crouches over harder, trying to keep the smell and the whiskey contained in himself.

"But there is release, and the release is now. Make the choice, brothers and sisters. Open your hearts and receive Him here, tonight, this minute, and you will have your release. He asks so little of you. Open your heart to Him, and He will open His heart to you. The heavenly release is yours for so little. Step forward and take Him for your savior and have your release. Know that your trials, your pain, your suffering, will find release and you will be free. Step forward now. Accept Him. Let Him accept you. Step forward now."

His sister's elbow catches him in the arm and straightens him up. As she rises, he rises, and she pushes him out of the pew and into the aisle, where the people are beginning to move forward. Around him, they move, their eyes locked forward, up toward Brother Randall, up toward the salvation and release, and the smell and the whiskey push upward at him and spin him around until he is facing the people moving forward, all people he knows, who do not show any sign of recognition but keep their heads forward, eyes locked toward the front. He begins pushing his way through, easing past a woman in a cotton dress with small light-blue figures, and then square into a man in white cotton shirt and Cant-Bust-Em overalls. He pushes past and runs into more, as the congregation starts moving forward. He pushes and pushes until he is running, down the aisle and out the door and onto the dirt in front of the church.

The air is suddenly chillingly cool on his sweating skin, and he runs a few more yards toward the maple tree before he lurches forward onto his knees and begins to puke whiskey. It keeps coming, more than he could possibly have drunk, burning his nose and throat. Finally, he is convulsed. The waves coming up from his stomach bring nothing with them. He pushes away, then falls again and rolls onto his back, looking up at the stars that burn forever.

And then his mother is standing over him, her jaws clenched in fury. "How dare you," she says, "how dare you come into the House of the Lord like that. You get out of here, get. You are no better than him. You are no better than your father. You don't care about anything but liquor and women. And you are growing up just like him. Neither of you are any better than a damn nigger. You're going to spend your life nigger poor, just like he done."

When the phone rings, Bad does not know where he is. "Mr. Blake," the familiar voice says, "hold for Mr. Greene." Bad rolls over for his watch, then a Pall Mall. It is eleven o'clock.

"Bad," Jack says, "how are you?"

"It's eleven o'clock in the morning, Jack. I'm dead."

"How's Santa Fe? It's a great town. You been to the Palace of the Governors yet?"

"Jack, it's eleven o'clock in the fucking morning. I haven't even been to sleep yet."

"Wake up, Bad. I've got great news. You're going to like this. Get out of bed and get a pencil and paper."

"Shit." Bad rolls out of bed and stumbles to the dresser. In a drawer, he finds a postcard of the motel. He looks for a pencil, but he can't find one. He can't find his glasses, either. He goes back to the phone. "Hold on, I can't find a goddamned pencil." There are pencils out in the van, but it is downstairs and a couple of hundred yards away.

He lights another match and lets it burn. Then he blows it out, and goes back to the phone. "O.K., what do you have?"

"Cancel Benson, Arizona, on your itinerary."

He still hasn't found his glasses, so he scrawls in big letters on the back of the postcard, "CAN BEN," with the burnt match. "What the hell is so great about canceling another stop?"

"Wait till you hear what I've got for you instead. Are you ready for this? Are you writing this down?"

Bad looks at the burnt match. He figures it's good for a few more letters. "Yeah, I'm writing this down. What am I writing?"

"You won't believe this. I busted my ass for this. Write it down—the twenty-ninth, Phoenix, Arizona, Veterans Memorial Coliseum, eight-thirty."

Bad writes "PHO, VET MEM," before the match gives out.

"Well?" Jack says.

"Well what?"

"Bad, for Christ's sake. I just called to tell you you're out of the Horseshoe Lounge in Benson, Arizona, on the twenty-ninth, and instead you're in a goddamned arena in Phoenix. For Christ's sake, Bad."

"An arena?"

"A goddamned arena, Bad. Ten thousand seats. I got you opening a major show in Phoenix."

"Opening? Shit. I don't open."

"Cut the crap. This is ten thousand seats we are talking about, and in slack times. Where the hell else are you going to play ten thousand seats? Bad, this is the biggest damned thing you've done in years. Don't tell me you don't open. There are acts up the bedudah that would kill to open for ten thousand seats."

"Opening for who?"

"This is the best part. Tommy Sweet."

"Shit." He can't think of anything else to say. "Shit," then, "Fuck," then, "No. No goddamned way."

"Bad. Look. Think about this. You want to do another album with Tommy. This is a step in the right direction. Open for him, get together, talk with him. I haven't been able to convince him, but I got him to agree to this. It's a first step, damn it. You can convince him. Let him hear you. Hell, you can pull it off. It's ten thousand seats, Bad."

"Goddamn it, Jack, I won't do it. I'll open for someone else. Find someone else and I'll open, but not Tommy."

"Who else are you going to open for? Who's playing are-nas these days? Willie Nelson, Kenny Rogers and Tommy Sweet—that's who. Who the hell are you going to open for? Springsteen? You want to open for Springsteen? How about Madonna? Should I try Madonna? This is it, Bad. This is the break we've been waiting for. Don't get stubborn and blow the whole damned deal."

"Oh, goddamn, Jack. I don't know. Tommy. Hell, I can't open for Tommy."

"This is a grand and a quarter for one night. This is ten thousand seats. A quarter of those never heard of you, an-other quarter figure you're dead. That's five thousand people you can bring around, and another five thousand that haven't been thinking a lot about you the last few years. This is exposure, Bad. This is the best exposure you're going to get."

"I just don't know, Jack."

"Look, Bad. I'm talking business here. That's what you pay me for. I went out and busted my ass for this, and damn it, I got it. You got it. We beat a couple dozen acts on this one. You better start thinking business here and forget pride for a while. Besides that, Tommy wants you. He really does."

"Jack, the dream of every sideman in the whole fucking world is that someday the front man whose ass he's been staring at for months, for years, is going to open for him. I don't owe that dream to Tommy Sweet. I don't owe Tommy Sweet one fucking thing."

"That's right, Bad. You don't owe Tommy Sweet a damned thing. You and I both know that Tommy owes you. Well, he's making a payment here, Bad. He's offering you the chance to open for ten thousand seats. He's offering you the biggest audience you're going to get right now. He's offering you a grand and a quarter. Maybe he's thinking of offering you another album. Don't be so damned stubborn. Let him pay off a little bit. You've tried to take your damned pride to the bank before, Bad, and you and I both know exactly how much it's worth."

"Goddamn. Goddamn you, you motherfucking, cock-sucking son-of-a-bitch."

"You'll do it?"

"I don't know. Goddamn it, Jack, if you were here right now, your lips would be on the back of your head. Let me think about it. I'll call you back."

"No. Tell me now."

"I need time to think. I'll call you this afternoon."

"There is no time. Tell me now."

"Jack, let me think. Goddamn, please let me think."

"Yes or no, Bad."

"Goddamn . . ."

"Yes or no?"

"Yes. Goddamn it, yes."

"Good. Now listen. I'll get you a good backup band. I promise. You'll have the best available. You'll be billed in all the ads that run from now on. Be at the coliseum by twelve noon for rehearsal and sound check. Check with Ralphie. He's Tommy's road manager. He'll have everything set up for you. You getting all this?"

Bad looks at the stub of burned match. "Yeah, right. I'm getting all this. Have Brenda send me an itinerary."

"Don't mess this up."

"Jack," he says, tired now, "I told you. I'll do it. Have I ever backed down on a promise to you?"

"No, Bad. No, you haven't. And you'll do a good show. And it's going to come off well. I know you. Have a good time, Bad."

"Right. It's like I get great seats for a Tommy Sweet show, right? And I get to go backstage and meet him in person and everything?"

"You'll be great. I know you will."

"You bet your sweet ass."

"So how are things in Santa Fe, anyway?"

"I've got a piano player. He's good. He's fucking good."

"A piano player? That's nice, Bad. That's real nice. Listen, I have another call on the line. I'll be talking to you."

"Right." When the line is dead, he hangs up the phone. Tommy Sweet, Jesus Lord, you got me opening for Tommy Sweet.

He has opened before. He has opened for Ray Price, Jim Reeves and Roy Acuff. When he was still in Louisville, the Kentucky Bluebirds opened for Hank Williams. He shook Hank Williams' hand, he took a drink of bourbon from Hank Williams' bottle. Hank Williams, a skeleton in a Nudie suit, said to him, "You can pick some guitar there, Slim." Now he will open for Tommy Sweet, who used to back him.

Chapter Five

After he picks up his laundry, folded and wrapped in brown paper, his suits, red, yellow and orange, under clear plastic, he drives into the middle of town. The streets are narrow and lined with cars. The Palace of Governors is a long, flat building built from mud and braced by cedar posts. Along the sidewalk, under the portico, Indians display their jewelry, baskets and trinkets on blankets. There must be some joke here, Bad thinks. How the white men got so much away from the Indians by giving them beads and trinkets, and here they are trying to get some of it back by selling the white folks from Iowa and Connecticut and Pennsylvania beads and trinkets. When he looks closely at the faces of the old Indian women, he decides there is no joke here of any kind.

Down from the palace is the cathedral, hundreds of years old, built by Spanish monks. He walks around the garden, marveling at what these people were able to accomplish with mud and cedar. On impulse, he opens a side door and walks in. Inside, the cathedral is huge and empty, except for pews and altar. It is painted in earth tones, tan, pink and turquoise. Rows of columns support a vaulted ceiling of pink squares edged with thin lines of turquoise. At the front is the altar, behind a cedar railing. On one side, a large white marble Virgin; on the other, a crucifix with a twisted, tortured Christ. His Baptist upbringing has never prepared him for this graphic representation of Christ in agony. Around him, the columns begin to soften and slowly bow. The vaulted ceiling trembles and begins slowly to lower. The outer walls follow the ceiling, leaning in at the top, down toward him, until the whole church is beginning to lower around him, to enfold and smother him. His heart begins its awkward race, missing beats here and there, and his breath comes in hard, wheezing gasps. He is cold, and his shirt is wet with sweat. Around him, the bright room darkens. He is suddenly outside, in bright sunlight, unsure what has happened, struggling to control his breathing. The wall of the cathedral behind him is cool and solid against his wet back. He lurches away from it, and into the garden.

East of Santa Fe, he revives. He is less than twenty miles out of town, on a plateau of the Sangre de Cristo Mountains, overlooking the Mora River sliding slowly past, fifty feet below him. Also below him, cars wind past on the snaking blacktop. From the top of the plateau, he hears only wind pushing through the leaves of scrub oak. His boots crunch softly through dirt and dry brush as he walks past. Ahead of him, a jay scuttles from bush to bush, quietly watching him, tilting its head from side to side.

He has his heartbeat under control, his breathing is regular. The sweat has cooled and dried on his face and neck.

He squats and plucks blades of dry grass, braiding them together. Once in 1967 in Nashville, he went to the wedding of one of Lee Stoner's sidemen. Before the ceremony, he felt the eyes of Jesus, twisted on the cross, unlock from their upward imploring and take hold of his own, augering into him, until he had to brace himself on the pew in front of him, locking his elbows and gritting his teeth, straining not to be pulled straight forward and up toward the bleeding Jesus for some accounting he was not, would never be, prepared to give. Then the cross and body started to torque, twisting loose from the marble base to come at him and for him. Christ twisted at the horizontal arms of the cross, trying to wrench it free, to free himself to get at Bad, and Bad pushed his way down the pew and into the aisle, running past ushers and guests to get to the fresh air and sunshine, where he fell on his knees, breath coming in long gulps.

Until today, he has not been in a church since. The churches of his boyhood, the plain and simple white wooden shells filled with wooden chairs, where the sermons of damnation were smoothed over and softened by the singing of dozens of voices in praise and thanksgiving, have given over to the tall, angular structures of blame and redemption. Bouquets of wildflowers have been replaced by statues of Jesus, racked and bleeding, looking upward as if asking who has done this to Him. As soon as he walks into one of these churches, Bad can feel Jesus' eyes break loose in their plaster sockets and swivel toward him, claiming, I know. What a friend we have in Jesus.

The wind picks up. To the south, over the tree-topped hills, gray clouds are starting to build. The wind has an edge to it. If he doesn't look down toward the river and road, but off toward any horizon, he can see only trees and sky. Voices rise around him and he is lifted into the rhythm of singing: "With my Jesus on high, / Where we never shall die, / In the land where we'll never grow old."

The Friday night house is nearly full. Sureshot has been playing for over an hour when Bad, wearing black slacks, white shirt and black hat, climbs up onto the stage. While the band is working through a verse of "Last Cheater's Waltz," Bad crouches behind the amplifiers, plugs in and checks his tuning. As Rocky Parker begins the chorus, Bad walks up behind him and sings a bass harmony. From the bar, there is scattered applause. He tips his hat. At the end of the chorus, he simply joins the band for the rhythm. It has been months since he has enjoyed playing enough to just walk up and join the band before his own set begins. He plays two more numbers with them, trading licks with Wesley Barnes on "Funny, How Time Slips Away," and then leaves the stage to the band until they are ready for his set.

He sits at the bar and while the band plays "Every Time Two Fools Collide," he sips his drink, nodding and smiling to customers who catch his eye. No one comes up to shake hands or talk. As the band breaks into the final number of the set, "Rocky Top," he impetuously slides off his barstool, takes the hand of a woman at the table next to him and leads her onto the dance floor. They do a quick, nearly graceful shuffle with lots of spins as the tempo of the song increases incrementally. By the time the song is over, he is huffing and wheezing, dizzy, his face burning from the exertion. Around the bar, people stand and clap. Bad and his partner bow to each other and the audience. He is actually having fun.

During the break, he gets surrounded, handshaken, patted and pounded. Across the room he catches a glimpse of Jean, but people crowd toward him, blocking his view. Behind him on the bar, half a dozen drinks are lined up for him. He takes a couple of sips from each before it is time to hit the stage.

"Thank you, Santa Fe," he says from behind the light. "My God, what a beautiful place you've got here." He moves into "A Cheatin' Night Tonight," and the first set moves by quickly. A woman in jeans and T-shirt brings a beer to the bandstand for him. "Darlin'," he says, "that's just real sweet, but I just can't drink that beer." He turns sideways, so they can see his profile. "I got to protect this fine figure I worked so hard for."

Drinks keep appearing through the break. Bad keeps chatting with people who come up to meet him, and he manages to get only a couple of mouthfuls down. He keeps looking for Jean, but he can't find her. When the stage lights are on, his vision is obscured by glare and dark; when the house lights are on, people are up and milling around.

"What do you all think of Sureshot?" he asks to open the second set. When the audience breaks into applause, he says,

"Aren't they a fine bunch? I think so much of them, I think we ought to kick out the play list this set and play a little Stump the Band, don't you?" More applause. "What would you like to hear?"

"Slow Boat" comes up several times, a couple of other standards, before Bad hears the oddball he has been waiting for. "Sir?" he asks. "Did you really call for 'White Lightnin'? Do you know that's George Jones's song? Do you know I'm not George Jones?" The guy keeps grinning and clapping. "Do you know which side of you your chair is on?" The guy grins and claps. "Well," Bad says, "I guess he's passed the sobriety test, and I guess we better do 'White Lightnin'.'" The drummer gives him the tempo. "Hold it, hold it," he says. "We didn't rehearse this, but if we're going to wing it, let's really wing it." He counts the beat back to the drummer, sped up by half.

In the song, he forgets the last verse, but in the chorus he pulls the "White Lightnin'" refrain up basso profundo, and in the break, he and Wesley just start to cut. He plays runs he hasn't played in years, and Wesley keeps pushing him, finding new phrasings of the melody that demand answers. All in all, they stretch the song to over five minutes.

After "White Lightnin'," the crowd begins asking for odder, and faster, stuff—Elvis, Hank Cochran, Jerry Lee Lewis, Hank Thompson. By the time they get to Bare's "Marie Laveau," he has the audience whooping into the chorus with him. After the song, Rocky Parker surprises him, telling him they have only ten more minutes to get offstage before last call. They bring it down on "Slow Boat."

"Wait," he says. "One more, let's do one more." Then to the band, "'Satisfied'?" Wesley Barnes nods and leads it off. "I got that old-time religion," Bad sings, "that old-time religion, / And that is why I'm satisfied." Wesley Barnes has moved into boogie, and the audience, bewildered at first to hear gospel in a bar, has begun to clap along with the band. "I'm satisfied, / No trouble will ever get me down. / When my eyes are closed in death, / With my Jesus, I'll be at rest, / And that is why I'm satisfied." He follows with a double descending run, going suddenly and surprisingly sharp on the last note, and he is out. "Thank you, good night, and God love you all."

He is packing up, winding the guitar cord, hand to elbow, stowing it in the back of the amplifier, when she moves forward. "That was wonderful," she says. She is at the edge of the bandstand in a straight white dress cinched at the waist by a concho belt. She looks different, more handsome than he remembers.

"Hey," he says, "more questions?"

"A couple, if you don't mind."

He picks up the guitar and amplifier. "Which one do you want?"

"Since I have a choice, let me stick with the guitar."

"Drink?" he asks again when they get to his room.

"Sure." She unpacks her recorder and sets it on the dresser.

"That's a real nice dress."

She smiles, starts to respond, then begins again. "Why did you do that?"

He stops pouring the bourbon. "Do what?"

"Sing that gospel song. I mean, a gospel song in a bar."

"Did you like it?"

"Of course. It was wonderful. But I've never heard any-body do anything like that. It was terrific. I mean, how did you know you could get away with something like that?"

He lights a cigarette. "I knew. I knew I could get away with anything tonight. I just decided to do it. Sometimes it works. Maybe it's you, or maybe the audience, or the stars or vibrations or whatever the hell you think it is. Sometimes it just works. Tonight it worked. 'Satisfied' is a great song. It's not a great gospel song, it's a great song, period. It feels real good. I felt good, so I did it."

"Are you religious?"

"I was. Maybe I still am, I don't know. I don't go into churches if I can help it. I don't say my prayers at night any-more. But I guess I believe there's a God, and I guess I believe He keeps track. If that's religious, I'm that. You religious?"

She shakes her head.

"But you liked the song. See, it doesn't make any differ-ence, it's a great song. It's sort of the way with country music. There really isn't any forbidden territory. You can sing about anything. I mean, we got all these drinkin' and fightin' and lovin' and cheatin' songs. As long as it's something that people feel, it's O.K. for country music. So it's O.K. to sing gospel in a bar. I felt happy, and it's a happy song that makes other people happy, so I wanted to play it. I don't say this stuff very well. Maybe you can fix it up so it makes sense in your paper."

"I think you did O.K."

"You know I don't know much about books and stuff. I know movies, mostly. But books and movies, they make life glamorous, you know? Lives come out better, or bigger, than they are. But in books they write about special kinds of people. Country music is about people who aren't real special, who are never going to be. They grow up, work, get married, slip around, and they die. And the music is the glamour of that kind of life. Maybe slipping around on your wife or husband ain't the best thing in the world, but for a lot of folks, it's what they got. And the music, it helps."

"What about your songs?"

"I try."

"I mean, where do you get them?"

"Out of living. Where else? What else can you write about?"

"Like 'Slow Boat.' Where did that come from?"

"Marge. My second wife. The one that run off. That's her song."

"Did you write songs about all your wives?"

"All my wives and a bunch of others."

"Like which?"

"Songs or others?"

"Songs."

"Well, let's see. 'Love Came and Got Me,' that was with Evelyn, my first wife, then 'It's Strange' was Kathryn, number three, and 'Love Like That' was for Suzi, my last wife."

"Number four."

"Number four, the last. It's the same thing."

"It's funny. You know, those are all happy songs, real love songs. Yet you've broken up with four different wives. Didn't you write any of the sad ones?"

"Hell yes, only you've never heard them. I only recorded a couple of them. I don't write those songs very well. I do a lot of them—'Faded Love,' 'Please Release Me,' 'Crazy Heart,' things like that. But the ones I wrote just don't work. Hank Williams wrote better about endings than beginnings. With me it's just the opposite. Hank's songs are really pretty. Mine are like endings—ugly."

"What do you mean?"

"Well, maybe this has happened to you. I hope it hasn't. But there are times you are in bed, you know, I mean making love, and something's wrong, and then you realize that for the other person, this is just practice. I mean, I can't make a song out of that."

"That means you've tried?"

"Yes. Yes, that was Suzi. She was twenty-three and I was forty-six, forty-seven, and she started out thinking I was something pretty wonderful—a genuine country-western star. It didn't take her a whole lot of time to figure out what she had was a broke-down singer and picker who wasn't ever going to take her to Hollywood or New York City."

"I don't know. You don't seem that broke down."

He looks at her, really looks at her. Besides trading in the jeans and denim shirt for the dress, she is wearing her hair down, and a trace of makeup. She looks younger than last night, softer, and she smiles, not more but more fully. "Is this what you really want to talk about?"

"No. I guess not."

"You got a babysitter tonight?"

She nods her head. "He's with a friend."

"You stay?"

"If you still want me to."

He moves toward her, and she meets him halfway. As he starts to put his arms around her, he realizes he has a drink in one hand, a burning cigarette in the other. Somehow, in all the years, this has never stopped being awkward. By the time they break their kiss, he has dumped ashes in his drink, and she has dribbled hers down the back of his leg.

"That pretty white dress," he says, "would still look pretty on that chair there."

After the urgency of snaps and buckles, hooks and zippers, comes the urgency of unfamiliar skin and contours. When she is naked, he can't let go of her and holds her close while she tries to get his clothes off. She unsnaps his shirt and works it over his arms, works his belt buckle open, then tugs down his pants and shorts, only to realize he is still wearing his boots.

"Let me," he says. His pants are around his ankles, and he can't bend down to the boots without losing his balance and falling.

"Here," she says, and pushes him back until he is sitting on the bed. Then she begins to wrestle off the boots. He does his best to help her, trying to straighten his foot so the boot will slide off. But that only raises his instep, wedging it tighter in the boot.

She had begun gracefully, bending over to tug at the boot. He had watched the soft sway of her breasts. Now she is doubled over, not tugging, but pulling at the boot, turning and working her arms around it, like a pipefitter working on a froze-up valve. She swings one leg over his and pushes at the boot, then swings the other over and keeps pulling until it slides off, and she ends up on the floor, sitting facing him, legs spread, arms full of cowboy boot, hair in her face, and a smile of triumph.

In spite of himself, he is laughing. On the floor, she doesn't look naked or sexy, but like a child who has just completed a simple chore.

"I think I better do the other," he says.

"You're damned right," she says, then, noticing his withering erection, "Oh hell."

"You come here. Everything will be all right, as soon as I get this damned boot off."

After the initial rush of passion, they slow and luxuriate, then grow shy. He gets up for drinks and a cigarette and puts on his shirt to walk the eight feet to the dresser. She pulls up the sheet and tucks it around her.

"That was nice," she says.

"That was something more than nice." She leans into his arm, and he touches her hair with his fingers. "You're very beautiful."

"No," she says. "But thank you. I'm a lot of things, but I was never beautiful."

"You are," he insists. "And I would bet you've gotten more so over the years."

"Is this the famous country charm I've heard so much about?"

"I guess I wouldn't know a whole lot about that. I've never been real famous for charm. Country or any other."

"But you're famous. What's that like?"

"What's being a reporter like? Sometimes it's nice. A lot of times it's a pain in the butt. When people know who you are, they think they know who to ask for whatever they think they want. I never figured out whether I liked it or not. I started out wanting to be rich and famous. Then I was. Then I wasn't. I guess I want to be again. I don't know. I'd like to have another hit. I'd like people to know I can still do it."

She raises her glass. "I'll testify to that."

"Reporter's charm?"

"Reporters aren't famous for charm, either." She tilts her head up to kiss him.

He eases the sheet down from her breasts. She grips it and then relaxes. "I guess I don't have anything to hide anymore, do I?"

"That's maybe the best part, not hiding for a while." He continues working the sheet down, following it with his lips and tongue, over breasts and ribs, belly, over the lateral scar. "You really are beautiful," he says.

"Don't talk."   . . .

He wakes from dreamless sleep. Her head is cradled on his arm, her breathing regular and shallow on his chest. Love starts this way always, waking, his arm pleasantly numb from being slept on all night. And it always ends trying, in sleep, to get as far away as possible, until no bed is big enough to get the necessary distance. It always starts in sleep before it works its way into waking and consciousness.

It is still early, he knows, the room full of deep shadows. He gently lifts her head and eases his arm out from underneath. She stirs and groans, but her breathing eases and flattens out. He gets up and puts on his pants. He calls room service for coffee to be left outside the door. He lights a cigarette, moves their clothes from the chair and sits, watching her sleep.

"You could call in sick," he says.

"Don't think I wouldn't like to. I don't exactly have seniority on the paper. If I let up, I'm going to end up out on my ass. Besides, when you stick around, you get the good stories. I'm tired of movie reviews and interviews with the county agricultural agent on thrip control."

"And fading country singers."

She is sitting on the bed, in her slip, eating toast. She stops to lick a drop of butter from the side of her hand. "I worked to get this interview. It was my idea—well, Wes's actually, but I pitched it and got it. I thought it would be fun." She smooths strawberry jam over the toast. "My God. I had no idea how much fun it was going to be."

"Best damned interview I ever got."

"No one can say Jean Craddock doesn't throw herself into her work, or at least at her work."

"I got something else you can use if you still need something."

"I haven't put it together yet. What is it? Something salacious, I hope."

"Actually, no. I'm opening for Tommy Sweet in Phoenix in a couple of days."

"That's great." She looks puzzled at his expression. "That's not great, is it?"

"It's great," he says. "My agent has told me how great it is. It's good money, it's exposure. But hell, it's a hard thing, you know, opening for the guy who used to be your sideman. Hell, I gave that kid his start."

"What is it between you two?"

"It's that. I taught him how to sing and I taught him how to play. I got his teeth fixed. I got him exposure, I even helped him go out on his own. Son-of-a-bitch won't return my phone calls. Next time you see him grinning at you from one of those album covers, think about this: those teeth are mine. I bought and paid for them. Soon as things started to pop for him, he never looked back. Not a thank you, not even a damned Christmas card."

"But you did an album together."

"We did a hell of an album together. My agent did that. Tommy was cutting duet albums right and left. Jack just convinced him that that was the logical thing to do. He got sixty-five percent of the son-of-a-bitch, too. I put that album together. He cashed most of the checks."

"He is good, though."

"He can be good. He used to be good. He doesn't work at it hard enough. When he started out, he was the hardest damned worker I ever saw. I really liked that. But now he just sort of slides by. You noticed how flat he is on the new albums?"

"No. I guess I haven't really noticed."

"Most people don't. They hear the voice, recognize the phrasing, that's Tommy Sweet and they're satisfied. Yeah, he's always sung flat. In the old days, he used to work past it. He used to work and work until he found the notes, and he'd push himself to stay there. Now he just slides along. On the last album he wasn't close enough to most of the notes to hit them in the ass with a double handful of rock salt. And his playing is sloppy as hell. He got himself famous and quit trying. That burns me. There are too many people working too damned hard for him to get away with that crap."

"Like you?"

"Like me and a lot of others. This business uses talent like paper. Most of it is wasted. There are all sorts of talented people out there who are never going to get anywhere. And here's old Tommy just sliding by."

"Why'd you work so hard with him?"

"He was good. I could tell that. And he wanted it so bad. I needed a guitar player, and he was on the way to being one. I figured I could teach him right. And I liked him. He was a good kid. And old Eldon Morton. He took a chance on me. I figured I owed for that. One day when I needed a picker, there he was. He wasn't a hell of a lot better than a hundred, five hundred, kids trying to break in. I mean, he could play. Damn, he was quicker than a hiccup, but he didn't know the instrument very well. Neither did I when I started. I taught him the way others taught me. He sang flat, so I worked with him. I made him sing with me. I made him reach for the notes until he got them. And he worked. He worked like the devil."

"But people taught you, and then you moved on. You got famous. Eldon Morton never got famous."

"Right. But I never turned my back on them. I mean, people move on. That's the way it works. But you don't forget where you came from. Tommy never looked back. He acts like he did it all himself. Hell, I don't want to talk about this any-more. Anyway, I'm opening for him in Phoenix."

"Well, I don't know what to say. Good luck, I guess."

"Why don't you say you're coming back tonight?"

"I'd like to. Believe me I would. But I have a child. I've left him with someone two nights in a row now."

"How about your ex?"

"My ex doesn't have anything to do with him. Besides, that's not really the problem. I don't think you should go run-ning around, shuttling your kid from house to house. I need to spend some time with him."

"I'd really like you to come back. This is my last night here."

"I want to, Bad. I really do. Let me see what I can do.

Maybe Barbara can keep him just one more night. I don't know. Can I call you?"

"Please. Please call."

She calls. It is three o'clock in the afternoon. He is watching television. But he can't get interested. He turns up the sound. In a courtroom, two grown men argue over cookies. "What I ordered," one man explains, "was four gross of three-and-one-half-inch-diameter oatmeal cookies." Bad gets up and turns off the sound. The phone rings.

"Bad, listen. I'm really sorry. I have to stay home tonight."

"This is my last night. I'm in Las Cruces tomorrow night."

"I know. I know. I really want to. It's my son. I really have to stay home with my son. You understand that, don't you?"

"Sure, darlin', I understand."

"No, no, of course you don't. I just can't go off and leave him again. I have to think of him before me, before us. I just can't."

"Look. Do you really want to see me?"

"Yes, Bad. Yes, I do."

"Can I come over there? I don't get off until one-thirty. He'll be in bed."

There is a long pause at the other end. "You can't stay. I mean, you have to be gone before seven."

"I can do that. I can't do it pretty or graceful, but I can do it."

"O.K. Come on over."

"How do I get there?"

"Well, when you leave the motel, turn right and go about a mile and get back on the interstate, then it's about three miles. . . ."

"Is this north or south?"

"It's north, for about three miles, maybe more. Oh hell. I'll sneak out and come and get you. Will you be ready at one-thirty?"

"I'll be ready."

"Promise me. I've never left him alone."

"I'll be ready. I promise."

Chapter Six

The Saturday house is not as good as the Friday house, but it's crowded and the audience responds. He sticks to the play list, working his way through it. He fights the feeling he should hurry this up. The band isn't a new treat anymore. He has become comfortable with them. He plays easily and concentrates on singing. They remain steady behind him, and there are no surprises. It is a work night, the way it is supposed to be.

At the break, Wesley Barnes comes up to him. "I want to thank you," he says, "for helping Jean out. She's a real nice girl. I mean, she's not a girl anymore. But she's real nice. She hasn't had an easy time of it. Her divorce, the boy, and all. But she's solid as a rock. I think the world of her. She's just real nice, you know?"

Bad looks at him, unsure what this means. "She is real nice," he says. "You're right to be proud of her. She's just real nice."

Wesley gives him a big smile, like he has just got something settled, something that was gnawing on him. There are little drops of sweat on the top of his head.

"And," Bad says, "thank you. For playing with me. You're real fine. Better than a lot of professionals I've played with. I wish I had a road band again. I'd like to have you with me. This is the most fun I've had in years. You, and the rest of the boys, you're all real good."

"We just do it for fun."

"That's the way it's supposed to be. It usually isn't, but it's supposed to be. You all have made it fun for me. God, I hope I get to come back and play with you again sometime."

Wesley Barnes grins. "Yes. Yes, that would be fine. We'd like that."

"You all just keep having fun."

By the end of the last set she is not there. By the end of the encore of "Slow Boat" she is not there. He packs up and says his goodbyes to the band, the barmaids and the manager. As he is loading up, Rocky Parker comes up behind him and hands him a picture. It is an eight-by-ten, an old public-ity still. Bad remembers the picture. It must have been '63 or '64. In the picture he is wearing a blue suit with silver sequins and a white scarf knotted at his throat. He has a Stetson 4X beaver pushed back on his head. He is holding the Guild archtop he lost years ago. He remembers. It was a sweet guitar.

"This is kind of embarrassing," Rocky says, "but would you sign this for me?"

"To Rocky and Sureshot," Bad writes, "Bad's Boys in Santa Fe. With my thanks, Bad."

"I really appreciate it," Rocky says. "I've always been a big fan."

"Tell you what, old buddy, now I'm one of yours."

He has been sitting in the van, smoking, lighting them off the butts, hoping no one notices he is still sitting in the parking lot like he has nowhere to go and nothing to do. The bar is closed and he needs a drink. He considers going back to the room for his bottle, but he is afraid he'll miss her. It is a quarter of two when she finally pulls into the parking lot.

"I'm sorry," she says, "I was out of gas. You know how hard it is to find a gas station at one o'clock?"

"I get off work at one o'clock. I know how hard it is to find everything at one o'clock. I'm just glad you found me."

She knows how to drive with someone following her. She slows to make sure they will both make the lights, and he stays right with her. They wind through a complex of apartments, twenty or thirty two-story buildings with six or eight apartments in each.

"Sweet Jesus," he says when they are inside her apartment. "You read all of these books?"

"Most of them. I was an English major in college. I love to read. We'll have to keep quiet. I don't have men over. I'm not going to have him wake up in the morning and find a stranger in his house."

"Did you know I have a boy, too? He's twenty-four. Name is Steven. He lives in Los Angeles."

"You get to see him very often?"

"No. Marge took him when he was four. I never got her tracked down. Here, look at this . . ." He takes a gold money clip from his pocket. "This is his. I bought it for his eighteenth birthday. Somehow I figured I could send it to him. But I never knew where he lived. I carry it with me. Someday I might run into him. I want him to have it."

"You've never heard from him in twenty years?"

"Not once. His mother took off and left. I tracked her down to L.A. Then, I don't know. I just couldn't figure she was really mad enough to try so hard to get away from me. I figured she'd cool off and call me. You know, want alimony or something. I never heard from either of them again. But kids, you know, they're all trying to find their mothers and fathers these days. I keep hoping he's going to find me."

"Why Steven?"

"It's a real name. I wanted him to have a regular name. One that wouldn't embarrass him like mine did me."

"I don't know your name. Goddamn. I don't believe it. I don't know your name."

"Otis. Otis Arthur Blake. Otis Arthur Blake, Junior, as a matter of fact. I loved my daddy, I really did. But ain't that a damned awful thing to do to your own kid? I sure as hell wasn't about to do it to mine."

She is trying to keep a straight face. "I don't know," she says. "I mean, it was your father's name. That's nice. Oh hell. You're right, Otis Arthur is a damned awful name."

"Worse. At home they all called me Otie. Soon as I left, I

became Art. That lasted a couple of months, then I was Bad."

"I promise," she says, "I'll never call you Otie."

"We'll get along just fine."

On top of the television is a framed color portrait of a boy about three or four. "This is him?"

"Daniel Rawlings Craddock. Buddy."

"Fine-looking boy. Fine-looking mother."

"How about you and that fine-looking mother going into the other room? I hate to bring this up, but you've got to be out of here by sunup."

He had a fiddle player, Cletus Young, who said he played his fiddle like a woman's body. That was only one sign Cletus was a jerk. But there's something about love that's like music. It's a way that your body begins something and then becomes what it does. Their lovemaking, still a little strange, a little nervous, is like playing. It's the counterpoint of single note and chord. It's the tonic, dominant, subdominant, and the sudden ascent to relative minor. Their bodies are the same chords played an octave apart, the movement familiar from hundreds of times before, but still unexpected. Pleasing in the familiar strangeness of it all. He has the feeling, tangled into her, of being where he belongs, like a progression that takes an unexpected turn and ends up not where he thinks it is going but where it has to go, as if he has known, without knowing he did.

He dreams of water. He pumps it up from the well in Judah, pushing the pump handle in long, steady strokes. The water comes into his cup, copper green, then clears. He draws a drink from the chrome faucet. In the glass, the water is copper green. It clears from the bottom. He considers trying another faucet, though he doesn't know where the next one is, only that the water will come out copper green and then clear from the bottom up.

It is barely light. He doesn't know what time it is. There is a clock on the dresser, but it is several feet away, and he doesn't have his glasses. Jean is asleep beside him, her hands in fists, curled under her chin. They have, he suspects, only a little time. He moves his hand down her back, across her hip and down her thigh. She stirs and turns away, moving her back into him. He is working on getting the angle, when something smacks against his butt.

"Read?" a voice asks.

He rolls over, pulling the sheet over himself. Next to the bed is a small boy, wearing only a pair of baggy briefs. In his left hand he holds a blue bowl made of soft plastic. Milk and Cheerios slosh over the edge. In his right hand he holds a thin paper book by its cover. He smacks the book against Bad's leg. "Read," he says.

"Read?"

"Read."

"Well, old buddy," he says, trying to regain his composure, "what's your name?" He shakes Jean's shoulder, trying to wake her.

"Buddy."

"That's right. What's your name?"

"Buddy."

"O.K., little buddy, you want to watch TV or something?"

"Read?"

"I'm not too good at reading. You sure you don't want to watch TV?"

"What's your name?"

"Bad. What's yours?"

"No. Buddy."

"Right. Buddies." He looks over to Jean, then back to Buddy, holding his finger to his lips. She doesn't wake.

Buddy turns and walks out of the room. He stops at the door. "Read?"

By the time he finds his glasses and clothes, Jean has stirred awake. "What time is it?"

"Early," he says. "Stay in bed. I'll take care of myself."

In the living room, he stops at the sofa to pull on his socks and boots. Buddy watches from around the corner of the breakfast bar. Bad pats the sofa cushion next to him. Buddy walks slowly over, sits down next to him and hands him the book. *Bernie and the Firetruck.*

When Jean comes into the room in her robe, Buddy is on Bad's lap, explaining the story of Bernie and the Firetruck to him. Bad looks up at Jean. "Sorry, I guess we kind of overslept. You care for some breakfast?"

Her expression is one he can't quite read. "Buddy," she says, "this is Bad. Bad, this is Buddy."

"No," Buddy says. "Buddies."

"Let's go make your mom breakfast."

While she is in the bathroom, he finds most of the ingredients he needs. Buddy hands him spoons and packages. He is almost done, when he realizes he is missing one ingredient. He walks to the bathroom door. "Where do you keep the cream of tartar?"

"I don't have any. What the hell do you want cream of tartar for?"

"Biscuits. Don't you use cream of tartar in your biscuits?"

"I don't make biscuits."

"And here I thought you were such a good woman."

They eat biscuits and eggs while Buddy plays on the living room floor. "That's a real nice boy you got."

"I know. He likes you, that's for sure. He's not around men all that much. I'm kind of surprised."

"Doesn't he spend time with your ex?"

She shakes her head and takes another biscuit. "Buddy's not his. I had him two years after the divorce." She waits for a response, gets none, and goes on. "You get older, you get wiser, but you still make mistakes. Only sometimes mistakes don't turn out that way."

"Mine usually do. But I know what you mean. He's a good boy. Good mom."

"Good biscuits."

.   .   .

It is five hours due south on I-25 to Las Cruces. Past Albuquerque, the heat builds steadily. He sweats and drives, his
heart beating evenly and slowly. He has tonight in Las Cruces
and then it is on to Arizona, and Phoenix.

Between sets, he stands at the bar and pumps hands. Yes,
yes, he says, that's just wonderful. Tommy's like my own
son, he says to a couple who want to know what Tommy is
like.

"How about 'Let's Get Drunk and Screw'?" This from a
young woman who has appeared in front of him. She is in
her early twenties, thin and blond, in tight jeans and a cotton
chemise top that shows her nipples. She wears a tooled belt
with a large silver buckle. He knows the belt is carved in back,
"Debbie" or "Robin." Debbie, he decides. She has a longneck
in one hand and a cigarette in the other. She is also chewing
gum.

"Pardon?"

"'Let's Get Drunk and Screw,' you do it?"

"The song or the mistake?"

"The song. Mostly."

"I know it. I've done it. I don't do it anymore."

"The song or the mistake?" She cocks her head and takes
a drag on the cigarette, closing one eye. Bad watches the shirt
tighten across her breasts.

She smiles and tilts her head in the other direction, her

eye still closed, though the smoke is more in his face than hers now. "It ain't always a mistake, you know."

"I sure as hell used to believe that. Every once in a while I can still convince myself of it. Mostly it's a mistake, though."

"Have it your way," she says, shrugging her shoulders. "'The Wrangler of Love,' huh?"

"I made a whole bunch of mistakes in my life, darlin'. That's why I know so much about them."

She shakes her head and turns away. The back of her belt reads "Jackie."

He's made enough mistakes in his life, he thinks, to know about all there is to know about them. He's also made enough to know that he hasn't made one for a long time now.

He is on I-10, fifty miles out of Tucson, watching a blue Pontiac that he has been following for four or five miles. It is a late sixties model, with Georgia plates and a broken left taillight. There are two people in the front seat, a man and a woman. For miles the woman has been moving closer to the man. Occasionally their heads merge and seem to become one. Then she will pull back, nuzzle, and begin the process again.

What interests Bad is that now her head has disappeared completely. This can mean only one thing, he thinks. Actually, it can mean any number of things, but only one is worth considering at the moment. It is hot and the road is threatening never to end. He pushes down the accelerator, pulling up closer to the Pontiac. He can see the man's head clearly now. He has brown hair, but not a lot of it. This pleases Bad. He cannot see the woman. He signals and pulls into the right lane, where he can get a better look.

He remembers a night in Minnesota, 1959 or 1960. He let the rest of the band have the bus and he and the new backup singer rode alone in a rented De Soto, on ahead of the bus into blackness that turned into snow. He drove with one hand, trying to coax her head into his lap with the other. Both of them were giggling, lustful, too drunk to be afraid of snow and slick roads, too happy to quit drinking. When the bus finally caught up with them and pulled the De Soto from the snowbank where Bad had driven it, both he and Marge were so deep in sleep they had to be helped onto the bus.

When he pulls up even with the Pontiac, he can see the woman's foot resting on the window frame and the bunch of her shoulder on the front seat. He pulls up a little to see if he can get a better angle on the couple, when the opening bars of "Slow Boat" come whining out of the radio speaker. He has never grown tired of hearing the song come at him from a car radio or, less often, from the jukebox of a honky-tonk. Being caught by surprise by the song is like letting memories come at him shotgun. The song has been part of his life—on the worst days, his whole life—for twenty-five years.

Because he has already been thinking of Marge, he gets a twinge, a memory of him and Marge in L.A. in 1960. Twelve bars into the song, he is driving his new Cadillac convertible around the twists of Mulholland Drive in the middle of a radiant afternoon, with his wife beside him. "Slow Boat" is on the radio, and he turns it up, letting the music ricochet off retaining walls that line the road, suddenly the most intensely beautiful sight he has ever seen. The air is clear and dry in the afternoon sun. Plants atop the retaining wall burn with color. "Slow Boat" has been to number one on *Billboard*'s country chart, has stayed there nine straight weeks and now is off but still getting decent airplay. He cannot write a bad song, and he has corrected, in this second marriage, the mistakes of his first. He doesn't get tongue-tied anymore when he has to talk to men who wear suits and neckties. In short, he has stopped being a jerk.

He is now half a car length ahead of the Pontiac, angling the outside mirror so he can see into the car's front seat, and singing along with himself on the radio. He has a better view now, but he still can't decide whether he is watching sex or nausea. When he decides that he really doesn't care anymore, and pulls up another car length ahead of the Pontiac, the DJ announces that they have been listening to "Slow Boat" by "the late Mr. Bad Blake, one of the great ones." He slows down, and he can feel the sweat soaking his shirt against the vinyl of the seat. In the rearview mirror, his face is fish-belly white. He begins to look for a place to stop and get a drink. The blue Pontiac moves past him on the left. The woman is sitting upright now, and as the car passes, the driver gives Bad the O.K. sign, finger to thumb. Bad reaches for a cigarette. Here he is, sweating his way through a state where they think he is dead, on his way to be an opening act for Tommy Sweet. Yeah, I know, buddy, he thinks, ain't none of us ever stop being jerks.

· · ·

His drink wavers in his hand, rattling the ice. He is in a tiny bar just outside Tucson, a square stucco building that stinks of piss and disinfectant. "Would you like to contribute to my next dance?" a woman in a transparent negligee asks. He shakes his head.

"You want to see, you want to pay," she says.

"Darlin', the only thing I want to see is the bottom of this glass, and the bottom of the next one, too."

"Fuck you."

"Better not, darlin', I'm a dead man."

Chapter Seven

In Phoenix, the traffic begins to slow and stop. There is a rhythm to traffic that he loves. On the open road, it unfolds and plays slowly, gracefully. In the city, the tempo quickens, but it begins a series of variations, off the beat, an irregular pattern but still a pattern that can be followed. He has lost his itinerary and instructions. He exits the freeway and stops at a Shell station for directions, gets back on the freeway and heads north.

He exits on McDowell, heads east to Nineteenth. There is the sign. "Veterans Memorial Coliseum. August 29. Tommy Sweet. / Special Guest, Bad Blake." Jack, you cocksucker, thank you.

It takes him twice around the perimeter before he finds the one gate that is open. He pulls the van in, up to where two tractor trailers sit next to the coliseum. "Tommy Sweet" is written in script on the sides of both trailers. Beyond the trailers in the lot is a Silver Eagle bus. "Tommy Sweet" is also across the side of the bus. Below that, "Lovin' You."

At the rear door of the coliseum, a security cop lounges in a lawn chair. "Howdy," Bad says. "Bad Blake." The cop looks up, mirroring Bad in his glasses, two Bad Blakes grinning down.

"You got a stage pass?" the cop asks.

"Hell no. I just got here. I'm Bad Blake."

"I can't let you beyond this point without a pass."

"Get me a pass. I'm on the show."

"I just check passes. You're supposed to have one."

"Get Tommy, then."

"No sir. I can't do that."

"The hell." He starts to move past the guard and into the coliseum.

"I'm sorry, sir." The guard puts his hand on his gun. "You don't move past this point without a pass."

Bad goes back to the van, looks for his notes in the glove compartment, until a vague memory stirs. He goes back to the cop. "You know Ralphie?"

"Yessir."

"You go find Ralphie. You tell him Bad Blake is here. Then you tell him Bad Blake is waiting five more minutes, then he is out of here. Then you better go buy yourself a newspaper and start reading the want ads, because, buddy, your job is over here."

The cop scowls, gets up and walks inside the coliseum. Bad follows. "You wait here," the cop says. Inside it is dark and cool. He hears the cop's footsteps echo off the concrete.

In the distance he can see stage lights and spots being turned off and on. The cop comes back. "Ralphie will be right here."

Bad takes a cigarette from his pocket. The cop offers him a light.

"This is my job," the cop says. "You understand that. No one gets in without a pass. No one ever gets hassled when I work a show."

"Yeah, we all got jobs."

"They should have sent you a pass. That's their job. I just make sure no one gets in without one."

"Yeah. Right."

"I work all kinds of shows here. I like these country shows. You guys are all right. Willie Nelson, he slipped me a fifty-dollar tip two years ago. I hate those damn rock-and-roll shows. All a bunch of stuck-up little shits, you know? Treat you like dirt. And then all those little girls around here. Hell, I don't let them in. I got a girl of my own. How's some guy going to feel, his daughter running around in the middle of the night, trying to put out for some faggot in pink pants and mascara? God, it makes me sick."

"Yeah. Hell of a thing. Any of those girls come around looking for me, let 'em in. I don't wear mascara."

"And the Ice Capades. I bet every one of them is queer. And some of those girls in the show. Jesus Christ. And it's all wasted on a bunch of queers in tight pants. Oh, I get them all, believe you me."

"Bad Blake. Good to meet you." A little man in jeans and red satin jacket shakes Bad's hand. He is wearing a wireless headset with earphones and a pencil-thin mike. "Ralph Martin. I'm with Tommy. Call me Ralphie. We expected you two hours ago. You have trouble?"

"Long trip. I left Las Cruces at five this morning. Played last night. Car trouble in Tucson."

"Shit. You're tired, then. Listen, Jack Greene's got you set up at the Holiday Inn right down the road here. Soon as we're done, I'll have someone take you over. We're in sound check right now, so things won't be too long. Come on up, take a look around."

"I got a band here?"

"Yeah, yeah. They showed up about eleven. We're running a little late, you know. All the union guys trying to run into the double bubble here. Your guys are downstairs, I'll take you down in just a minute. I think they're having lunch. You hungry?"

"Well, now that you mention it."

"We got the food downstairs. Just a minute. Come on up on the stage. And here. Put this on." He takes a cloth patch and sticks it to the leg of Bad's jeans—"Tommy Sweet, Lovin' You."

They climb up ten wooden stairs, onto the stage. Roadies in undershirts are busy taping wires to the stage. At both ends of the stage, amps are stacked—Altecs, Fenders and Marshalls. At the back of the stage is a Rogers drum kit with double bass and two synthesized drums. At the far end is a Baldwin grand piano. Around the stage are stacked blue Anvil crates on casters. Stenciled on the sides is "Tommy Sweet." From above, beyond the basketball scoreboard in the middle of the arena, baby spots sweep across the floor. "Bear," Ralphie says into his microphone, "stage, please." Then, to Bad, "Bear handles our sound, he'll help you set up."

Bad looks out across the arena. There are two tiers of seats, which run in a horseshoe from the stage to about a hundred yards back. On the floor, plywood covering the basketball court, chairs are set up in two sections all the way back to the first tier of permanents. "How are tickets?"

"Not bad. No sellout, but we were at ninety-three at noon. Maybe ninety-six or ninety-seven by showtime. It's not great, but it's O.K. We're running radio spots until seven tonight."

Sweet Jesus. Last night in Las Cruces, they estimated the house at one-fifty. He looks back out at the seats. Ninety-six or ninety-seven hundred people here tonight. "Where's Tommy?"

"Back at the hotel. He'll come in for final check about five-thirty and then he'll head back to the hotel until showtime. He said he's anxious to see you. Maybe he'll be by early."

A huge, fat man in a sleeveless cowboy shirt moves across the stage toward them. "What's up, man?"

"Bear, this is Bad Blake. You'll need to get him set up. How's this going?"

"Fucked up the butt, man. We got buzz on channel eight we can't get out and monitor three's dead. The usual. Fucked right up the butt. How you doin', man? What's your equipment like?"

"Roland Cube."

"That's it? A Roland Cube? Well, that ain't going to bounce

off the back wall. No sweat. We'll run you through one of these.
You got a preference—Marshall, Fender? Like it don't matter.
Those boys with you got a god-awful mix of stuff—Mesas,
Peaveys, heavy rock-and-roll shit. Suit yourself."

"I like my Roland."

"Well, that's no sweat, either. I'll mike it through the PA.
What else you need?"

"Just time to rehearse."

"Give me thirty minutes to get this stuff untangled, and
come on up. Where's your stuff?"

"Parking lot. Black Dodge van."

"Give me the keys. I'll take care of it. Go on downstairs
and chow down. I'll call you when we're clear up here."

On their way down the stairs, Ralphie runs through the
program. "You go on at eight-fifteen. You got forty-five minutes. Stay on that. I'll be stage left and I'll give you your time
remaining. You can't run over more than three minutes.
Tommy goes on at nine-thirty. Tommy's off at eleven-thirty.
We're torn down and out of here by one-thirty. May be some
party at the hotel around two or so. You're welcome." They
are on a winding corridor that leads past the locker room.
"This is your dressing room. Tommy's is the next one down."

When he opens the door, Bad walks into a room that
looks like a bus station john, white tile floor and wall, mirrors
and sinks along the length of one wall. Beyond the sinks, five
men sit on folding chairs, eating and drinking. "Maverick,"
Ralphie says, "your backup." Bad walks over and introduces

himself. Beyond the band, on the shelf in front of the mirror, are four plates of cold cuts, cheese, bread and relishes, cans of beer, bottles of wine, soft drinks, glasses, ice, and a case of Jack Daniel's with a note. "Save some for me. Tommy."

While they eat, Bad goes over the play list with Maverick. He has cut three sets down to one, keeping to big stuff, keeping it simple. He has a drummer, bass player, two guitars and pedal steel. He would like to keep the stuff he tried in Santa Fe, but they have two hours onstage before they play before ninety-seven hundred people. The band knows most of the songs by sight, and have "Slow Boat," "Faded Love," "I Love You (A Thousand Ways)," "Love Came and Got Me" in their repertoire. What they don't know, they are intelligent enough to ask about.

"What we are doing here," Bad tells them, "is opening. It's Tommy's show. We go out, we play our forty-five minutes straight. We don't get cute or fancy. We do our work, nothing more."

"Jesus, Lord," Ray, the bass player, says when they get on the stage. "This place is about twice as big from down here as from up there."

"You ever played an arena before?"

"Hell no. We played five hundred at a barbecue once."

"Not a hell of a lot of difference," Bad tells him, "except the sound. It's going to crunch you when you first hear it. Get used to it, and remember, it won't be as loud when there are people here."

The band is competent enough. The guitars can't resist moving up to the front of the stage to try rock-and-roll licks. Bad lets them go. Tonight they will stand stone still behind him.

"Bear," he says into the microphone, "bring up number one mike, the bass, and tone down the guitars."

"Mix is good," a voice responds.

"Set it the way I tell you, and leave it."

"I've got a good read out here. Your mix is fine. Trust me."

"Bear, I'm an old man. I get grumpy. Bring up the lead mike, the bass, set the guitars down, and humor me."

"You want one of us to go there and check the mix?" Nick the rhythm guitar player asks.

"We're going to get a shit mix," Bad tells him. "Opening acts always do. One of the sound man's jobs is to fuck up the opening mix. It makes the headline act sound that much better. We can send the whole band out there. It won't make a hell of a difference. What we're doing here is negotiating just how bad a mix we're getting."

"You've got another fifty minutes of stage time," Bear says.

"We're going to be on this stage until the mix is where I want it. Give me my mix or we may rehearse right through Tommy's first set."

When he has pushed Bear as far as he thinks he is willing to go, Bad moves them through the rest of the play list, and comes back and works the rough edges off "Slow Boat" and "Cheatin' Night Tonight."

"You're off in five minutes," Bear calls.

"Fifteen," Bad responds, and takes the band through three more numbers. He is off in fifteen minutes. He can't let the sound man push him, or the sound man will run the show. On the other hand, he can't throw the sound man too far off, or the mix will sound like the track to an auto wreck.

"Sounds good, Mr. Blake."

"I like the mix, Bear. I appreciate it."

"What do you think?" he asks Ron, the pedal steel.

"Sounds good. Simple enough. We can handle it."

Just wait, Bad thinks, until you walk out here and realize that there are nearly ten thousand people in those seats. Then you handle it.

"I'll drive you to the hotel now," Ralphie says. "I'll send someone by at seven to pick you up." Then, to the band, "You need to be in the dressing room at seven-fifteen. Your instruments will be onstage. They'll be tuned for you."

"No," Bad says. "Have them down here. We'll tune ourselves."

"We'll tune them on the scope. We'll have them under the lights so they'll stay in tune."

"I'll tune. You can take them up fifteen minutes before, but we tune to me."

Ralphie turns and walks away. Bad breaks open the case and takes a bottle out for the hotel. A couple of the guys take them, too. "Hold it," Bad says. "You're welcome to the booze. That's no problem. But now you're working for me. You be real careful with that stuff. Anyone shows up drunk, I'm personally kicking his ass up between his ears."

At the hotel, there is a message for him. "Call me, #647, Tommy." Bad folds the note and puts it in his pocket. In his room, he undresses and climbs onto the bed. He needs an hour or two of sleep. His stomach is churning, and his heart is pounding like an engine about to throw a rod.

It is 1951, in Lexington, Kentucky. He is sitting in the bus with the rest of the Kentucky Bluebirds, waiting. Out the window, beyond the fence, he can see cars pulling in, people milling around. It is over two hours to showtime, but they are lining up outside the armory, waiting for Hank Williams.

He has seen Williams twice before. Once in Louisville, once in Ohio after driving all night with Leon, just for a chance to see Hank, to watch him work, to see him in person. Tonight he is opening with the Bluebirds for Hank Williams. He is going to walk onto the same stage Hank Williams will walk onto. He is going to play for the same people Hank Williams is going to sing for.

He keeps looking out the window. Beyond the fence are only cars and people. He can see only a few yards down the road, to where it curves behind the trees. He really doesn't know what he expects to see—another bus, a procession of Cadillacs, a golden cloud. "You nervous?" Leon asks him. No, he lies, no, he is not nervous. It's another date in Kentucky. He has been playing them for nearly two years now. What he wants to know is whether Hank is nervous about having to follow him.

They play their first set, leave the stage, and ten minutes later are back on for another set. Hank is still not here. They play nearly every song they know and repeat a couple. They have been playing for nearly two hours when the word comes, "Hank is here."

He is off the stage, putting his guitar in the case, when Hank Williams walks past him, nearly as tall as he is, but thin as a guitar string, smoking a cigar that seems as thick as his arm. He is wearing a white suit decorated with quarter notes up the leg and down the arms. And he is wearing the fanciest pair of black-and-white boots Bad has ever seen. Bad watches Hank move up behind the stage for the intro, grind out the cigar, and take off his hat and wipe the sweat from his head. Bad is stunned. Hank Williams is going bald.

After he is done, Hank moves around backstage, smoking his cigar and swigging on a bottle of bourbon. He is not very old, not out of his twenties yet, but he is balding and he looks drawn and weary, even while he ambles through the backstage crush, shaking hands and chatting, smiling all the time. Hank stops and chats with Eldon, and then moves through the other members of the band. Bad sticks out his hand and Williams takes it. "I heard you. You can pick some guitar, Slim." He holds out the bottle. "Want a slug?"

Chapter Eight

When the knock comes at the door, he is between sleep and waking, unsure what time it is. He finds his glasses, but there is no clock in the room. It must be, he figures, time to leave for the coliseum. He gets out of the bed and gets dressed, his heart heaving and skipping beats. "I'll be right there."

"Hurry up, goddamn it, we run a tight ship here."

Goddamned efficient little shit. Runs a show like a fucking space mission. He runs a comb through his hair and opens the door.

"I got booze, you got ice?" Tommy says, holding up a bottle.

"You son-of-a-bitch."

"I always admired that in you, Bad. You always know the right thing to say. How the hell are you?"

"Worse."

"That's about right, I guess. Can I come in?"

Bad steps aside and lets Tommy into the room. Tommy holds up the bottle. "I could use some ice."

"None here. Try room service."

Tommy plops down in a chair next to the bed, where

he rests his feet. His boots are made of thin strips of leather, sewn together so they form a series of V's pointing down to the toes. Bad estimates six hundred bucks, maybe seven. His jeans are crisp and new, his starched white shirt is mono-grammed at the pocket. On his right hand he has a diamond ring in the shape of Texas. "I can do without ice," he says, "but a glass would help. A couple of them."

Bad finds glasses in the bathroom, brings them in and sets them down on the dresser. Tommy pours three fingers of Wild Turkey in each one.

"You give up on the Southern Comfort?"

"I still drink it onstage. It's good for the throat."

"So they tell me. Damn stuff was always too sweet for me."

"When I started drinking, it was the only thing I could choke down. I didn't like it much, either. But hell, if you're one of Bad's Boys, you got to be able to put away the whiskey. Hell, those were good times, weren't they, Bad?"

"Yeah. We had some good times. You remember Bob Glover? I ran into him a couple days ago in New Mexico."

"Bob Glover. Bob Glover. Oh, hell yes, I remember Bob. Remember, one night in Arkansas, he had some girl in his room, and you started banging on the door, screaming like you were her husband. And I was yelling, 'Don't shoot, please don't shoot our drummer.'"

"No. That was Will Samuels."

"Will Samuels, hell yes. We had him so scared he crawled out the bathroom window bare-assed. Who the hell is Bob Glover?"

"Bass player. About sixty, sixty-one. Came over from Lee Stoner's group."

"Yeah, maybe I remember him. Kind of a quiet guy."

"He's a grandfather."

"You don't say. You remember Kelly, my little girl? She's seventeen now. Going to college next year."

"I'll be damned." Bad takes a long drink and lights up a cigarette.

"Bad. It's good to see you again. I'm really glad you agreed to do this for me. It'll be great to be working together again."

"I need the money. If it wasn't this, I'd be playing Benson, Arizona, tonight."

"Benson? Where's that?"

"Real damn close to Tombstone."

"Listen, you remember that time we broke down in the middle of west Texas? Two hundred miles from El Paso? We sat out there all goddamned day waiting for the wrecker while Ted Randolph sat in some bar getting shit-faced. It must have been a hundred and ten out there. I thought old Paul was going to die. Why the hell was Ted at the bar?"

"The guy who owned the wrecker was at lunch. Ted went to get a drink. He kept on drinking. Is that why you wear the ring?"

Tommy looks at the ring on his finger. "Ain't that a bitch? You ever try to buy a diamond ring in the shape of Kansas?"

"Kansas is square."

"See what I mean? Nobody knows what the hell it looks like."

"So how's the tour going?"

"It's O.K. Fifty dates in two months. It's a grind, but it'll pay for Kelly's college, a few other things. How about yours?"

"I'm out for a month. Six states. I'll be off next week."

"Pickup bands?"

"Yeah."

"Jesus, that's a ball buster. Hell, we should have gotten together earlier. We could have done this whole tour together."

"We tried that once. It didn't work."

"Yeah. I know. The *Memories* tour. Hell, there were just too many things going on. I had that movie shooting in Mexico, and Jill wanted me to spend some time at home. I was on the road almost all that year. I wanted to do it. It would have been a hell of a tour."

"Yeah. A hell of a tour."

"Oh, come on, Bad. I'm sorry. It just didn't work out. I was trying to keep my marriage together. Don't hold that against me."

"I got a career, too. And I had a marriage or two I wanted to keep together."

"Goddamn it. You gave me my start. I remember that, Bad. You taught me most of what I know that's worth knowing. O.K.? I haven't forgotten any of that. But goddamn it, I have a life to live, too."

"Yeah. Well, hell. Those are the goddamned ugliest boots I ever saw in my life."

"You ever see a boa constrictor? Ugly damn snake. Ugly damn boots."

"Salesman threaten to shoot your dog?"

"Kind of like the idea of wearing snakes on my feet. Besides that, they were expensive. Real expensive. I like that. When I spend my money, it means that no one else is spending it."

"So why the hell won't you do another album?"

"Hold up. I never said I wouldn't. J.M.I. doesn't think it's the right time to do another duet."

"I think it is."

"You might be right. But over at J.M.I., marketing says it's the wrong time. Hell, they got those guys over there making all this money, my money, and they call the plays. They want a couple more solos, then we can do a duet. You got first shot. I already told them that."

"I don't have a lot more time. I need some money now."

"Look, even if we go to the studio—say I front the money to cut the album—they won't release it. They'll sit on it until they think it's right. You won't make any money with tape sitting in the vault."

"Shit, Tommy. I'm fifty-six years old. My career isn't going anywhere. I need something to get it moving again. I can't get a solo album. I need this. Goddamn it, I really need this."

"I hear you, Bad. I really hear you. But I can't get them to budge on this one. There is a way you can make some money, though."

"Which is?"

"Songs. I need some songs. I'm supposed to be in the stu-

dio in two months for a solo album. I don't have new material, and the stuff I've been hearing is just crap. Give me some
new songs. I'll deal straight with you. You publish and I'll
give you three cents for the mechanical rights, the others on
line, above going rate. I've been moving one or two million on
every album. And I'd take up to five songs."

"I haven't written a new song in three years."

"Think about it. I need some material. I want some from
you. Jesus, you write some of the best material around."

"I used to."

"I tell you what. If you can get me some new songs, and
I take them, we'll release at least one as a single. I can guarantee that."

"Look, like I told you, I don't have any new songs."

"Write me some. I don't have to be in the studio until October. You've got a couple of months."

"I'm not a songwriter anymore. I haven't been in years. It
doesn't matter what kind of figures you come up with. You're
really not offering me anything. I'm a singer and a picker. We
can do an album, but I can't write you any songs."

"Do it, Bad. You're not the only one who's hurting. I could
really use a hit right now. I haven't put a single to the top in
over a year."

"Scary, isn't it?"

"What?"

"Staring at nothing. You got any of that whiskey left?"

"Oh hell, it's just a little dry spell. But yeah, it gets wor-
risome."

"It gets to be a whole lot of fun later on."

Bad's into his third drink when the phone rings.

"Mr. Blake, it's Brenda. I have a message from Mr. Greene."

"If he wants to know if I'm here, tell him I am."

"No. He wants you to know he's sent you five boxes of product and he's cleared it with Sweet Productions so you can sell them at the concert."

"Sell? What the hell are you talking about?"

"He's bought five hundred units of *Memories* from J.M.I. at two dollars. He says you're supposed to sell them for five dollars each."

"What the hell is going on? I don't sell anything. I sing. I play. I don't sell my goddamned records at concerts."

"Mr. Blake, all I have is this message. He wants three dollars a unit. You're to keep the rest."

"Son-of-a-bitch. Let me talk to him."

"He's out of town. On the Coast. He just left this message for you."

"That motherfucking prick. Where is he? Get him for me."

"He's not here, Mr. Blake. I can't reach him. I'm sorry."

"You find him. And when you do, you tell him to get his fat ass to Phoenix and pick up his goddamn albums. Because this is where they are going to stay. You tell him that. And you tell him he's a worthless son-of-a-bitch with more nerve than brains."

"I'm just delivering the message, Mr. Blake."

"Hell, I know that, darlin'. Nothing against you. You just deliver that message back is all."

"I'll tell him. Mr. Blake, I'm sorry."

"Yeah, darlin', I know. Me, too."

Bad slams the receiver down, ringing the phone.

"That," Tommy says, "was not your basic good news."

"Fucking jackass wants me to hawk copies of *Memories* after the show."

"Well, hell, Bad, that's no problem. We got concession-aires working at all my shows. We'll just turn the records over to them. They'll sell them for you. No sweat."

"I don't sell albums at my shows."

"Well, damn it, I do. I mean, the concessionaires do. Everybody does it. How many you got?"

"I ain't got any. Jack Greene's got five hundred. And if he wants them sold, he's going to have to do it himself."

"What do you get off each one?"

"Two dollars."

"That's a thousand bucks. Hell, for a thousand bucks, I'll go sell them."

"You're welcome to them."

"Think about it. I mean, that's the business, right? Selling product? One way or another, you're selling the stuff. I got to go. It's getting on showtime. Listen, I've got all day in Phoenix tomorrow. What do you say we go play a little golf in the morning? I'm better than I used to be. Hell, I break ninety every now and again."

"I got to get back on the road early."

"That's too bad. You used to hit a good ball. I remember."

"Ain't remembering wonderful?"

• • •

The band is already there when he arrives. There is a new arrangement of food on the dressing table. The air is acrid with marijuana. Bad finds a roach in an ashtray and lights up.

"You all eaten yet? Eat some if you can, but don't overdo it. A little bit will help settle your stomachs. Have a couple of drinks, but no more. It's O.K. to be nervous. It'll go away. You get drunk, that won't go away. You blow a couple of notes early on, it doesn't make much difference, but the end of the show has to be tight."

"This is fucking living," Nick says, building a ham sandwich. "A couple more years, we're going to have shit like this every night."

"Yeah, I hope you do," Bad says, working on the roast beef. "But let's get through tonight first."

"You get this kind of stuff all the time?"

"I work clubs mostly. I get dinner and drinks."

"You work on the gate?"

"Flat fee."

"We get thirty-five percent over a guarantee of two hundred dollars."

"I travel alone. I can't check the gate. My agent sets a flat fee. I never have to deal with the money."

"What does your agent take?"

"Fifteen percent."

"Damn, is that worth it?"

"Agents are a pain in the butt. They're bastards, all of them. And you're damn right they're worth it. If you're going to do anything at all in the business, you better get yourself one."

"Half an hour." It's Ralphie at the door. "Anything you guys need?"

"I guess we're O.K."

"I'll be back in twenty minutes. While you're on, I'll be stage right. Any problems, let me know. Broken strings, that sort of stuff. Anything goes wrong, anything, make sure I'm the first to know."

"Let's tune them up," Bad says. He tunes his and then gives the band each string, thumb up for flat, back down for sharp. "You all remember the intro?"

"Of course," Nick says. "We've got it cold."

"Play it for me."

"Aw, for Christ sakes, we know it."

"Play it for me."

They go through the intro, the guitars and bass, the drummer tapping out the beat on the bottom of a chair. "Like I said, we know it."

"Don't come unwrapped. Things change out there. I know you know it. I want you to remember you know it."

"Ten minutes," Ralphie says. "Give me the instruments. We're doing the last stage check. Problems?"

"Ready to work."

"Good. Listen. I got your boxes of albums. Tommy told me to put them with the concessions up on the concourse. You can check with me later on tonight for an accounting, or we'll just send the receipts along to Greene and Gold, whatever you want. Let me know after the show."

"Shit."

Ralphie leads them back up the ramp toward the stage. Along the way, they pass a couple of Tommy's boys heading for the dressing room. When they make the final turn toward the stage, they can see the horseshoe of seats nearly full. The noise of the crowd is like a low grinding.

"Holy fucking shit," Nick says.

"Just breathe," Bad says, "get your breath steady. You're fine." His own heart is thumping like a broken cam. He inhales hard and holds it.

"In ninety seconds the houselights go down," Ralphie says. "Get a good look at the stairs. There will be two guys at the side to help you up, but you got to climb yourself. Six steps, remember that. Count as you go. It's going to be dark as hell until you reach the stage."

When the lights go down, the crowd noise comes up, as if they were wired on the same switch. Noise rolls over them.

"Go," Ralphie says.

The band moves up the steps to the stage. From the bottom of the steps, Bad can see them moving slowly across the dark stage, sees the instruments being lifted. From the corner of his eye, he sees Ralphie's hand move, and the stage lights come up. Bob taps out four beats on his sticks, and the band moves into "Wildwood Flower." Two bars in, Nick misses a chord.

"Shit," Ralphie says.

"They're O.K.," Bad says, and starts up to the stage. When he moves from behind the stacked amplifiers into the clear stage, the crowd noise intensifies, and he feels his knees begin to wobble. At the edge of the clearing, he picks up his white Gretsch and moves to the center, the microphone pulling him like a beacon. When he reaches the mike, he picks his guitar cord from the stage, while Nick makes the intro: "Ladies and gentlemen, 'The Wrangler of Love,' Mr. Bad Blake."

They are running a couple of beats behind what they have rehearsed, and when they reach the chorus, Bad is not ready, and has to just count the beat into the turnaround before he can start playing. The notes come back at him through the monitor pure and crisp. At the end of the song, the applause is politely enthusiastic.

"Thank you, Phoenix, Arizona," he says. "It's real good to be here tonight. Of course, at my age, it's real good to be anywhere." Applause and a little laughter. "This is a song I had a hit on a long time ago," he says, "called 'Love Came and Got Me.'" He will announce every song, just to make sure the band doesn't get confused.

They stay with him for the whole set. They are not as sharp as Sureshot in Santa Fe, but they are steady and dependable. The steel guitar covers the ragged edges at the ends of the progression with long, sweeping wails.

They are three quarters of the way through the set, moving into "Faded Love," when the crowd begins to stomp and cheer. Finally, he has struck some response in them. From the corner of his eye he can see someone moving up toward him. As he moves into the chorus, Tommy is up to the microphone with him, singing harmony.

> I miss you, darling,
> More and more every day,
> As heaven would miss the stars above.
> With every heartbeat,
> I still think of you
> And remember our faded love.

At the next verse, Tommy picks up his blue Adamas guitar and plays rhythm behind Bad. At the choruses, he moves up and sings the harmony. Halfway through the break, Bad steps back and offers the rest to Tommy, who plays it through his way, quickly hammering and pulling, trilling the final notes. He gives Bad a grin and a nod, and Bad takes it back and runs it through once more, duplicating Tommy's moves, but elaborating on them, substituting triplets at the end. They harmonize the last chorus and bring it down.

"This is the man," Tommy says, "who taught me to play that and just about everything else. I guess he can still teach, huh?" The crowd begins to cheer and Tommy steps back and waits, careful not to step on any of Bad's applause. When it starts to die down, he says, "I'll see you all in a little bit. I'm going to go back and listen to this man play."

When they have finished "Slow Boat" there is no question of a curtain call. The band unplugs and waves. "You all know,"

Bad says into the microphone, "that Tommy and me did an album a couple of years ago. You can't get it at the record stores anymore, but we got some copies of it up at the concession stand. I'll be up there in a little bit, if you'd like to have me sign some of them for you. Come by and say howdy. Thanks, and God bless you."

As he's leaving the stage, Ralphie grabs him. "Tommy would like you to join him in his set for 'Please Release Me' and 'Cold, Cold Heart.' I'll cue you."

"No," Bad says. "This is Tommy's show. I got records to sell."

He moves through the crush of people on the concourse easily for a bit, until heads start to turn and people move up to pat him on the back and shake his hand. By the time he reaches the concession stand, people are waiting with copies of the record in their hands. He puts on his glasses and starts signing them on people's backs. "Best Wishes, Bad Blake."

"Is Tommy going to come up and sign them, too?" a couple of people ask.

"No," Bad says. "I don't think Tommy's coming up."

When the houselights start to flash the five-minute warning, there is still a sizable crowd waiting. A few move back toward their seats. "The show is about to start," Bad says. "Why don't you all get back to your seats and enjoy it. Maybe I can see you afterward." Thirty or forty remain, stubbornly waiting for him to sign their albums. He stays and signs even after the houselights go down and Tommy's band starts up.

The sound is crisp as new beans, and as he listens, he knows Tommy has paid a lot of money for these arrangements—piano, horns, strings, as tight and methodical as Muzak.

He still has his back to the stage, signing albums, when he hears the reaction of the crowd, and then the repetitive hammering on the guitar. There is not even an introduction. He turns his head to the stage as Tommy, still in the same jeans and white shirt, with a high-crowned straw hat, begins his version of "Lost Highway."

Back in the dressing room, the band is eating and drinking, listening to Tommy's show through the intercom. From somewhere, girls have appeared, and the band is having its own little party. Bad makes his way through a couple of dancers to the bar. His case of Jack Daniel's is well broken into. He pours a glass and leans back against the mirror to watch.

"I blew that intro," Nick says. "Jesus, I'm sorry. I got out there and started shaking so hard I thought I was going to fall down."

"It's no problem. You're not the first to do it. I wasn't the first, either. Just forget it and have a good time."

"I don't think I've ever had this much fun in my life. Jesus, backing Bad Blake and Tommy Sweet on the same night."

"Yeah," Bad says, "it's a goddamned bunch of fun, isn't it?"

While the boys party, Bad eats Tommy's food and drinks Tommy's booze. He listens, through the intercom, to Tommy's show. Even through the six-inch speaker, he can tell this show is as smooth as a baby's butt. Though, my God, what a mess Tommy can make of good material. On "Bright Side," his first hit, Tommy has cluttered the song with horns and strings until it is nearly a new number. He thinks of Marge and the things she used to do with Jell-O. She put fruit and nuts in it, whipped cream and ice cream, she whipped it and chopped it in pieces. She served it in bowls, cups and glasses, but it always came out Jell-O.

"Excuse me," a red-haired girl in cowboy shirt and jeans says. "I want to get to the food here." Bad smiles and steps aside. "You were very good. I enjoyed it. A real nice show."

"Thanks, I appreciate it."

As she bends over to get at the relishes, she shows off the Tommy Sweet patch on the rear pocket of her jeans.

"You with the tour?" Bad asks.

"Local radio," she says. "I hit most of the shows. Linda Fuller."

"Bad Blake. Linda, you a DJ?"

"Advertising."

"Here for the party?"

"Mostly. Sometimes they can be pretty fun. I bring clients sometimes. It builds goodwill to let them meet a few stars. Usually it's a way to pass the time."

"The boys seem to be having a pretty good time."

She shrugs. "The real party will start after the band gets off. I'll check it out, I guess."

Over the intercom, the band stops and the crowd noise comes up. "You know when they're planning to get off?"

"Eleven-thirty."

"That'll be three, then."

"Three?"

"Curtain calls. About seven minutes each, I figure."

"You been to a few of these shows."

"It beats television, usually."

The crowd noise intensifies. He hears a familiar intro, but he can't place it."

"'Coming Home for Keeps,'" she says. "He'll end up with 'Lovin' You.'"

"You seen the show before?"

She shakes her head. "Not this one. But they're all about the same. Save the biggest one for the last encore. I always figure that's how they guarantee the curtain calls, by holding out the big one."

"I guess that's just about the way it all works."

When Tommy has finished his last encore with "Lovin' You," Bad wanders over to the next dressing room. It is already packed. Cans of beer shoot up from the corner of the room like mortar shells into the crowd of people. He finds Tommy in the corner, changing his shirt.

"You're pissed because I cut in on your set."

"No," Bad says, "I'm not pissed at all. Thanks."

"You were welcome in mine. I would have appreciated it."

"I figured you had it covered. I had albums to sell."

"Goddamn it. Why are you busting my hump, Bad?

What exactly is my fault here? What the hell do you want from me?"

"An album. Nothing more. I ain't asking for a damn thing. You did real well on the last one."

"I told you, you got the album. But you've got it when J.M.I. says they're ready for it. I can't do a damn thing about it."

"Then I don't want anything. Except to say thanks and good night."

"Damn it, Bad. I'm trying to be friends here. Stick around. Tomorrow's a rest day. We'll probably have a pretty good party here. There's booze, there's girls, somebody's got some pretty good blow around here. Get off your fucking high horse. Stick around and have some fun."

"I've got to drive tomorrow. I'm playing Utah tomorrow night. I believe I'll get my gear and go back to the hotel."

"Shit. Suit yourself. Ralphie's around here somewhere. Check with him. He'll take care of you."

"Right. Well, take care of yourself, Tommy."

"You, too, Bad. I'll be in touch on the album."

Bad starts to work his way through the jam of people. A couple slap him on the back and say, "Good show."

"Bad." Tommy is behind him, still shirtless. "Write me a couple of songs."

"Think you can walk through one without all the damn horns and strings?"

"I might manage."

"I'll see what I can do."   . . .

He is on his way out the back of the coliseum, carrying his guitar and amp, heading toward the parking lot.

"You packing it in for the night?" It is Linda, sitting on an amp crate, smoking a cigarette.

"I believe I've pretty well had it for tonight."

"You want some company?"

"You don't want to stick around for the big party?"

"They're all pretty predictable, too."

"Come on."

In the hotel room she lights a cigarette, takes one long drag, sets it in the ashtray and begins to undress. When she is naked, she takes up the cigarette, takes another drag, sets it back down, and steps up to and begins undressing him. When she has his clothes off, she gently pushes him back to the bed, sets him down and kneels down to his cock.

He runs his fingers down her neck and back, as far as he can reach, fingering the red marks left by her underwear. She raises her arms a little so he can get to her breasts. Her body is lean and young, her skin rich and smooth, nearly white where her bathing suit has blocked the sun. Her breasts are small and firm. It has been years since he has touched a body like this, unlined, unscarred, not dimpled with fat.

The smoothness of her skin makes him conscious of his own body, the sagging belly and hairy breasts, nearly as large as hers, the sweat chilling under the air-conditioning. Under the semicircles of her buttocks, he can see the bottoms of her feet, the pink toes, and next to them, his own, white as death, his toes twisted and callused from years of wearing cowboy boots. She is methodical, urging and coaxing him on, running her fingernails gently over the skin of his inner thighs.

He leans forward, trying to get his face into her red hair, but as he leans, his belly forces her head back, her teeth scraping him. She gently pushes him back. What, he wonders, does someone as young as this, with a body like this, want with someone like him?

Later, when she is asleep, the covers pulled up to her chin, her hair splayed over her face, he eases out of bed, lights a cigarette and moves to turn out the light. He stops to look at her. She is probably twenty-five, if she is that old. He can't remember how long it has been since he has held someone this young. He may never hold another. And beyond that, the other thought, that he misses Jean, scar, lines and fat. Given the choice, he guesses, he would trade.

Chapter Nine

He has four hours to kill before the show. He turns on the television. A thin man in a striped apron is pounding a piece of veal between pieces of plastic. "You want a larger portion? Just pound it longer." He turns off the television.

He sits down with his guitar. He begins chording through the standard progression in E, hoping he will find a note here that will lead him to something. "Home cooking," he thinks. There might be something there. He runs the scale a couple of times. Home cooking and home loving. Getting fat is like getting loved. He goes to the relative minor. There is something here, he is sure of it. He is also sure he doesn't have the patience to go through all the crap he is going to have to wade through to find it.

He puts down the guitar and picks up the telephone. It is not until the desk clerk answers that he knows exactly what he is going to do. "Long distance, please. Information."

"What city?" the operator asks.

"Santa Fe. New Mexico."

It never occurred to him to get her phone number, and now he realizes that it may be unlisted. By the time this has settled in, the operator is back on the line, giving him the number.

"Hello," a small voice says.

"Buddy, this is Bad, your old buddy."

"Buddy."

"Right. How are you doing, Buddy?"

"Watching Big Bird."

"How's Big Bird?"

"He talked to the policeman."

"That's good. Do you know the policeman is your friend?"

"Yeah."

"That's good, too. Is your mom there?"

"Yeah."

"Will you go get her so I can talk to her? Then you can go back and see what old Big Bird is up to."

The line goes dead for a few seconds, then Jean's voice.

"This is Bad."

"Bad?"

"Yeah. It's Bad. How are you?"

"Where are you?"

"Utah. Cedar City."

"What . . . ? I mean, I'm sorry, Bad. I didn't expect to hear from you. You caught me by surprise."

"Yeah, me too, as a matter of fact. I was thinking about you. I just decided to call."

"How was Phoenix? How was the show? And Tommy Sweet?"

"It was O.K. It was a show. It was nothing special."

"You and Tommy get along all right?"

"We had some drinks, talked. We're going to do an album, but I don't know when."

"That's nice."

"I've been thinking about you lately."

"Lately? It's only been a couple of days."

"Yeah, but damned funny thing, it seems long, I mean since I saw you. I've been thinking of you since."

"It was nice."

"You think any about me?"

"A lot. I've been finishing the article."

"That's not what I meant."

"I know. I'm sorry. Yes. I've thought about you. I had a good time."

"Listen. I get off the road in another week. Then I have four days before I go back to Houston. I want to stop off in Santa Fe. I want to see you."

She pauses for a long time. "You could do that."

"Hell. You're not making this easy. You want me to stop by or not? You don't want me to, I won't."

She pauses again. "Yes. Yes, I guess I want you to."

"I guess I'll be stopping by in about eight days, then. On the ninth. I think I can be there by early evening."

"The ninth?"

"That's a Friday."

"Friday. That's good."

"Maybe we could take Buddy to the zoo or something. Is there a zoo in Santa Fe?"

"I'll look forward to it. We both will."

"Me, too. So I'll see you next Friday."

"I miss you."

When she has hung up the phone, he holds on to it for a moment. Say that once more, he whispers.

There are still a couple of hours until he has to get ready. He pulls on his boots and a shirt, and heads across the street to the bar. It is still fairly early in the afternoon, and the bar is quiet.

Bad walks to the back of the bar to check out the action at the pool table. There are three guys, two playing, one watching. They are playing straight eight ball, and they are playing respectably, calling their shots, making enough of them. The man in the plaid shirt is obviously the better of the two. He has a steady hand, and as Bad watches, he sees that he has enough knowledge of the game that he is setting up shots in advance and moving the game quickly. Bad walks over to the table and places a quarter on the rail, then goes through the rack until he finds a twenty-three-ounce cue that is pretty straight, not too worn at the tip. When the game is finished, he picks up his quarter, runs it and racks.

"We can play for drinks if you want," Plaid Shirt tells him. "Or not, it doesn't matter. But that's as high as we go here. It's a friendly game."

"That suits me just fine."

Plaid Shirt breaks and takes down three stripes before he misses. When he does, he doesn't leave much. Bad takes out his glasses, surveys the table and takes the hardest shot, working for position. "Three ball, off the cushion." The cue ball comes off the cushion slowly and nudges the three ball into the corner pocket, easing behind the twelve. The shot leaves him a straight shot at the six. He hits it low for backspin so the cue ball stops dead on impact, leaving him a line to the far end of the table. He sinks the four and the seven before he misses the one on a side carom.

Plaid Shirt takes two more before he misses. This time he mishits and leaves Bad a clear table. He runs it.

"Nice shooting," Plaid Shirt says. "What are you drinking?" Bad looks around at what the others are drinking. "One of those drafts will be just fine."

He takes the other two players easily. He hasn't played on the road, but at home he plays for five or six hours a week. When Plaid Shirt brings his beer, he sips at it, playing conservatively but pulling away from the others easily. He begins taking harder shots than necessary, just trying to play against himself since neither of these guys is providing any competition. When Plaid Shirt is up again, he gives Bad a tight smile and puts his quarter into the slot. "Is this going to hurt again?" he asks.

Bad smiles and breaks. He likes the sound of that. "Is this going to hurt again?" He could do something with that.

"Mr. Blake," Brenda says, "hold for Mr. Greene."

Suddenly the earpiece of the telephone oozes recorded music. Ten million strings play Dolly Parton. The business has gone to the dogs.

"Bad, how're you doing?"

"I'm not going to play another date, Jack. I'm off tomorrow night and that's it. No more, damn it. No more."

"Bad. Bad. No more. No problem, you're done after tomorrow night. I'm not going to overbook you. I want you to get some rest."

"Jack, if you found out your sister was turning five-dollar tricks, you'd overbook her."

"Cute, Bad. Remind me, next time I'll put you in a couple of comedy clubs."

"Might as well, the clown bands you've stuck me with."

"You ever tried to book bands in New Mexico?"

"New Mexico you did O.K. It was all the rest you fucked up."

"That's the first time you've ever admitted I did anything right. You're slipping, Bad."

"No. It's the first time you did anything right."

"Hell. That means I'm slipping. Anyway, I've got some news from Tommy. Apparently you actually did yourself some good for a change."

"Yeah, I refused to whip his ass at golf."

"Whatever you did, you did well. I got a check for twenty-five hundred for the albums you sold."

"You cocksucker."

"I know, Brenda told me."

"Bless her heart."

"Ditto. And I have a contract here, offering you a five-thousand-dollar advance for an album to be recorded at a future date, to be specified by the end of this calendar year. Plus another two thousand for first refusal rights to all songs written or cowritten by you over the next two years."

"Holy shit."

"Ditto."

"I'll sign for the album but not the songs."

"It's the same contract."

"X out the song part, and I'll sign."

"I don't think we can do that."

"Hell, you're a lawyer; of course we can do that."

"I mean, I think they did it this way to make it a package deal, take it or leave it."

"I'll leave it."

"The hell you'll leave it."

"I don't write songs, Jack."

"Of course you write songs. Almost half of your income over the last ten years has been off songs you wrote."

"Wrote, Jack, wrote. I don't write songs."

"According to this contract, you don't have to. All they are asking is first refusal rights."

"No dice. If I write another song, it's my song, not Tommy's."

"Bad, you don't have a label anymore. If you write a song, how are you going to record it?"

"I don't give a good goddamn whether I record it or not. If it's my song, it's my song. I'm not going to work for Tommy Sweet."

"All he's asking is the right to see everything you write.

It doesn't mean everything you write belongs to him. This is first right of refusal, not indentured servitude."

"I don't have dentures. They're my own teeth, they're my own songs."

"This is seventy-five hundred dollars. I believe you could use that kind of money."

"I'm working on a song, Jack. I want it for myself."

"So we'll negotiate it with Tommy. I'm sending the contract to Houston. Sign it."

"You sign it. You've got power of attorney. At least sign the damn thing for me."

"Right. Think about this, Bad. Tommy has just kicked in nine grand in the last two weeks. Maybe you could ease up on him."

"He's a bastard with a nice checkbook."

"Have it your way, but this is now your best year in the last seven. Brenda has some messages for you. Get some rest and I'll talk to you when you're back home."

"Right."

There is a pause, a couple more bars of market music, then Brenda's voice. "Mr. Blake. You've had a few phone calls. Let me give you the numbers."

"Did you really give Jack my message?"

She laughs, "It was a bad day. I gave it to him word for word."

"You sweet thing."

"It was my pleasure. You ready for these numbers? Terry

in Houston wants you to call him right away, he says you have his number."

"Right."

"Then there is a message from a Mr. Wilks in Dallas; his number is—"

"I don't know Mr. Wilks. Who is he?"

"I don't know; he just wants you to call."

"It's somebody who wants something, an interview or to listen to his new song. Can it."

"You've got it. You have a good trip home."

"I believe I will. I do believe I will. Wait, Brenda, hold on a second. What's a nice perfume?"

"For who?"

"For a woman. What would you want someone to give you?"

"Serious or just fooling around?"

"Maybe serious."

"I like Opium. It's expensive, though."

"That's O.K. Tell Jack to wire me some money this afternoon."

The perfume is the easy part. That only takes a good portion of his cash. By his reckoning, it would cost about five hundred to get even the beginnings of a buzz off it. The hard part happens in the toy store. He has not been in a toy store in over twenty years. The last time he was in one, it was small and filled with dolls, cap guns, balls and bats, games and stuffed toys. This one has all of those plus computers, tape recorders and stuff he can't even recognize. The salesman points out the favorite toys: Gobots, Transformers, He-Man, G.I. Joe, Star Wars or Rambo. What it all comes down to, no matter how many guns, knives, bows and arrows, or muscles, is dolls. He considers a plastic guitar, but toy instruments seem wrong to him. He ends up with a riding fire engine and a foam basketball with a hoop that hangs over a closet door.

When he has finished the final set, shaken hands with the people who have stayed for last call, packed up his equipment and said goodbye to the band, he is tempted to get in the van and head out of Utah. He has about six hundred and fifty miles to drive. If he left now, he would end up in Santa Fe about two o'clock in the afternoon. He has told her early evening. He goes back to the motel and leaves a wake-up call for five o'clock. That will give him a little over three hours of sleep.

By noon he knows he has chosen the worst route. He has driven more vertical miles than horizontal. As soon as he hits a stretch of straight level road, the brush at the roadside grows coarse and dense. The van starts to knock in third, and he is climbing again. He tries to calculate the hours it will take to drive another three hundred miles in second gear.

He is weary of scenery, and his legs are starting to cramp. In the last six weeks he has driven three thousand miles, most of it on three or four hours' sleep. He drives straight through, stopping only for gas and coffee. Food he buys at drive-ins where he does not have to get out of the van or even stop the engine.

Near the New Mexico border he stops for gas in a small station and gets the mileage to Santa Fe. Inside the station, a mongrel dog, part shepherd, raises his head and wags his tail. "Nice dog," Bad says to the guy who is charging his gas.

"Damn good dog," the guy says. "He might not look like much, but he's a goddamn killer. He likes you. Course, you're white. Let a goddamn nigger or Indian come in, and you'd better believe it's a different story."

The dog wags his tail. The guy comes around the counter and takes a swiping kick at the dog, who jumps back and bares his fangs. "You was a nigger, he'd tear your throat out. That's a good dog. He hates niggers and Indians."

The dog is backed into the corner of the wall and counter, his fangs still bared, watching the owner. "I don't know about that," Bad says. "Looks like a good judge of character to me."

"He hates niggers. I got him for my wife. A damn nigger comes around her, that dog'll kill him."

"Must be a big disappointment to your wife."

"Yeah. What? Hell no. My old woman's a good woman. She hates niggers and Indians."

"If she is a good woman, I'd get me a pack of those dogs if I was you."

"Hey, what the hell are you sayin'? You sayin' my old woman's got a taste for niggers? That what you're sayin'? You get back here."

As he climbs into the van, the dog follows him out. "You poor son-of-a-bitch," Bad says.

As he drives, images from a dream come back to him, a dream that never got finished but was cut off by the wake-up call. He is in a small bar, not one he has played before but one that might be all the bars he has played before. He cannot quiet the crowd, who keep getting up from their seats, heading for the door and coming back in again. He has this new song, and he is going to sing it for them, but only if they won't tell anybody what it is. If he can get them to stay in their seats, Tommy won't find out about it. "You have to be real quiet now," he tells them. Half of them get up from their seats and head for the door, where Tommy is waiting. He keeps tuning the guitar and trying to hold the song in. Before he can sing it for them, the phone rings.

The song he was about to sing is called "Is This Going to Hurt Again?" As he drives, he works with the one line, trying others with it. That line is a chorus, he figures. He tries it as a first line, putting it to the melody of the fragment he came up with between Colorado and New Mexico: "Is this going to hurt again? / I can't take any more / Long, lonely nights, walking the floor." Then he tries: "I can't take any more / Of saying goodbye, and slamming the door." And other fragments: "I think about love every now and then / But then I stop and ask myself / Is this going to hurt again?"

What he needs is a guitar. If he could hear the music, test the possibilities on the guitar, he could find his way through

this. Once he has a line or two, the phrasing of the music always suggests the rest of the lines. Trying to sing the song
and invent the words at the same time is like trying to paint
a wall as you're building it. He has always believed that he
never wrote songs anyway, he just copied down songs that
already existed somewhere in his mind.

He has the feeling that if he stopped, he could do most of
the song in about a half hour. But it is nearly sundown and
he's still a hundred and fifty miles or so from Santa Fe. The
light is failing, he is sleepy and his back is beginning to stiffen
on him. He keeps shifting position to try to put the pressure
on different muscles. If he shifts to his right and pushes forward on the seat, he can stretch the cramping muscles, but he
keeps slipping back. Finally, he hooks his left foot under the
brace of the seat and lets the angle of his leg hold him in the
position he wants.

He keeps working those phrases again, trying to hear
the melody, the phrases that move it from verse to chorus in
the attempt to work backward into the song. From what he
knows, he tries to build an intro. A quick run from E to A to
B^7 and backward through A to E. He tries tuning the guitar,
hearing the notes and running a quick E scale. "You'll have
to be real quiet," he tells them. "I can't sing this song unless
you're real quiet, stay in your seats and promise not to tell
anyone what I have done." But they don't stay quiet and they
don't stay in their seats. He keeps tuning, but they won't settle
down. He keeps looking toward the door.

He hears the crunch of the tires on gravel and then an

easy thump. He sees grass and brush and a wire fence coming at him in slow motion. He moves his foot to the brake and turns the wheel, but he is moving in slow motion, too, and the van is bouncing across the scrub brush at the side of the road, rocking slowly from side to side, over the fence. He hears the wire of the fence scraping the side of the van and pulling brush with it until the tree is in front of him. He turns the wheel as hard as he can, but the impact sends him across the wheel and into the windshield.

For a minute, he does not know where he is or why he is sitting here. His head is cold and his hand hurts. He sees his hat on the floor next to him in a pile of sheet music and a Styrofoam hamburger box. Around him, everything is wet and sticky. He bends over to pull his hat away from the mess of paper and spilled Coke, and pain blooms in front of his eyes like a Chinese firecracker. Things spin and the world implodes.

When he comes to again, his leg feels like it is strung with hot wires from ankle to hip. He tries to move it, and pain sends hamburger and bile burning up his throat. He eases himself back upright. Now his head is beginning to throb. He checks his face in the rearview mirror. He has a bump and a small cut across the top of his forehead. There is a thin trickle of blood in a winding stream down to his eyebrow.

What worries him is his leg. He can see that his foot is still hooked behind the seat brace. He tenderly runs his hands down the calf of his leg, over the tops of his boot until they reach his ankle. Slowly, gently, he pulls at the ankle to free his foot. A wave of cold splashes up from inside him and the inside of the van darkens to black.

"You O.K.?"

There is a hand on his shoulder, and a face at the window of the van.

"You O.K.?"

Bad leans his head back against the top of the seat and slowly nods his head. "Yeah, I'm O.K. Accident. Fell asleep."

"Can you get out?" The man opens the door of the van slowly, holding on to Bad's shoulder with his other hand.

"My leg. I think I broke my leg."

"Try to get out. Grab on to me."

The man, Bad is aware, is much smaller than he is, but when the door is open and he has turned around in the seat so he is facing the door, the man's hands grip him hard under the arms and lift him from the seat. Bad reaches out, and puts his arm around the man's shoulder. They do a slow, intricate waltz out of the van, lean up against it, and then spin heavily across the grass to where a pickup truck idles, its taillights flashing red.

"It doesn't look too bad," the man says when he comes back to the truck. "Crunched your right fender, busted a headlight. You got a flat tire. Not too bad. And you got about twenty yards of fence, too." He hands Bad the keys. "I locked it." He starts the truck.

Bad hears the crunch of gravel under the tires as the truck noses out onto the road. "Wait," he says. "Wait. My guitar."

When the man comes back with the guitar, Bad remembers. "Fire truck, get the fire truck, too."

"Ain't no fire, buddy. It's all O.K."

He wants to explain about Buddy's fire truck, to go back and get it, but he feels too tired to speak.

He rides huddled against the door, shivering, trying not to move. His ankle has begun to throb. The man keeps poking him in the shoulder.

"You got a bump on your head. You might have a concussion. I don't think you should sleep. Talk to me. You a musician?"

"Yeah."

"What kind?"

"Guitar."

"I know that. Come on, talk to me. What kind of music do you play?"

"Country."

"Yeah? You know Kenny Rogers? I really like him. You know 'Lucille'? Come on, sing it with me."

"My ankle," Bad says.

"'You picked a fine time to leave me, Lucille,'" the man croaks. "Come on, 'With four hungry kids and a crop in the field.' Come on, you know it."

Bad tries to mumble a harmony behind him.

The hospital is light and full of angles that spin past him. Every time he looks up, lights shine in his eyes. He closes them tight and Tommy is there with golf clubs, asking him if he wants a drink. He reaches for the bottle and Tommy pulls it away and laughs a sharp, brittle laugh. As Tommy laughs, he runs his hands through his hair, drawing his ears out to long red points. He runs a hand across his face and pulls it sharp and covered with red fur. His nose is small and black above the long red whiskers. His tongue lolls over the rows of small white pointed teeth. The yellow eyes shine and dart. His upper lip wrinkles and pulls up away from the little teeth. Tommy darts forward, sinking his teeth into Bad's ankle. Then he runs, skittering across the tile floor of the hospital and under the root of a tree and gone.

Chapter Ten

When he wakes he is in bed, but he is not sure where. The vertical blinds, the bed rails, the curtain, slowly come into focus. He is in the hospital, he knows that. He has had an accident. There is someone in another bed, next to him.

"Where am I?" he asks.

"Hospital," the man answers. "You got a busted ankle. They brought you in late last night. You were gone, man."

"Where? Where are we?"

"Taos. That what you mean? You want a nurse? I can call one for you."

Nurses are in and out all morning. He is questioned and poked. He drifts in and out of dreamless sleep, waking to thermometers, needles to the inside of the elbow, and the puffing sleeve of the sphygmomanometer. "Where am I?" he keeps asking them. "The hospital," they assure him confidently.

When he remains awake, he checks the damage. There is a bandage on his forehead and a plaster cast on his left ankle, about as long as the shaft of a good boot. His neck, shoulders and back are all sore and tight. He has pain, but more, he has questions: what is wrong with him, where is he, where is his guitar, where is his van, and when can he get out of here?

"I'll call the nurse again," the guy in the next bed says, "if you can stay awake long enough to talk to her."

"Call," he says. His throat is parched and his lips are cracking.

"Simple fracture of the fibula," she tells him. "Broken ankle. A minor concussion. You are in the hospital, Taos, New Mexico; your guitar is in the closet with your clothes. About your van, you'll have to contact the New Mexico Department of Public Safety, and when you can leave is up to the doctor."

"Soon?" he asks.

"Probably."

"Today?"

"Probably not."

"Get me the doctor."

"If you can make it down the hall, you can call from the pay phone, it's cheaper," the guy in the next bed advises.

Bad considers the white cocoon around his ankle and the pain that seems to squeeze up out of it and spiral up his leg. He calls the DPS from the phone beside the bed.

After he is forced to spell out his name, his whole name, his legal name, over the phone, he is told his van is at the impound lot in Taos. He needs proof of insurance, and two hundred sixty-eight dollars to cover impound fees and forty yards of wire-mesh fence and six fence posts, plus labor. He is also being cited for Failure to Control Vehicle. He gives them Jack's phone number.

The doctor, the nurse tells him, will be in to see him before long. In the meantime, she wants to know what kind of medication he is taking for his blood pressure.

"None," he says. "An occasional whiskey. But only once in a while."

"Terrific," she says. "Your blood pressure is one eighty-five over ninety-five."

"That's not good, huh?"

"That's not real good."

"I could drink a couple more, I guess."

The problem, the doctor explains, is not really the ankle. It's a pretty clean break and should heal without undue complication, though at his age, who really knows? He will have to stay off it for at least six weeks, but he can leave in the morning. The problem, as the doctor sees it, is his general condition, or lack of condition. His blood pressure is way too high, his heart has a fairly pronounced arrhythmia, and there is considerable chest congestion. And from the responses he gave the nurse earlier in the morning, it is clear that his drinking and smoking have slipped to something beyond excess.

"I was still asleep then," Bad says. "I didn't know what I was saying. If I'd been awake, I would have lied. Then we'd both be happier."

The doctor is young and sweet-looking. He has short brown hair, a neatly trimmed beard and wire-rim glasses. He wears a western shirt and a bolo tie below the open collar. He wears corduroy jeans, and Bad knows that he wears rounded shoes with crepe soles. He is sincere, and sincerely trying to be kind. But Bad figures that anyone who is willing to stick two fingers up your ass and poke around like that enjoys his work. The pretense of kindness doesn't go very far.

The real problem, the doctor tells him, is not that he is going to die. That's not a problem, that's a simple fact. The real problem is that he probably is not going to die for quite a while yet. Bad does not consider this a serious problem.

"Let me explain it to you this way," the doctor begins. "If it was simply a matter of life expectancy, you might decide that it is worth the gamble. You go on living the way you are, the way you seem to think you want to live, and then in a couple of years, four or five angels lift you up into heaven with a lot of harp music in the background. That would be great. You've paid your money, you've taken your choice. You've traded ten or twenty years of your life for the right to live any damn way you choose. Good enough. The only thing is, it doesn't work that way. The kinds of stuff we're talking about here—emphysema, congestive heart failure, cancer, an extremely good chance of stroke—are more debilitating than quickly and cleanly fatal. They will kill you, there's no mistaking that, but they're going to do it slowly, painfully, and humiliatingly. You're going to end up helpless as a child, in all probability.

"Mr. Blake, are you going to talk to me?"

"About what?"

"Look, Mr. Blake, I have other patients to see. Obviously, you don't want to hear any of this. You've got a broken ankle, you want to go home. I understand that. But when I see something like this, I have to say something. You don't want to hear it, and I don't particularly want to say it, but I've got to. You come in here from an auto accident; after I set your ankle, I find a fifty-six-year-old man who is rapidly starting to wear out. You smoke two packs of unfiltered cigarettes a day; you are a good thirty pounds overweight; your blood pressure is way too high; you obviously get no exercise; you clearly eat anything at all; and let's not kid ourselves about this one: you're an alcoholic.

"What you want is to get rid of the pain in your ankle and get out of here, then you'll feel better. But don't you see you're not going to feel much better, even without the pain? I'm telling you: stop smoking, stop drinking, lose twenty-five pounds. You do that, you'll feel better. I can make recommendations for ways to do that. Your own doctor can help you. But that's what you've got to do. It's your choice, but you don't have any real options. In the meantime, stay off the leg."

"He didn't give you cholesterol and salt," the guy in the next bed says. "That comes next. Give up all that, and then it's cholesterol and salt. It's always something."

"I'd give up cholesterol and salt and kiss his ass for a drink," Bad says.

· · ·

"Bad, where are you?" He tries to gauge the distance in her voice.

"Taos," he says.

"Taos? I waited up most of the night for you. I thought you were going to be here last night."

"I'm in the hospital."

"Oh, my God."

"I had an accident. I'm sorry. I broke my ankle. I wasn't drinking. I just had an accident."

"Are you O.K.?"

"Well, no. I broke my ankle."

"Oh jeez, I'm sorry."

"No, look. I'm sorry. I was about an hour and a half out of Santa Fe last night and I fell asleep. It was my own damn fault. And it's not all that bad. I get out of here in the morning."

"Are you still going to come here?"

"If I can. If it's all right with you."

"I'll come and get you."

"I can drive. My van's O.K. as far as I can tell."

"I'll come and get you. I'll take the bus in the morning."

"You really don't have to."

"I'm coming. I want to."

"That's wonderful."

He likes getting pushed down the hall in the wheelchair, his left leg stuck out in front like a cowcatcher. He is still in his gown, but he has his hat, stained at the brim from the spilled

Coca-Cola. He nods and smiles to the people he passes. In 1963, he rode in the Rose Bowl Parade, two cars behind the grand marshal. This is oddly similar.

In the physical therapy room, he is held up by two orderlies, while he is measured and crutches are adjusted for him. The crutches are not as easy as they look. He keeps dropping down and catching his armpits on the braces. He is having trouble getting the rhythm of swinging the heavy cast ahead of him as he goes. He stops and sits on the therapy table. "Shit," he says. "This would be a hell of a lot easier if I had a drink."

"Walk ten times across the room," the therapist says.

"Hell, I can't walk that three times, much less ten."

"O.K.," the therapist says, "we'll send the chair back. You can walk back to your room with your butt hanging out. One way or another, you'll learn to use those."

Bad slides off the table and starts swinging himself across the room.

When she arrives, he has been sitting in the wheelchair for an hour and a half, ready to go. He has dressed in the clothes he was wearing when he had the accident. The left leg of his jeans is slit up to the knee. He has his guitar and left boot on his lap.

"I'll only stay a day or so, then I'll head back to Houston," he tells her in the taxi on the way to the impound yard. "You don't need some old gimp hanging around being a bother."

"Nonsense. You won't be a bother."

"If I'm as good at being laid up as I think I'm going to be, I'll be a hell of a bother."

The van is worse than he has expected. It's drivable, but the right front fender is smashed and there is a small crack at the lower corner of the windshield. The bumper is twisted on the right, and the grille is pushed in. The headlight is gone, and there are long scratches down both sides, where he has dragged the fence along with him. It looks like three or four hundred dollars' worth of damage.

The impound bill has been taken care of out of Jack's office. He has to sign release forms and a citation for Failure to Control Vehicle. He has a court date in two weeks to answer the charge.

"Can I just pay this?" he asks.

"Call the district court," the trooper tells him. "They'll take a plea over the phone and assess the fine. You better get that headlight fixed right away. The second you are off this lot, you are in violation. You could pick up another citation for Faulty Equipment."

"Jesus, Lord. You aren't going to pull that kind of shit on me, are you?"

"I'm here at this desk. I'm not going to cite anyone. I can't speak for anyone else, though. I'd get it fixed right away."

"Yeah. Damn. I'll get right to it." He swings away from the desk on his crutches, holding himself stiff with his forearms, careful of his already tender armpits. "I got a flat tire there. Anyone here to change it for me?"

"I'm sorry, sir, we're not staffed to take care of those items."

"I'll pay."

"Sorry, sir. No can do."

"I'll do it," Jean says. "Don't worry about it."

"Mr. Blake," the trooper calls, "it was nice to meet you. I've always liked your songs."

"Khaki bastard," he says to Jean when they are out the door.

"That was sort of nice. I mean, to say he likes your songs."

"My ex-wives all liked my songs, too. They tried to cut my heart out. There isn't anything as treacherous as a fan."

Jean jacks up the van and pulls the bad tire and wheel with little difficulty. Bad hobbles around her, looking for something to do. He keeps fluttering his hands and saying, "Hell, you shouldn't be doing this." She gets the spare, mounts it and runs the lug nuts tight.

"Is there anything you need?" she asks as she wheels the van into the street. "Did you have breakfast?"

"Yeah. I had something in the hospital."

"What did you have?"

"Food. That was as close as I could identify it. What time is it?"

"Quarter after eleven."

"Could we stop for a drink?"

"Isn't it a little early for that?"

"Depends on how you look at it. To me, it looks like about two days late."

"Can't you wait until we get to Santa Fe?"

He is trying to light a cigarette, his hand shaking so hard he has to brace it with the other. "I don't think so."

He is flat on his back in Jean's bed. His foot is propped up on two cushions from the sofa in the living room. Both of the pillows from the bed are behind his head. On the table beside him are his cigarettes and a bottle of Jack Daniel's. At the foot of the bed is the television, wheeled in from the living room. On the television, lives tangle and knot into ruin. He can hear Jean moving through the other rooms.

On the television, two women talk. One fights back tears. The other keeps talking, hesitates, then turns and leaves. In the hall, beyond the door, she stops. "She needs someone to talk to," she says to no one Bad can see. She moves back to the door. Talk, Bad thinks, is not what she needs. She's going to need someone to walk to. He repeats that. Then he throws back the covers and slips out of bed. He hops to the other side of the room, where his guitar is propped against the chair.

It comes as easily to him as an old song recalled after years, in E flat: "She's going to need someone to walk to, / When she walks out on you. / She's going to need someone to talk to, / When she finally says she's through." It slips like grease on a skillet from E flat to A flat, back to E flat and up to B flat.

He calls Jean in and sings it for her. "She's going to need someone to walk to, / And it's going to be me instead of you."

"You know that song?" he asks.

"I think so," she says. "I'm sure I've heard it."

"Yeah," he says, "that's the way it is. The good ones are the ones you're sure you've heard before. That's the next hit for Tommy Sweet."

"You wrote that?"

"Just now. Just fifteen minutes ago. I'm afraid that's going to be about all I'm going to be good for for a little while here."

"No," she says, slipping back the covers. "That's not why you're here."

"So how the hell did this happen?" Jack asks.

"I fell asleep. I'd been driving for fifteen hours."

"Drinking?"

"No. Goddamn it, no. I fell asleep."

"O.K., O.K. What are you doing in Santa Fe?"

"Visiting a friend."

"Friend?"

"A friend. People who aren't so goddamned suspicious have them."

"You have any idea how much your marriages have cost you over the years? You've spent more on alimony than some folks make in their whole lives."

"I ain't marrying anybody. I'm visiting my friend."

"When are you going to be back in Houston?"

"In a couple of days. Terry is auditioning new bass players. I'll be back in time to get started. It wouldn't go any faster with me there."

"O.K. Have Brenda give you the insurance policy number.

Call the office and get them working on getting the van fixed. Can you drive?"

"Yeah. I can drive. I will drive. I'll be there by the first of the week."

"Take care of yourself, Bad."

"I wasn't drinking."

Jean comes into the room with two cups of coffee. "You want me to call him?"

"Why?"

"To tell him that I'm not about to marry you."

"You might have waited until I asked before you turned me down."

"Oh God, don't even joke."

"I'm not all that bad. They weren't all my fault. I think it was Kay Starr said, on the occasion of her fifth or sixth divorce, 'I guess it can't always be the guy's fault.' I've taken a lot of comfort from that."

"No, you're not bad at all, but I think you've missed the point there somehow."

"No. I just got a different one than she intended. I mean, it wasn't always my fault. I finally figured that one out. Most of them were, but not all of them."

She puts the coffee cups down and sits on the bed with him, pulling his head into her lap. "You worry about that a lot, don't you?"

"I got a twenty-four-year-old son. I haven't seen him since he was four. I don't know what he looks like. I don't know what he's doing. I don't know how he did in school. I don't know if he played baseball or had trouble with geography. I didn't see him ride his bike or teach him how to drive a car. I think about that a lot. That's my fault, that's all my fault, and that's a hell of a goddamned price to pay. It's a hell of a thing to be fifty-six years old and not know a damned thing about your own son."

"I couldn't live if I lost Buddy."

"That's the goddamnedest part. You do live."

"Why didn't you find them after they left?" They are sitting propped up in the bed, naked. He is smoking. She toys with sweated strands of hair at the back of his neck.

"I tried. I tracked her down to L.A. Even in L.A. she kept moving around. She knew I'd be following her. Then the record company got involved. They convinced me that I had to give up. I guess they were still thinking about Spade Cooley and all of that. Anyway, they told me it was either keep chasing them down or keep making records and money. Records and money seemed real important then."

"Who's Spade Cooley?"

"Spade Cooley was one of the best bandleaders in western swing. Maybe he was the best. All during the forties, he and Bob Wills were always about neck and neck. He wrote the song 'Shame on You.' It was really top-notch stuff. Anyway, in about nineteen sixty, sixty-one, he got the idea that his wife was cheating on him. That she was having an affair with Roy Rogers, as a matter of fact. So he killed her. Only it was worse than that. He got his little girl out of bed and took her into the living room and told her he was going to stomp her mother to death, and she was going to watch. Then he did it. He stomped her to death.

"It made the guys in the suits real nervous. I mean, this was a guy who was like you or me, and suddenly he snaps and beats his wife to death. So when they found out they had a two-hundred-and-twenty-pound drunk running around L.A., looking for the wife that had run out on him, they got pretty worried. They sent three guys after me. I woke up in a sanitarium, where they were supposed to be drying me out. First two days, I was in a straitjacket; after that, every time I woke up I took another needle in the ass. I didn't wake up for days."

"They locked you up?"

"It's true. I was worth a lot of money to them. Things were a lot different then. I mean, we all know about George Jones and his drinking, and people love it. But back then, they wouldn't let anything like that get out. I mean, when Hank Williams died, they got the official death certificate to read 'heart attack.' We all knew what killed him, but they didn't let stuff like that out.

"So Marge got smart. When she took off, she went to L.A. and went right to the boys in the suits. She convinced them that I was going to kill or at least beat her when I got to L.A. She let them know that if they didn't want another Spade Cooley on their hands, they better protect her from me. And the sort of reputation I had been building up went a long way to back her story.

"When they finally let me out, they gave me the word. I got the hell out of L.A. and didn't cause any more trouble, or I was back in the ward again. I don't scare real easy, but that scared the piss out of me. Those boys knew where the button was and how to push it.

"Anyway, I lost track of Marge and Steve. I got the divorce papers from the record company. By the time things had loosened up, it was all too late. I guess they're still in L.A., but I don't know."

"You could probably find them. I mean, if you looked."

"What the hell am I going to say? 'Hi, how you doing? What's been going on the last twenty years?' No. They don't need to see me now. They were better off without me, and I guess they still are. Marge was a good woman with a good head on her shoulders. They did all right. I'm sure of that."

"You could find them for your sake. Don't you think they owe something to you?"

"No. She was right. Marge was right to do what she did. I was a rotten father and a worse husband. They really were better off without me. Maybe that's what I would tell her, that she was right."

"No. I don't think so. I think you deserve better."

"I didn't. I'm not sure I do now, but I know I didn't then. There was the drinking, and there were pills, too. And I was on the road all the time. I mean, I couldn't stand being home for very long. There were no lights, no one applauded. That was out on the road, that and lots of women, lots of good times. I just figured that was all mine, I mean I had it coming, and a wife and a baby shouldn't change what was rightfully mine, and goddamn it, I didn't let it."

"Look. I won't even pretend I understand how someone could let a child go. And I think you owe it to both of you to try to find him again. Don't let what you've done stop you from being what you are."

"Most of my life anyway, that's been being a son-of-a-bitch."

"Well, I like you. I won't marry you, but I like you."

"If there's one thing in the world better than a pretty girl, it's a pretty girl who's gullible."

"If there's one thing better than a good man, it's a good man who's too crippled up to get away," she says, nestling up against him.

"You're welcome to break the other ankle."

In the morning, he is up before she is. The road has changed his rhythms. He wakes ready to get into the van and drive on to the next stop. He tries to be quiet, but as he swings his legs out of the bed, the cast on his left ankle clunks heavily on the floor. He bites his lip against the pain. Jean stirs but doesn't wake.

His crutches are across the room, leaning against the dresser. He stands, weight on his right leg. Slowly, he shifts it to his left. He is able to transfer only part of it before the pain flashes up from the ankle to the pit of his stomach. He shifts back to the right leg. He tries to calculate the furniture's strength to see if he can move from piece to piece across the room. Most of it is wicker. He sinks to his knees and crawls across the floor on hands and knees.

When he reaches the dresser, he gets the crutches and moves the five feet to the wicker hamper where she has draped his pants. He gets the left leg on, snaking the pants over the cast. Then he realizes that to get the right leg on, he will have to rest his weight on his left leg. He maneuvers back to the hamper and tests it with his weight. It seems sturdy enough. By sitting gingerly on it, he can work his right foot into the pants leg and start working the pants on. When he pulls them up, though, the cuff is still caught under his foot. He shifts his weight to the center of the hamper and lifts up his foot. When his foot clears the floor, his weight shifts backward, the top of the hamper gives and he goes in, butt first.

"Jesus," Jean screams, sitting suddenly upright. Then, "Oh, my God, Bad, are you all right?"

He is on the floor, his left leg up, sticking out of the broken hamper, his right leg splayed out and resting on top of an aralia palm in a ceramic pot. His pants are caught around his knees.

"Tell me you're all right," Jean says. "Please God, tell me you're all right."

"Help me up," Bad says. "I'm goddamned all right. Help me up."

"Thank God you're all right," she says, " 'cause I'm going to bust something if I can't laugh. That's the funniest goddamned thing I've ever seen. Where's my camera?"

"Help me up, goddamn it."

Bad is trying to get out of the smashed hamper, and Jean is rolling in the bed, when Buddy walks in. He watches wide-eyed as Jean pulls the sheets up and Bad tries to wiggle his jeans up to his hips. He walks over to where Bad is on the floor and pulls the palm plant off Bad's foot. "Can we have pancakes?" he asks.

In the kitchen, Bad gives orders and Buddy fetches for him. "You like apples?" Bad asks. Yes, Buddy nods. "Get some apples, then. I'm going to teach you the right way to cook. Let's see, you're four?" Yes, Buddy nods. "You married yet?" No. "Then you better learn how to cook. You know how to cook, you don't have to live with some mean old witch just because she keeps you fed."

Bad peels, cores and slices apples, then dices them and sets them aside. He sends Buddy to the refrigerator for milk and eggs, to the cupboard for flour, oil and a skillet. He sets Buddy on the counter and mixes the batter, explaining every step. When he has beaten the batter smooth, he adds the diced apples. When he drops the batter into the hot skillet, he shows Buddy how to wait until bubbles form, first at the edges, then in the center, before flipping the pancakes.

"I've got to go down to the paper for a while this morning," Jean says at breakfast. "I'll drop Buddy off at the day care center. You want me to take you somewhere, or do you want to stay here?"

"I don't know what I could do with this ankle. I'm not much for libraries and museums. Why don't you leave Buddy here with me?"

"You don't want to babysit. Besides, Buddy will want to see his friends today."

"I want to stay here," Buddy says.

"There you go. We want to stay here."

"And do what?"

"Man stuff," Bad says.

"Man stuff," Buddy says.

"You play cards?" Bad asks when Jean is gone.

"No."

"You know any good fishing stories?"

"No."

"Then maybe we ought to go take a walk and see what kind of trouble we can get into."

"Yeah."

He has difficulty negotiating the steps down from Jean's apartment to the sidewalk, but by stopping often and leaning his weight on the railing, he learns how to work the heavy cast gently from step to step.

The apartment complex is made up of several two-story buildings, each containing eight apartments. To avoid a look of monotonous conformity, they have been set at oblique angles to each other. The sidewalk that connects them curves and angles off around buildings and landscaping. Buddy runs ahead, out of Bad's sight, and then comes running back when Bad doesn't catch up. They have been walking only about five minutes. Bad does not know exactly where they are, but Buddy keeps leading him on.

Finally, Bad turns a corner and finds himself in the playground. There are swings, teeter-totters, and lots of telephone poles cut in odd lengths and sunk into the ground. Bad can handle the swing, braced on his crutches and pushing Buddy with one hand, and he can, awkwardly, do much the same to keep Buddy going on the teeter-totter. What Buddy really wants to do is play on the telephone poles. Bad has a rush of panic. They look dangerous, full of sharp edges and splinters. Why the hell do they give kids such artsy-fartsy stuff, stuff that could bust their heads open in a second? He has visions of Buddy's small body bent and crumpled at the bottom of the log pile, smeared with blood. How could any creature be as delicate and fragile as a child? He thinks back to what he played on as a kid. Rocks, trees and farm machinery, vines, a creek and a wooden footbridge over the creek—a miracle that any of them lived through it.

When Buddy is through with the telephone poles, he pulls Bad over to the swimming pool.

"The concrete pond," Bad tells him. There are two women next to it, in bathing suits. "It's a concrete pond, and they've got the thing stocked."

While Buddy runs around the fence surrounding the pool, Bad chats with one of the women. She is young and friendly, and her skin glitters with drops of sweat. He tells her about his accident, about the tour. She tells him she is a student at the university, studying business administration. He watches a drop of sweat run from her collarbone, around the curve of her breast and under her swimsuit top. Become a booking agent, he tells her; there is a fortune to be made off other people's work. When Buddy wearies of running the fence, he comes back to Bad and they head for the apartment.

"Take good care of your grandpa," the girl says.

"Turn on the sound," Buddy says.

"No," Bad says, "it's better to watch it this way. We can make up our own story."

"She's bad," Buddy says of the woman in the red dress.

"How do you know that, Bud?"

"I can tell. She's a bad lady. She has funny eyes."

"I wish I could figure it out that easy. O.K. She's a bad lady. What are we going to do about her?"

"Shoot her," Buddy says.

"No. You can't do that. That's the code of the West. You can't shoot a lady. What should we do?"

"You tell."

"I suppose, if it was me, I'd marry her."

Buddy puts his hands over his face and begins to giggle.

"That would fix her little red wagon, right?"

"You're silly."

"I guess you got that right, little buddy."

"You didn't even put him down for a nap?" Jean asks later that evening. "Even the day care center makes him take naps."

"We were having a good time. If I made him take a nap, what would I have done? Who would I have played with?"

"He really likes you. It's amazing."

"It's not. I'm a good guy. He knows that. Kids can tell."

She curls into him on the sofa. On the television, Shane has traded in his guns to be a peaceful farmhand for Jean Arthur and Van Heflin. "That's bullshit," Jean says. "Maybe it's right bullshit this time, but it's still bullshit."

"What are you going to do?"

"When?"

"Anytime. From now on. What are you going to do from now on?"

"Write. It's what I do. I'm going to keep on doing it. What are you going to do?"

"There's only one thing I can do. But you've got a boy."

"That's right. And I'm doing O.K. He look underfed to you? Look, I ended up at thirty-four divorced and alone. I started writing, and I took care of myself writing. Then Buddy came along, and now I take care of both of us. I guess I can keep it up. Buddy and I are doing all right. There will be better jobs, better papers, magazines."

"But kids are expensive, and they get more expensive. They want clothes, cars and college."

"Hold it just a minute here. Are you suggesting that I need a man to help me, that I can't raise my own son? The only thing I really needed a man for is over and done with. I can do the rest quite well by myself, thank you."

"I'm not suggesting anything. I'm not going to give you

advice on how to run your life. I sure as hell didn't do so great with my own. I like you. I like Buddy. I was just wondering, maybe worrying a little. No harm meant."

"You want to do something for me, help me out?"

"What?"

"Hold me, touch me. That's what you can do. That's nice. It's been a while since I have really had someone to touch and touch me back. I miss that part. Help me out."

On the television, little Joey persuades Shane to bring out his guns, to teach him to shoot. Shane looks moody, regretful, but he brings out the guns. In the yard, he shows Joey how to wear them, not too low, but up on the hip so they come out cocked and ready. Then he draws both and sends a rock spinning across the yard, firing the six-guns with both hands.

Jean Arthur comes running into the yard, terrified of the gunfire, furious that Shane has shown little Joey how to use a gun. "A gun is just a tool," Shane says, "like any other. A gun is as good or bad as the man using it. Remember that."

"Remember that," Bad says.

"Why?"

"Damned if I know. He said it, not me."

Later, as Shane has strapped on the guns for real, ridden into town and killed Jack Palance and the rest of the outlaws, then ridden away, leaving little Joey behind, crying, Jean reaches up and touches Bad's face. "Is that the kind of crap you believe? That you're going to ride off and me and Buddy are going to stand here crying, wondering how we are going to live without you?"

"What the hell is that for? I just asked you a goddamned question."

"You're right," she says. "I'm sorry. It was stupid."

"Besides," Bad says, "every time I see this picture, I kind of figure I'm Joey, standing there watching him ride off."

"Can you tell me something?"

"About what?"

"The road. What keeps you going back?"

"I don't know. I guess I just like pissing in gas stations."

"I mean it. Why do you do it? Why have you done it all your life?"

"Well, it's my life, at least the only part of my life that makes any kind of sense. Musicians are like patent medicine sellers. They got to keep moving or folks are going to figure out what's going on. So you see, we really haven't got a choice. We do what we have to."

"Yeah, but you like it."

"Most of the time, anyway. I know what you're asking, and I'm trying not to answer mostly because I don't know. It's good on the road, I know that. Every night it's a different town, different folks, and they're always interested in what you're doing. Maybe you're tired of it, but they're not, and that keeps you interested. It's like starting over all the time."

"Like love?"

"Maybe. It's like part of the excitement of being with someone new. They're different, and you feel different. You get to tell about yourself and you come out a little better than you did the time before. You got a few more good things to say, and you get to leave out more of the bad stuff."

"It's like running away."

"I don't know. I haven't run away since I was seventeen."

"I know. I did a few years ago. It was exhilarating. I left my problems behind. I didn't care that there would be new ones; the old ones weren't my problem anymore."

"Yeah. I guess that's part of it. It's all about freedom, I guess, only don't ask me what that means. I don't know. It's a lot better and more complicated than 'nothing left to lose.' I know that much."

"Freedom doesn't last, though. It's not supposed to last. I was free when I left my ex, and that was good. But then I had Buddy, and that was even better. The best thing about freedom is that it doesn't last."

"On the road you got it both ways. You're free while you're out, and then you go back home. When that starts to chafe, you're back out again. It's the best of both."

"Or neither. You lost your home, your wife, your son. Maybe there is no best of both. Maybe you always have to choose."

"You never have to choose. Choices get made for you. What the hell started all this, anyway?"

"I was just thinking. I was thinking it must be nice just to climb into a car and take off and see new things and new people. But then I thought being here with Buddy is better. I guess I don't have what it takes."

"You're a good mom. I was a rotten dad."

"Come here to Momma."

The van looks better than it did before the accident. The fender and grille and headlight are new and the entire van has been re-painted. "Looks real good," Bad says as he signs the ticket.

"Yeah," the guy agrees. "It looks real good. It left about a half a quart of oil on my floor, though."

"What do you think?" he asks.

"Don't really know. My cousin's a mechanic, though. He could tell you. I can call him if you like."

"Come visit me," he says. "I'm booked in Houston for the next four months, Wednesday through Saturday, but you could come, and I could show you around. I'm off all day. I don't go to work until eight-thirty. That and rehearsals on Thursday afternoons. Otherwise, I have lots of time."

"That would be nice," she says, "but I have my work here, and there's Buddy."

"You could bring him along. He's no problem. I could take him down to NASA. He'd like that. He'd like all those rockets and things. Hell, I want to see it."

"We'll see."

"That means no."

"No. It means I'm not sure. Maybe. I'll try."

"There are newspapers and magazines in Houston. A bunch of them."

"That's more than a visit. We are talking about a visit. If I can get the time. If things work out."

"Well, you can visit the newspapers and magazines, too."

"Maybe we'd just better be Alan Ladd and Jean Arthur for a while here. You ride off, and I'll watch longingly and cry a little."

"She was in love with him."

"She was hot for his body."

"I don't think that's the way it was."

"You write country and western songs. You're a professional romantic."

"Women like those songs, too."

"Sure. But I'm a professional nonromantic."

"I'm going to miss you."

"I hope so."

Chapter Eleven

Nearing Houston, the landscape flattens and the humidity builds. His ankle throbs. He has tried to take it easy, stopping often, but at rest stops he has to swing clumsily along on the crutches. He goes a few yards, then has to sit down at one of the concrete picnic benches. Sitting there, he realizes that he might as well be back in the van, moving forward instead of sitting still. Worse yet are the rest rooms, which are treacherous, the floors slick with piss and spilled water. He has to test the crutch tip for purchase before he can take another step or rest his weight.

When he reaches the western outskirts of Houston on I-10, the traffic begins to crowd. It is eight o'clock at night, and still it is overcrowded and backed up with construction. For hours he has driven a nearly straight line, changing lanes only occasionally to pass a poky car. Now he is moving constantly from lane to lane to maintain something like a steady speed.

At the interchange to 45 North, downtown Houston is directly in front of him, vertical light. At night, the city is stunning. In the years he has been here, it has completely changed, gone straight up. There is a song he has heard of the city: "The buildings aren't constructed, / They erupt from the ground."

As he exits 45, he is nearly home, and the neighborhood is close and familiar, full of signs in Spanish: *Bodega, Taquería, Dos Hermanos*. This, at least, hasn't changed much. The streets are narrow and tree-lined. He has lived here for twelve years. After Judah, Indiana, he has lived here longer than anywhere else. The neighborhood feels close, intimate, but threatened. Old houses are being restored, painted, added to, decorated with gingerbread, glass and brass. The Mexicans and blacks are being slowly pushed out by young whites with suits, briefcases and BMWs. Front yards full of corn and chilis are being replaced by mowed lawns and brick driveways. The Mexicans next door sold out a couple of weeks before he left.

When he pulls into the driveway, Terry's Plymouth station wagon is parked there, and in the house the lights are on. He cuts the engine, gathers up his Dopp Kit and crutches, slams the door loudly, and thumps his way up the wooden porch. He unlocks the door and pushes, but it is stopped by the chain. "Terry," he yells, "it's me. I'm home." He hears thumping and rattling from the back of the house. He moves back down the steps and sits on the bottom one, lights a cigarette and waits.

The porch light comes on, the door opens and Terry sticks his head out. "Bad—hey, Bad. Welcome home. I'm glad to see you."

Bad struggles back to his feet. "I'm interrupting something?"

"Jeez, Bad." Terry steps out on the porch. He is wearing only jeans. "Let me help you. I heard about the accident from Jack. I'm really sorry."

"It's O.K. Do I need to smoke another cigarette?"

"I'm sorry, Bad. I really am. I thought you were coming back tomorrow night."

Bad reaches out and touches Terry's shoulder. "I'm sorry, son. What you do is your own business. You take care of my house for me, you're welcome to use it, but I been driving all day, and I haven't slept in my own bed for over a month."

"Bad, we were going to be leaving in just a bit anyway. Let me help you get your stuff out of the truck."

"I'd appreciate it. I can't carry stuff very well. It's O.K. if I go in?"

"Sure. Sure. You might want to stay in the front part of the house for a little bit, though."

On the coffee table in the living room, there are stacks of mail. Most are advertising fliers, with a few letters, a couple of bills. There is one brown envelope he recognizes without looking at the return address: IRS. Around the room, the plants look healthy. The furniture is dusty, and there are beer cans on the end tables by the sofa. It is just as he left it. The television is quietly pulsing light in the corner.

"Hi, Bad." A small young woman in a T-shirt and jeans walks shyly into the room. She brushes long dirty-blond hair away from her face.

"Kim. What the hell?"

"Oh, your leg. It's awful, Bad. Does it hurt a lot? Can I help you?"

He rejects her with a shake of his hand.

"Bad. It's not like it looks. I mean, Terry and me, we were just . . ."

"Yeah, I know what you were just."

"It's just that there's this other guy. He's real scary. Terry was protecting me. He brought me over here . . ."

"Where you know the mattress."

"Oh, Bad. I feel just awful."

Terry comes in the door carrying a suitcase and the guitar. He sets them down quietly in the corner. "Look, Bad . . ."

"Just get the rest of my stuff, will you?"

"Sure. Sure."

"Kim, get me a glass of ice. Get enough for all of us."

When Terry comes back in with another suitcase, the Roland Cube, and a case full of sheet music, Bad finds the bottle of Jack Daniel's and pours three glasses. "So," he asks, "how are we coming on finding a new bass player?"

"I got three for you to listen to. They're all O.K. None of them are as good as Dave, but they're all right. Jim Mitchell from Autumn is one of them. He's having trouble with Marty and wants out. He's probably the best of the bunch. He's a great jazz player, real innovative but very knowledgeable, too. He could really be good for us, even better than David was. Then there's a kid who's played in a lot of rock bands around town. He's rough, but he's got some talent, too. Then there's

an older guy who's just down from Michigan. He's traditional, steady. You can listen to them as soon as you're ready."

"And how about Wayne? How's he handling this?"

"Wayne's kind of on the rag."

"Wayne's always on the rag," Kim says.

"He was going to do a big promotion, you know. Newspaper ads, radio spots to let everyone know you're back. And
the band he had covering for us had booked another date, so
he had to scrounge a little for a one-week fill-in. But he understands about the leg and all. Are you going to be able to play?"

"I don't pick with my foot, and I tap with my right. I'll be
O.K. We'll get a stool or something. We'll work it out. Maybe
I better call Wayne and get his feathers smoothed. Hell, I'll do
it in the morning. I'm really beat."

"We better get out of here," Terry says, "unless there is
something you need."

"Unless you got a spare ankle, I guess there ain't much to
do until tomorrow."

When Kim is out the door, Terry stops and tries to apologize again. "She's been going out with this heavy Harley kind
of guy, and he's got her spooked. I was just trying to help out.
I wasn't cutting in on you or anything."

"No," Bad says, "Kim is Kim. I know that. We aren't married, for God's sake. But," he adds, "you are, buddy. You be
careful what you do. Don't mess that up. It ain't worth it. Take
it from me. And Kim sure as hell ain't worth it. Think on that
a bit."

The sheets haven't been changed, but he is too tired to

care. He locks the doors, turns out the lights and undresses, and crawls into bed. As he settles into the pillow, he smells a familiar, homey smell. He gets up and goes to the closet for fresh sheets.

He has to hold for Jack. Sometimes he suspects Jack needs the time to pull a file and remember who he is.

"Welcome home," Jack says. "How's the leg?"

"Son-of-a-bitch itches like a widow."

"You going to be ready to work again Tuesday?"

"I'll do it. I was just fixing to call Wayne. I thought I better hear it from you first."

"I'd rather you didn't call. Let me handle this. You just get the band ready."

"Wayne's my friend."

"That's what I mean. You let me handle it. Keep friendship and business separate. You know that."

"He's still my friend. I've got to call him."

"Don't discuss figures with him. Don't even apologize for being a week late."

"Why the hell should I apologize? I broke my damn ankle."

"Exactly. Keep that attitude."

"What the hell is going on?"

"Here's the deal. We renegotiated the contract, up twelve and a half on the guarantee, but down on the base, allowing for inflation and general growth of business, without consideration of the entertainment. Basically, you should see a net increase of about five percent if things go the way they have been."

"That doesn't seem to be any problem."

"That's all fine. It gets sticky when we start talking about promotion. Wayne wants to increase his promotion allowance, including a splash for your return, which is now delayed by a week. We agreed to hold at the old figures for thirty days as our part of the promotion costs. But now he is out kill fees on the radio spots, and the expense of another band for a week, which is actually costing him less than you would, since he's paying a flat fee."

"Wait. Are you telling me the son-of-a-bitch is holding me up for money because I broke my ankle?"

"He's not holding anyone up. He wants an additional thirty days at the old figures as compensation."

"For what?"

"For rescheduling everything. Frankly, it doesn't amount to squat, and he knows it."

"That fucker is trying to screw me because I broke my ankle?"

"Bad, this is what I was talking about. This is business. He's looking out for himself, I look out for you. He does his job, I do yours; everything works just fine."

"Hell, I'll talk to him. That fucker will back off."

"Bad, damn it. You talk to him about the weather, about music, fishing or football, but don't you talk to him about business. Don't talk to him at all. Take the rest of the week off and just relax."

"Jack, that son-of-a-bitch is my friend."

· · ·

At the club, the front door is still locked, and Bad has to swing his way to the back door to get in. Wayne is in the back, checking stock. Bad makes his way past trash cans waiting to be emptied, and boxes of empty beer bottles.

"Jesus, Bad. You look like shit."

"I know. It's all on account of the toilets I have to play in."

"I heard about the wreck. It's a damn shame. Hurt much?"

"Not much. Makes it hell when you got to get your britches on in a hurry, though."

"Damn, it's good to see you. Come on into the office."

The office is a cell, filled with boxes and stacks of paper. There is a desk and two chairs. On the desk there is a telephone, adding machine, pictures of Wayne's wife, two kids, and at the other corner a framed picture of Bad. On the wall are beer signs, a pinup of a redhead holding up a towel that just misses covering her right breast, and a poster from 1977, "The Sundown Lounge, Bad Blake and Bad's Boys, appearing nightly."

"How's business?"

"Crap. I just figured out, I'm down about ten cases a night from July."

"You ever cleaned this office, you might figure out how to run this damn business."

"I clean this office, and I might find out we're both broke. So how was the road this time?"

"They don't get any shorter. It makes coming back to work look good."

Wayne takes a bottle from a drawer and sets it on the

desk. He goes out the door and comes back with one glass of ice. He hands it to Bad, who pours his own drink. "Cheers." He drinks it off and pours another.

"Well, come on. Something interesting must have happened."

"Yeah. I broke my ankle. I signed for another album with Tommy, opened a show for him in Phoenix. Met a woman in Santa Fe."

"That doesn't come as a real surprise."

"I met a good one this time. Better than my usual. Speaking of that, how long has this thing with Kim and Terry been going on?"

"Who knows? He's been hanging around the last week or so. I try not to pay too much attention to Kim. I wouldn't worry about her if I were you."

"I'm not. I'm worried about Terry. He's a good kid. Sandra's a good kid. I worry about them."

"You talked to Jack yet?"

"Yeah."

"What do you think?"

"I don't. If I did, I wouldn't have to pay Jack to do it for me."

"Right. So how long until we can play some golf?"

"Cast comes off in four more weeks. Soon after that, I suspect. We'll have to use carts, though."

"We always use carts."

"Yeah, but that's because we want to. Now we have to."

"Why the hell Santa Fe?"

"It's a nice town. A little artsy-fartsy, but it's pretty nice. Cooler than here."

"I think you need to talk to Kim about what she calls 'geographic desirability.' Santa Fe's a hell of a way from here."

"Eight hundred and seventy-nine miles."

"Tough trip for a man who has to work Saturday nights."

"Which reminds me. I have to audition some bass players this week. I'll need to come in a couple of afternoons and put them through the routine."

"No problem."

Bad gets up and sets his drink down. He bends over heavily to pick up his crutches.

"You put on a few pounds out there on the road?"

"Road food and long hours. I'll take it off when I can get back into a regular schedule."

"You really should. You don't need to be carrying any extra with you. Not good for the ticker, you know."

He is trying to straighten up a little, gathering and dumping ashtrays, picking up beer cans. He has unpacked. A pile of dirty clothes sits in the hallway, waiting to be taken to the laundry. Cleaning in the bedroom, he finds a ball of light-blue cloth in the corner, next to the bed. A pair of Kim's underpants.

When he answers the doorbell, a man in a lightweight tan suit smiles and opens the screen, extending his hand with an easy familiarity. "Mr. Blake, Marty Wilks, how are you today?"

"I don't want any."

Wilks grins and shakes his head. "I'm not selling anything. I've come to discuss a business matter. Can I come in?"

"Who are you?"

Wilks pulls a small leather case from the inside pocket of his jacket, takes out a business card. Martin Wilks, Personal Management.

"I've got a manager."

"Yes, yes, I know. I'm not here to try to sell my services. Actually, I'm not involved in entertainment at all. My field is political, really. Please, may I come in? I won't take much of your time."

"I was cleaning up," Bad says, pulling a stack of sheet music off the sofa for Wilks.

"I'm really sorry to barge in like this, Mr. Blake. I've been trying to call you for a couple of weeks, and I was in town, and I thought it might be easier just to stop by."

"I was just cleaning up."

"I won't keep you. I just want to talk to you about something I think you'll be interested in. Are you familiar with Larry Rounds?"

"I don't know. Maybe. He a singer?"

Wilks laughs. "No, not really. He's a state representative from Dallas. You've seen his name in the papers, I'm sure."

"Oh, sure. Right."

"I think you'll be pleased to know that Larry's a big fan of yours. And that has given me an idea."

Bad winces. He doesn't like ideas. They always come from

someone else, and they always cost him money. There doesn't seem to be a way to stop people from having ideas. "I'm trying to get my house cleaned up," he says.

"I'm imposing. I understand. But I think you're going to like what I have to say. This seems to be one of those fortunate situations where everybody stands to benefit. You know, of course, that Representative Rounds is running for a congressional seat this fall?"

Bad doesn't know. "Sure," he says.

"Well, it's a close race. We're five points behind in the polls right now, but we're closing. In these last two months, we are going directly to the people, where Larry's real strength lies. And that's where you come in. What I'm putting together is a series of old-fashioned rallies around the state, Sunday afternoon barbecues, really, to let the people meet Larry, get to know him, to understand that he is one of them—not one of those rich Harvard lawyer politicians, but a real Texas boy, just like them. And what I would like, what Larry would like, is to have you be a part of those rallies."

"Well, hell," Bad says, "I'm just a singer and a picker. I don't know . . ."

"Exactly. That's what we want. We want you to perform at the rallies, to entertain the folks, give them a good time, and to introduce Larry." Martin Wilks leans back, stretches his arm across the top of the sofa and crosses his legs. He is wearing the round, heavy loafers college students used to wear. His smile is broad and open.

Bad sighs and relaxes. He settles back into his chair. "Well, old buddy, the guy you need to be talking to is old Jack Greene of Greene and Gold Productions. He's my manager, he makes all the arrangements for me. I have his card here somewhere."

Martin Wilks pushes forward from the sofa and holds up his hand, palm outward. "What we're talking about here is not really something for your management. We're talking about a more personal kind of commitment rather than a strict business arrangement."

"I see. What does that mean?"

"Well, this campaign is not a business. It's a personal commitment on Larry's part. It is about ideals and virtues, traditional American values. We're conducting a real personal, Texas-style campaign here. And we are looking for the kind of straightforward, traditional people who will commit to our kind of political vision, and I think you're our man. So does Larry."

"You're saying you're not going to pay me?"

Martin Wilks laughs. "You get right to the point, don't you? I like that. I really do. No, we couldn't pay you as such, but we would make it worth your while."

"I'm a professional musician," Bad explains. "It's how I make my living." He motions to the wall to the left of Wilks. "I have gold records, four of them."

"Of course, of course. I understand you completely. Like I said, we are prepared to make this worth your while. We aren't trying to take advantage of you. We can pay your expenses, and you will be performing before thousands and thousands of people. We expect to draw nearly a half-million people to these rallies by the end of October. I'm not involved in music. I'm involved in politics. And that makes me uniquely aware of the value of exposure and publicity. While Larry is getting his message across at these rallies, you'll be getting yours, too. Don't you see? You'll be working together. You'll help us, we'll help you. Lots of musicians have thrown their support into political campaigns—Willie Nelson, Charlie Daniels, Linda Ronstadt, Jackson Browne—and believe me, it hasn't hurt their careers one bit."

"It sounds more like something for Willie," Bad says.

Martin Wilks shakes his head and waves his hand. "No, no. This isn't for Willie Nelson. That 'outlaw' business, the dope and all that. No, you're the man we're looking for."

"Well, hell, let me tell you, old buddy, I'm just not much for politics. I don't really think I'm the boy you're looking for."

"Bad. Can I call you Bad? I feel like I've known you for a while. Bad, everyone's involved in politics, whether they know it or not. Do you believe it's right to murder babies? Do you believe we should encourage deviates to go around raping our wives and daughters? Do you believe that when they do rape someone we should just slap their wrists and ask them, pretty please, not to do it again? Do you think I should take your money and give it to some wino dope fiend so he can just hang around and maybe break into your house and steal your television because he thinks you didn't give him enough? Do you think those things are right, Bad?"

"Of course not."

"Of course not. And do you think that we should let a bunch of Arabs and Communists go around murdering innocent people and not do anything about it? Do you think we should apologize to the Russians because we have weapons to defend ourselves with? Or that the Congress should just ignore the President that the people elected? Elected by the largest majority in history?"

"Well, no."

"Well, there you are, Bad. You are involved in politics, just like all the other people, and do you know what? You believe just what Larry Rounds believes. You see, Bad, what we are running here is a real people's campaign. We are standing up for the little guy, the guy who is the real backbone of America. You are a voice of that real America, and we want you to lend your voice to ours. Together, we are going to do great things. We can get America back to where it belongs, and when Larry is doing that, he's certainly not going to forget the help you gave him."

"I don't know. I'm not sure."

"O.K. I understand that, and I don't want you to join with us until you are really sure. I'm going to leave you some position papers. These are the same things we give our staff members and release to the press. We don't hide anything. Read these over, and when you have questions, you call me."

He takes out a pen and writes a number at the top of a sheaf of papers labeled "Foreign Policy." "It's my number in Dallas. Call collect."

The auditions serve as rehearsals, too. As good as his own bed and his own cooking is his own band. Even with the succession of bass players, rehearsing is comfortable. Howard is steady on drums, moving automatically to the correct tempo, pulling the rest along with him. Terry plays rhythm guitar exactly as Bad has taught him, and Ted is good enough on steel to move on to studio or road work, but he has no desire to leave Houston, and that suits Bad fine.

As they rehearse, they suggest songs, ones that are getting airplay and are likely to be requested. They have been together long enough that they know which ones they should consider and which ones to ignore. Terry brings tapes and they listen to each song twice and then play it through, stopping only to straighten out the lyrics or work through tricky bridges. Both Terry and Ted sing, and Bad is careful to let them bring in new material they want to do. They, in turn, suggest only things they figure will be acceptable to Bad.

They reject the kid bass player first. He is pretty good, but he's wrong for the band, a little too flashy, a little too punk. Howard and Terry favor Jim Mitchell, who has been playing in clubs around town for a couple of years. He is accomplished and serious. He has a good voice on harmony. Jim is a high tenor, and he can cover material that the rest of them can't. Even though he has been playing contemporary covers and a lot of straight jazz, he's interested and good enough to pick up their material easily.

"He's just not right," Bad says.

"You mean because he's black," Terry answers.

That has nothing to do with it, Bad insists. He is just too contemporary. He'll get bored and quit on them in a couple of months and they will be back where they started. He's a nice enough kid, but Bad doesn't quite trust him. He seems unreliable.

"Because he's black," Terry says.

"Listen, goddamn it, black doesn't have anything to do with anything. If it wasn't for Charlie Christian and T-Bone Walker, I'd still be playing pluck and strum, and you wouldn't be playing at all. I learned to play listening to the meanest blue-gum nigger blues I could find, and I'd drive all night to find it. I don't have a damned thing against niggers."

"But you don't want one in your band."

"My band. Remember that. My band. If I want it to be all white, it'll be all white, or all purple, or all green. But that's my decision, not yours."

Bad prefers Al Lovett, just down from Michigan, a welder who is out of work. He is in his late forties, and down on his luck. He has been playing honky-tonks on weekends for years and knows traditional material pretty well. His playing is unspectacular, but he keeps the beat and only misses an occasional shift. Rust, Al explains; he hasn't played in a couple of months. His voice isn't as steady as Jim's and he's a baritone, close to Bad.

That's a real problem, Terry points out. He can handle harmony, but if he wants to do solos, he's going to be walking in Bad's territory.

Still, he may be the right choice, Bad thinks.

"Amateur night," Terry says, "but he's white, that's a big plus."

"And that's a big mouth for a sideman," Bad says.

He is up early, in his underwear, trying to get the coffee brewed before his program comes on the television. He has taken most of the food from the lower cabinets and stacked it on the counter so he doesn't have to bend down to get it. He has the coffee and coffeepot at hand, but he doesn't have a lot of room to work. The electric can opener is behind a stack of tomato cans, and he's using a hand-cranked opener.

He gets the coffee started and turns on the television. There is a twenty percent chance of rain. Mostly that means hotter and more humid. The tomatoes in the backyard need rain, but he hasn't tried to walk with his crutches on wet pavement yet. Suddenly, the most innocent things have become treacherous.

He has a cup of coffee in front of him and a Pall Mall in his mouth when the sissy shrieks at him for the first time. He pulls the cigarette out of his mouth and tries to hide it. He is sure that if the sissy saw him smoking, his feelings would be hurt. It would be like hurting a puppy—a particularly obnoxious and ugly puppy, but a puppy. "What are you doing?" the sissy shrieks.

"Let's go. Let's get that fat. It's time to get moving." The sissy is wearing tight gray sweat pants and a purple undershirt. His face looks as if someone had tried to compress it in a vise. A bright-orange ball of hair surrounds his head, reminding Bad of a walnut wrapped in an orange pot-scrubber.

"Are you ready?" the sissy screams.

Bad takes a quick drag off his cigarette and snuffs it out. He has forgotten how much he hates this little person.

"Let's go, count it out: one, two, three."

The sissy is windmilling his arms and then twisting and bending forward. The windmilling Bad can handle, but the bending and twisting takes care and concentration. He bends tentatively forward, trying hard to keep his balance. He can only bend about forty degrees before his balance begins to give and his breathing is constricted.

"Let's go. Keep it up. Don't fall behind."

Now the sissy is hopping from one leg to the other. This one is out of the question. Bad falls back onto the sofa and takes a sip of coffee. Then the sissy is flat on the floor on his stomach. "Let's get that fanny, now. Firm it up. Come on."

Bad falls forward to the floor and lifts his head toward the TV. The sissy is lifting his legs from the floor, alternating left and right. Bad's right goes up, but the left is carrying five extra pounds. "One," he huffs, "two, three."

"Don't slow down," the sissy warns. "Keep those legs going. Now, on your back for some tummy work."

Bad rolls over onto his back and tries to catch his breath. The sissy is doing quick sit-ups, coming up to upright, his arms thrust straight forward. Bad lunges heavily up, and lets himself fall back to the floor. He lurches up again, and sees that every time he comes up, his cock slips out the fly of his shorts. He adjusts his shorts, embarrassed in front of the sissy.

"One, two, three, down. You're slowing down."

"You're speeding up, you little shit." Bad grunts. "Tempo, for Christ's sake." He settles back down to the floor. It is bad that they have a sissy doing this. It's worse that he has the personality of a Pomeranian that has eaten a Benzedrine inhaler, but it is unforgivable that he has no sense of tempo.

"Now for the bust." The sissy is swinging his arms from his sides, clapping them together in front of him. "Come on," the sissy shrieks, "let's fight those droops."

Bad keeps slapping his hands together in front of him, fighting his droops and imagining he is clapping his hands over the sissy's ears.

"You weren't born fat," the sissy tells him. "You weren't born with bad habits. You did this to yourself, so don't let up." The sissy jumps up and begins running in place. Bad fires up a Pall Mall and sends a stream of smoke toward the screen. He has a headache and he is wheezing. He wants a drink, but he hobbles out to the kitchen for another cup of coffee.

When he comes back, the sissy is gone, and a set of cars fills the screen. Little trucks and jeeps, with headlights that work, twist around a plastic track, up over a bridge, and then just miss each other at the intersection of a figure eight. Jesus, he bets Buddy would just love that. At the end of the commercial, he writes down the brand name so he can ask for it at the toy store.

The tomatoes are sad. Terry has put water on them, but he hasn't cared for them. Bad works his way through the rows, checking for flowers trying to set fruit in the September heat. It is starting to cool a little at night, and they should be setting again soon. He turns leaves over, inhaling their musty scent, tracing the dry, brown worm tracks until he finds the green cutworm and plucks it delicately from the stem, then with a snap of his wrist spins it splattering into the side of the house. He resets the stakes that have been pulled down in the dry ground by the weight of the plants. Then, gingerly, he eases down to his knees and begins to pick at weeds that have come up.

The dill hasn't held up, and the basil is starting to shrivel a little. The onions and garlic are browning at the tops, but should be about done by now anyway. Rosemary tangles through the edge of the garden. The peppers—bell and Anaheim chili—are tall and luxuriant in the heat.

Once, in Tennessee, he had a Japanese gardener who kept his two-acre yard clipped, cleaned and trimmed. There were flowers from spring through the first frost. When a plant started to brown and wither, it was pulled out and replaced. Bad had nothing to do with it. He walked with Marge sometimes in the evening, admiring the guitar-shaped rosebed in the middle of the backyard. Marge brought cut flowers into the house, but Bad never touched a plant.

He pulls up a carrot from the bed he has carefully cultivated, digging deep and working in sand and gypsum to break up the heavy clay gumbo soil. The carrot is pale and long, with clumps of black dirt clinging to its roots. He moves slowly over to the faucet and carries the hose back, running just a trickle, and sets it carefully at the base of a tomato plant. Guy Clark got it right, he thinks. "There are only two things money can't buy: / True love and home-grown tomatoes."

He thinks about the bass player. There is no question that Jim Mitchell is the best player. And he doesn't dislike niggers, he tells himself, he really doesn't. It just wouldn't work. One snappy black jazz bass player in a country band would change things. He likes the kid's technique and his style, and he admires his ability to understand the movement of a song and augment it well. Hell, there are lots of good black bands that would love to have a kid like that.

Bad decides on Al, and calls Terry about it. When it comes right down to it, Jim is the right choice. He's the better player, and his voice is a contribution, not a distraction. Bad's choice, he says, is based on wanting to hire the guy who is out of work instead of the one who just wants to change bands. "Sometimes you're just too sentimental," Terry says.

"You've got to stop sending Buddy all these toys," Jean tells him from Santa Fe.

"But damn, honey, you just got to see these little cars. The little boogers just scoot around that track like the devil was chasing them. He's just going to get a real kick out of them. I want to be there to see him when he runs them."

"Bad, you're spoiling him. He thinks you're Santa Claus and every day's Christmas. He's got to understand things don't work that way."

"But he's just a little kid. He's got to have fun. And hell, I'm having a ball buying this stuff. And he's got to know his Uncle Bad is thinking of him."

"You're not his uncle, Bad."

"Well, hell. Look, I think I'm hooked on toy stores. If I can't send these things to him, they'll just clutter up my house. I'll be playing with them all the time, and I'll never get any of my work done. I'm doing myself a favor, don't you see?"

"At least taper off, Bad. I'm serious. I don't want a greedy little monster on my hands who thinks he's just supposed to get toys for no reason."

"Jean, I got a reason. I mean, when I was a kid in Indiana, I had frogs, and pigs and chickens, squirrels, possums and rabbits to play with. What's poor old Buddy got there in Santa Fe? You got any possums for him to hunt? There ain't a single bullfrog in that swimming pool there, I checked."

"Bad, you're making me into the villain here."

"Aw, no, hon. I don't want to do that."

"Then just stop sending this stuff, please."

"The cars are already on their way."

"Then that's it, please?"

"O.K. But I was really having a good time with the toys. I

didn't mean any harm, really. It's been a long time since I had a boy to buy toys for."

There is a long pause before she says anything. "Bad, I've been thinking. Now, I understand that this is none of my business. And you can tell me that. I don't want to meddle, but I just have to say this. Don't get mad, but I think you ought to find your son. I think you need to look for him and find him. You need to know who he is."

His heart thumps. "I've tried, Jean. You know I've tried. I can't."

"You can hire a detective. You can spend some of the money you're spending on Buddy now, and you can find him. A detective in Los Angeles can go through court records and things and find him. It probably won't be that hard."

"It's not that. Oh hell. About ten years ago, I looked her up in the L.A. phone book. And I found her. She retook her maiden name. It was that simple. But I couldn't call her. I even dialed once. The phone rang before I hung up. I just couldn't do it. It's been too long. What would I say? What the hell do you say to the wife who ran out on you twenty years ago because you were a goddamned low-down drunk, so bad she couldn't stand to have your little boy see his daddy like that? What the hell do you say?"

"Say you want to see your son."

"But he don't want to see me."

"You don't know that. I think he probably does want to see you. He may not know it, but he wants to see you."

"I can't, Jean, I just can't."

"Bad. It's not my business, but I think you've got to."

"Yeah, well, we'll see. Listen, you understand these things better than me. There is this guy running for Congress named Rounds. You know him?"

"No. From Texas?"

"Yeah."

"I don't know anything about Texas politics since Johnson and Rayburn died. Why? What's up?"

"He wants me to sing at rallies for him. I think it might be a good idea. He seems pretty good. He believes in the President and the little guy."

"No. He can't do both."

"What? What do you mean? Sure he can. It's right here in his paper."

"Bad, think about it. This is the President who cut every major social program in the country and increased defense spending through the ceiling. That's not a people's President, Bad."

"But that's what the people want. And he's for women. He's against pornography and abortion because they both hurt women."

"Oh God, not that crap. Jesus Christ, Bad, stay away from that guy."

"But you're not for abortion. You had Buddy, you didn't . . ."

"I chose to have Buddy. Chose. I chose. I had Buddy because I wanted to, not because some self-righteous bigot waving a Bible told me I had to. I had the right to choose. Everyone should."

"But pornography. It says here that there is a direct link between pornography and violence."

"Maybe. I'm not crazy about it myself, but I'll tell you, I'm a lot more afraid of these right-wing politicians than I am of a bunch of guys sitting around a cheap theater with their hands in their pants."

"I don't know, it makes sense to me."

"How can this guy be for women on one hand, and against them on the other. That doesn't make sense. You can't have it both ways, Bad. You can't have it both ways."

In the Los Angeles phone book in the Southwestern Bell office, there is no listing for Marjorie Reynolds, but he finds two listings for Steven Reynolds. He copies both down.

He calls Al Lovett to tell him he has the job. Al embarrasses him with gratitude, even putting his wife on the phone to tell Bad how happy she is that Al is going to being playing with him. Bad understands that he has made the wrong choice, but he is willing to live with it. He will have to make Al understand that his vocals will be strictly harmony. He will have to make Terry and Howard understand that this is his band, and he makes the final decisions. Jim is the better player, but he has a job. When someone is hurting, you do what you can.

At rehearsal, Terry is cooperative, but Howard is reticent. Al is a little tentative, but that owes more to nerves than to ability. "You're not listening to me," Howard says, bringing his left hand down hard on the snare to emphasize the tempo.

"Howard," Bad says, "why the hell are you doing that? I

don't want to hear that Bruce Springsteen crap here. We play country music here. Grab ahold, son."

Howard looks off in the distance with obvious disgust.

"Al," Bad says, "I know this is hard. It's going to take you a little while to find the feel of all this. But you work with Howard back there. Never mind what we're doing on the top right now. You miss a little bitty move here and there, it'll be all right. But I want that bottom tight enough to bounce a coin off. Now let's all be a band here."

When they have run through two hours' worth of material, Al has settled down to a steady respectability. For two hours' worth of work, Bad figures, that is pretty good. Bad has brought him in for a couple of harmonies, having him sing a half beat behind on "Hello Love" and "Crazy Heart" so that the effect is like a bass echo. Al has shown no inclination to do anything more than he is asked, but it is still very early.

After the break, Bad introduces "She's Going to Need Someone to Walk To." It is a basic tonic-dominant-subdominant progression in D, with a shift at the second chorus up to E flat in 2/4 time. He has no lead sheets, so he just plays through once, and Howard and Al come in halfway through the first verse. Terry comes in at the second chorus, and Ted plays a basic rhythm pattern. Later they will add fills and augments.

"That's O.K.," Terry says. "I haven't heard that before. Whose is it?"

"Mine," Bad says.

"No shit? When did you write that?"

"A couple of weeks ago, up in Santa Fe."

"It's nice," Ted says. "I like it. Funny, we do all these songs of yours, but I just never thought about new songs."

"I'm writing for Tommy's new album."

"You ought to write stuff for us, too. We could do an album."

"You find the label, I'll write a whole goddamned album. Now, let's get back to this one."

They break their rehearsal at quarter to four to be out in time for the after-work crowd in the bar. They have two more practices before they get back to work on Saturday night. They won't be as tight as they should be, but they will be passable. In another week they will be a real band again.

Chapter Twelve

When he walks in the door of the house, the phone is ring-ing. It is a recorded message about time-share vacations. Bad lets it play for a couple of seconds, not listening, looking at the two Los Angeles numbers. He hangs up the phone. It is five-thirty, three-thirty in Los Angeles. No one is home at three-thirty.

He pours a long drink and starts to fix dinner. He scrubs potatoes under cold water, digging the eyes out with the point of a paring knife, sets them in a pot of water and puts them on the stove to boil. He has convinced himself he needs to start a diet, so he washes three leaves of lettuce, dries them on a towel, and tears them up into a salad bowl. Then he washes the carrot from his garden, slices it thin and adds it. He goes into the backyard for a green pepper and some basil, chops up both and adds that in. In the refrigerator he finds a chunk of cheese to crumble, two pieces of cold bacon, and olives—Spanish and black. He garnishes it all with slices of jalapeño peppers and a left-over anchovy he digs out of oil that has thickened into a salty gum. He puts this on the table with a bottle of Russian dressing.

By this time the potatoes are boiling well, so he takes two thick pork chops from the refrigerator. Each is ringed with a quarter inch of white fat, which he scores with a knife to keep the chops from curling in the pan. He coats them with flour, egg and bread crumbs, ladles a big tablespoonful of bacon fat into the cast-iron skillet, and when it is starting to spatter, he lays in the chops.

While the chops are cooking he mashes the potatoes by hand, adding in big slices of butter and splashing in cold milk. When the chops are done, he pours most of the grease off, adds a couple of tablespoons of flour, whisking it with a fork until it is blended and the browned pieces of breading are scraped from the pan, and then he pours in milk and keeps stirring, adding salt and enough pepper to speckle the whole mixture in the pan. When it is thick, he ladles it over the potatoes and chops and takes the plate into the dining room to eat with his diet salad. He puts some Les Paul and Mary Ford on the stereo and eats.

After dinner, he fixes another drink. When he has put the leftovers into cottage cheese containers and liver cartons, he scrapes and washes the dishes, wiping the iron skillet with a paper napkin to keep it seasoned. He wipes off the top of the stove. He starts a pot of coffee and pours another drink while it perks.

He looks at the phone, and then at his watch. It is seven, five in Los Angeles, still too early to call. He takes his drink into the living room and turns on the television. Young and beautiful people are busy solving crimes. In their few quiet moments, they fall into ill-fated love. On the other channels, their sisters and cousins are doing the same. He gets a cup of coffee, smokes a cigarette and watches.

When he can't stand another variation on this, he gets his guitar and Pignose amplifier and starts with scales, working his way up and down until a note opens some door and he touches a melody he faintly remembers. Still hearing Les Paul, he plays it blue, sliding chords with lots of bends and vibrato, keeping it harmonic. For a long while he just plays, letting one movement lead him into the next, not considering what he is doing or what he might do. He moves from harmonic to melodic and comes back, responding to signals he is not conscious of. It is as though his fingers have taken charge and all he needs to do, must do, is listen to what they are doing.

As he plays, a passage begins to repeat more and more frequently. At first he is dimly aware of it, later he seems unable to escape it. The more insistent it becomes, the more annoying it becomes, as if it is beating against the limits of the possibilities he finds to move it somewhere else. He keeps taking routes out of the progression, and none of them seems right. He gets up and pours another drink and walks out into the backyard. In the sky, a few stars are faintly visible against the overcast and the reflected lights of the city.

The simple answer is that the passage moves straightforwardly, I, IV, V, but then not back to I but up to II, then in half steps back down to I again, a three-beat descent. He goes back inside and tries that a couple of times. It is simple and clean, more from jazz than from country. He plays it again, adding lyrics as he goes: "Lately, I get to thinking of times back then, / And I ask myself, 'Is this going to hurt again?'" He jots it down and keeps working, getting up only for drinks. It's not, he knows, what he wants, but it is closer than he has been.

When he stops for the night, it is eleven-thirty. He turns on Johnny Carson. His throat is raw from cigarettes and he has drunk half a bottle. He feels empty, and the cigarette in his finger wavers.

He looks at the phone and then picks it up and dials. At the first number there is no answer. He has not considered that he might dial the right number and still not get an answer. He tries the second number.

"Hello," a man answers.

"Yeah," Bad says, "hello. Is this Steven Reynolds?"

"Yes. Who's calling?"

"Well, actually, buddy, I'm on kind of a hunting trip here. I'm trying to find a Marjorie Reynolds from Lima, Ohio, who lived in Nashville, Tennessee, from nineteen sixty to sixty-five. Are you related to her, by any chance?"

There is a pause. "She was my mother. She passed away two years ago. Who is this?"

Bad feels that his heart has contracted to the size of a walnut. His body goes cold. When he first speaks, his voice is between a croak and a whisper.

"I'm sorry, I can't hear you. Who is this?"

He whispers, louder this time, "Your father."

There is a longer pause. "Who is this?"

"Bad Blake, in Houston, Texas. I'm your father."

There is a pause. "I know."

Bad doesn't know what to say, so he goes to the obvious. "How are you?"

"Fine. What do you want?"

"I want to know how you are doing. You're my son."

"I'm doing fine."

"Marge is dead," he says as the realization sinks in. "When? How?"

"Two years ago in October. Cancer."

"Was it bad? I mean, did she suffer?"

"Yes."

"Oh God. I'm sorry. I am so sorry. I loved her. I swear I did."

"Yeah. What do you want?"

"I want to talk to you. I want to know who you are. I want you to know who I am." He begins to choke. "I want to say I'm sorry."

"Look. I know who you are. I know all about you, and I don't want an apology."

"No. You don't know who I am. I don't know what all you do know, but you don't know me. And I don't know a damn thing about you."

"My name is Steven Reynolds, I'm twenty-four years old. I work as an operations officer at PacifiTech. I'm six feet two inches tall, I weigh one hundred and ninety pounds. I have brown hair and brown eyes."

"And you're my son. My only son. You left that out."

"I'm Marjorie Reynolds' son."

"Haven't you ever wanted to know who I was? Haven't you wondered about me?"

There is another pause. "Yeah, some."

"I just want to talk to you. I don't want anything from you, I don't want to try to be your best buddy. I just want to talk to you, to see. I want to know who you are. I want to know that you're all right."

"I'm sorry. I really don't think I want to talk to you."

"How the hell can you not want to talk to me? You're six feet two and weigh one hundred and ninety pounds. You're that way because of me. Your mother was small and had red hair."

"And you left her."

"She left me. And she had reason to. I never would have left her. I don't blame your mother, and I'm not going to try to convince you that what she did was anything but right. She didn't owe me anything, and I guess you don't, either. Except you're my son, I'm your father. Maybe we owe each other something on that score."

"Why are you calling? Now? After all these years?"

"I can't explain to you why after all these years. Maybe someday, but not right now. And I'm trying to explain why I'm calling. Look, write this down." Bad dictates his address and telephone number and makes him repeat it back. "Think about it. Sleep on it. Then call me or write me a letter. We need to talk to each other. Call me collect. Come here, or I'll come there. But goddamn it, let's do something."

"I'll think about it, but I really don't think I want to talk to you."

"Right, you think about it."

He doesn't sleep. He sits up in bed, the lights off, with a bottle. He pulls the sheet up over his waist. The ceiling fan, turning slowly over his bed, evaporates the sweat that keeps coming. In the middle of September, it is eighty-five and he's cold. He keeps pulling at the bottle, trying hard for a good drunk that won't come. The clock next to the bed reads three-thirty.

Of the memories that keep at him, one is persistent. It is his wedding night, late August nineteen sixty, east Texas. It is early in the morning. He and Marge lie in the dark, exhausted and happy. But they can't sleep.

They're in a rented cabin, deep in pine woods, twenty miles from the highway. In the pines outside, a mockingbird is busy staking his territory, loudly moving from one call to another, trilling, rising and falling. Bad jumps up from the bed. Naked, he takes his guitar, a Martin D-28, and unpacks it. He sits on the edge of the bed and tunes it. "What are you doing?" Marge asks. "Just wait," he tells her, and heads for the door.

"You can't go out," she says, "you're buck naked." He stops and comes back for his boots, a pair of tooled black-and-white Justins, and his new Stetson 4X beaver, and then he goes out the door. Outside, he pauses, listening to the bird, trying to find the direction. When he has it, he moves slowly forward. There is a full moon that lights the ground in front of him.

About thirty yards from the cabin, he finds a large rock and sits on it, the surface cold and rough against his bare skin.

He waits until the bird has run through another round, and when the pause comes, he begins picking "Listen to the Mockingbird" in C. He plays a verse through and waits. The bird starts up, louder than before, runs through a series and waits. Bad gives it another verse, and for several minutes he and the mockingbird swap tunes back and forth, until Marge comes up behind Bad and wraps both arms around him, drawing herself into his broad back. "What in hell are you doing?" she asks him.

"Being happy as I've ever been in my life."

"I'd never be able to not love you," she says, "thinking of you out here, bare-assed in the moonlight, playing for a damn bird."

Somewhere near daylight he gives up and sleeps, dreamless.

When the phone rings, he does not know where he is, or what the noise is. When he leans over to take the receiver, pain thumps inside his head.

"Buddy, I made the cars go real fast. Real fast, then the jeep went around the corner and it went BOOM."

The noise hits the center of his head like a fist. "Buddy? You got the cars?"

"Yeah. I make them go faster than anybody. And then they go crash. I'm going to make them go again."

"Bad?"

"Jean."

"He didn't say thank you. That's why he was supposed to call."

"I think he did. I think that was thanks enough."

"He's going wild. He just loves them, Bad. You really shouldn't have. And you're not going to send any more, right?"

"What time is it?"

"Nine here."

"God. I'm hung over. I called him last night."

"Steven? You called Steven?"

"Yeah."

"How is he? What did he say?"

"Marge is dead. Two years."

"Oh Bad. I'm sorry."

"Yeah. God, my head. I think my skull is going to crack."

"What did he say? I mean, what did he say about you?"

"He didn't want to talk. I can't blame him, I guess. I wouldn't feel real good about me, either, if I was him. He's not real happy with me."

"Bad, I'm sorry. I think this is my fault. I pushed you into this. I should have minded my own business."

"No. It's not your fault. I did what I had to. You just reminded me that I had to do it. But listen, I can't talk. I feel like stepped-on shit. I'll call you later. I've got to go."

When his foot hits the floor, he figures out that he is still drunk. He can't make his knees carry him in a straight line. When he puts his weight on the cast, it throws him off balance and he lurches violently. He bangs into the dresser and then drops to the floor. He crawls into the bathroom on hands and knees. He is hanging on to the rim of the toilet, in the middle of his retching, when the crying starts, and he can't stop either of them.

He wakes still on the cold tile floor of the bathroom. His left arm is numb and his body is wet with sweat. He doesn't try to get up but crawls back to the bedroom and hoists himself back into the bed, pulling the still damp sheets and bedspread over him, so cold he's shivering, and falls back to sleep.

This time when the phone rings, he comes wide awake. His head still hurts, but it is clearer now.

"Bad," Terry says, "you O.K.?"

"What time is it?"

"Two-thirty. We're waiting on you here. We were supposed to start at two. You forget?"

"Shit. No. I didn't forget. You all started yet?"

"We're waiting on you."

"You get them started. Run through as many of the standards as you can. Run through all the songs you and Ted sing. Let Al and Howard get in as much work as they can."

"You coming?"

"Hell yes, I'm coming. I'll be a little bit yet, but I'm coming. Now you get everyone going. I'll catch up when I get there."

"Jesus," Terry says. "You had one hell of a time last night. Good or bad—one hell of a time."

"I hope to God," Bad says, "none of you ever feels like this. I really mean that. If you ever do, God help you, remember that I came to work and so will you. I really mean that, too."

When they have run through an hour and a half of practice, Bad breaks it up. The bar is starting to fill. When you rehearse in a bar, it's inevitable that people are going to be around, but he has never gotten used to rehearsing in front of an audience. You rehearse in private and you don't play for an audience until you are absolutely ready.

While the others are packing up and leaving, Bad goes to the bar for a beer to settle his stomach and clear his head. Kim is behind the bar, cleaning up. She draws him a draft. "Wayne says you got a girlfriend in Albuquerque."

"Santa Fe."

"Whatever. He said I'm supposed to explain to you about geographic desirability."

"Kim, darlin', I got a stove-in head. I don't think I want to hear this right now."

"It's simple, really," she says. She goes on to explain a complex mathematical formula, based on how much you want a person, divided by the number of miles away they live. It involves factoring in a number of variables including drinking patterns, drug use, number and ages of children living at home, and number and gender of roommates. "Now," she says, "let's say there's this guy—in your case, a girl—and he's about an eight and a half, because he's really good-looking and you figure you can have a pretty good time. Now, let's say he drinks a lot. A lot is enough so he gets down to serious partying but not so much that he can't follow through, right? O.K., that's another half a point. Now, he may be married, though he says he's divorced, but you're not sure, maybe,

maybe not—that's a half a point off. Anyway, he's got a place where you can go, so that's the half a point back on. So he's still a nine, right? And there are no children, so that's a full point added. But say there's a roommate. Only the roommate is also a guy, and he's cool, so that's only a half a point off."

"What if the roommate is a woman?"

"That's *beaucoup* points off. Unless she's cool, too, and you're into that sort of thing, and then you add points, how many is up to you. Anyway, now you've got yourself a nine and a half, and anything over an eight is a definite 'go for it.' Are you following all this?"

"Kim, I had a headache before you started this."

"Wait, wait. This is the crucial part. Now let's say that you live in the FM 1960 area like I do, and this guy, he lives in Bellaire. Now, that's about twenty miles. That's a good forty-five minutes when the freeways are clear, but a good hour to an hour and a half when they're not, like early in the morning when you're trying to get home. O.K.? So what you do is figure one point for every ten miles, so that's two points, and then you divide his value—nine and a half, remember—by two. Now he's only a four and three quarters. Do you really want to waste your time on a four and three quarters?"

"What if he's got a great car or a nice house?"

"You figure that in when you're figuring in his value. I mean, a really great car is worth two or three points all by itself, and a real house, that's really his, that can be five. I mean, this is all a real scientific formula. Now, how far away is Santa Fe?"

"Eight hundred and seventy-nine miles."

"Oh, my God, Bad. You've got to divide her by eighty-eight."

"Is Wayne in his office?"

"Yeah, I think so."

"I'm going back. Bring me another draft, will you?"

"Think about it. Eighty-eight."

Wayne is at his desk when Bad swings in. He doesn't look up. "New guy sounds pretty good from back here."

"He's O.K. He isn't top-drawer, but he's O.K. By Saturday night we'll be pretty close to full throttle again."

"How's the ankle doing?"

"Better. I figured out how to scratch under it with a bent-out coat hanger."

"Bad, she's got to be a minus number. She's just got to," Kim says as she sets the beer down in front of him, bending low, showing off the butterfly tattoo over her breast.

Wayne looks up and then waits until Kim is out of the office. "Geographic desirability?"

"Yeah."

"Ain't that a bitch? The first time she ran that one by me, I almost dropped my teeth. I mean, she's got a number for everything. And this is a gal who thinks Mount Rushmore is natural."

"Good head for a dumb girl."

"You'd know more about that than me. What's with the beer? You cutting back?"

"Hangover. Chocolate milk shakes and beer are the only things that work."

"Quitting works. I miss drinking every now and then, but I sure as hell don't miss the hangovers."

"I called my son last night."

"Your son? You mean, from back . . . from Marge?"

"Yeah. He wouldn't talk to me."

"How the hell did you find him?"

"I looked him up in the phone book. It was that easy."

"I'll be roped and doped. And he wouldn't talk to you?"

"No. He told me about Marge, though. She's dead. She died two years ago of cancer. I never knew. I never had any idea."

"Jesus, Bad, I'm sorry."

"I loved her, Wayne. I really goddamn loved her. And now she's gone."

"I know you did. I know. I'm not sure you ever actually said it, but I know. I always knew. Hell, what can I say? I'm sorry, really sorry. Is there anything I can do?"

"No. There ain't nothing anyone can do now. It just feels over, you know? I've felt bad before—hell, I've felt worse than I ever thought it was possible to feel—but I never felt over before. Jesus Lord."

"Oh, come on, Bad. You're not over. Hell, I know how you must feel, but you're doing all right. You're writing songs again, you've got yourself a new girlfriend. You've got a long way to go yet, buddy."

"No. I'm writing songs I can't get recorded. And I've got a

girlfriend who's eighteen years younger than I am. Hell, she's got a kid young enough to be my grandkid."

"Oh hell. My God, man, you were seeing Kim. She's twenty-eight. Maybe it takes a young woman to keep up with you. I'll tell you what. Let me call Larry to come in tonight. We'll go do something, you and me. What do you say?"

"No. That's O.K. I think I'll just go on home."

"Come on, Bad. I've been working my butt off here the last couple of weeks. I could use a night off. We can just go out to the house if you like. It's been a while since you saw Shirley. She'd like to see you. She's been asking about you. You ought to stop in and say hi. I seem to remember she was baking something when I left this afternoon."

"No. I suspect I wouldn't be real good company tonight. You tell her I'll be by to see her soon."

"Well, let's go to a movie or something. I haven't seen a movie in God's own green time. We'll go see Clint Eastwood or something. There's always a Clint Eastwood picture around."

"Wayne, I appreciate what you're doing here. But I'm O.K. I just need some time to myself, you know?"

"The hell you need time alone. The last thing you need is time alone. And I ain't going to leave you alone. You and me are going out and have us a good time. You can fuss about that all you like. But you ain't going home to pick at your scabs."

Bad protests and Wayne insists. "I'm right," Wayne says as he climbs into the van, "you'll see. If you go home, you'll just brood, and then you'll start drinking; tomorrow morning you'll wake up feeling worse than you did today."

"No," Bad says. "This morning I woke up a half step above dead. An hour later, I'd slipped back a quarter step. It's not possible to feel any worse."

"I never wake up like that anymore."

"I feel sorry for people who don't drink. They wake up knowing that's as good as they are going to feel all day."

"Jack Lemmon. *The Apartment*. Funny line as long as you don't believe it."

"No temperance lectures tonight."

"Right. What do you want to do?"

"I want to go home. You want to do something, not me."

"How about a movie?"

"No. No movies."

"Well, we can't play golf or go bowling. How about baseball?"

"I've seen baseball. The Astros don't play it."

"Hell, I know. Take a left here. Get on Forty-five and head north to the house."

"Wayne, I love you, and Shirley too, but I really don't want to sit around and visit tonight."

"No. No, Bad. We're going fishing."

"It's getting dark, I got a busted ankle. We can't go fishing. I don't have any equipment."

"We're going night fishing. We're going to stop at the house and pick up tackle, and then head for the lake.

It's forty-five minutes away, my boat's there. We're going fishing."

On the lake, the slight breeze moves across the water and cools them off. They are both rank with Cutter, but the mosquitoes keep at them anyway. Bad is in the prow of the boat, wearing the orange life jacket Wayne insists on. At first Bad objects, figuring that if they went over, the cast would take on water and pull him down anyway, but wearing it shuts Wayne up. He sips at a beer and looks up at the sky.

"Stars," he says. "That may be the best thing about the road. Jesus . . . Colorado, New Mexico, Arizona, Utah. You should have seen the stars."

"Right here," Wayne says, "right here there are the biggest damn catfish you ever saw." He pulls a chicken liver out of a plastic container and smells it. "Damn," he says, pulling his head back. "It's too fresh. I told that guy I wanted old. He gave me fresh." He works the chicken liver onto the hook, attaches a lead sinker on another ten inches of line below the hook and lets the line out overboard, then reels up the slack. "Here," he says, handing it to Bad, "that one's yours."

"You ever go froggin'?"

"Nope, never have."

"I used to go out with my daddy and later my brother. We'd go out when it got good and dark, with a lantern and gigs. You got to keep walking the bank with the lantern toward the water and try to see beyond it. All you see is the frog's eyes sticking out of the water. But as long as the light's in his eyes, he won't move. You aim the gig right under the eyes, and just pull him out."

"It doesn't seem hardly fair, sticking a poor damn blind frog."

"That's what the frogs keep saying. But it takes some skill. You got to be good to get close enough for the light to be right in their eyes. And they're damn good eating. I used to love that. I'd walk along behind my old man all night, and he'd never say a word to me. He'd gig the frogs, and I'd carry the croaker sack for him. He'd never say a word. I mean, even when we got back to the truck, the most he'd say was 'You got them frogs?' and I'd say 'Yessir'; he'd sling them into the back of the truck and we'd drive home. The next morning, he'd go out and skin them, and Momma would fry the legs for dinner. And every damn time, when he'd sit down at the table, he'd look at me and say, 'The boy got us a mess of frogs last night.'"

"You never talk much about your old man."

"There ain't a lot to say. He never had a lot to say. He spent most of his life listening to my momma rag on him about his drinking and being shiftless. He was just a dirt farmer, mainly, did odd jobs. We were stinking poor. But he kept us fed. I don't remember ever being very hungry. You know, the damnedest thing, he never talked much around the house, but he'd go down to the store and get with his cronies, and he'd tell these big windies all day long. I remember him telling this story about running shine with friends of his. I don't know whether he actually did it or not, but I suspect he probably did.

"Anyway, this one night he was tearing down the road toward Mitchell and suddenly there is this trooper right behind him. He was in somebody's car, some souped-up Ford, and this trooper was right on his tail, siren going, lights flashing, lighting up the woods on both sides of the road. They were going down these one-lane dirt roads nearly full out. When they got to the straight road, he says he just let that thing go full tilt, up over a hundred when the trooper finally got wise and backed out. He claimed he would have gone faster than that if he had to, just to spare the trooper the humiliation of it all."

"Humiliation?"

"That's right, humiliation. You see, he claimed that night they weren't running any shine, they were just having a race, and he was running fifth."

"Hold it."

"I didn't say it was a true story."

"No. I mean hold it. I got a bite."

Even though he can't see, he can feel movement as Wayne sets the hook, pulling up quickly but steadily with his body. Then he hears the slight whir of the reel. "He's on. I got you, you son-of-a-bitch." The fish breaks the water suddenly. Bad sees only a faint gleam, and the splash of the water. His foot is wedged under the seat of the boat, and he can't get up. He reaches forward to help Wayne with the fish. He can see it now, but not distinctly. He reaches for it. "Hold it," Wayne yells, "he'll cut you. Get the light."

Bad searches with his hand under the seat for the flashlight. He can see the blur of the fish in front of him, and he feels the spray of water on the exposed toes of his foot. When he finds the light, the catfish is on the floor of the boat, still hooked and flopping. It is a decent-sized cat, four or five pounds. Wayne is trying to work the hook out. A thin line of blood trickles down his hand as he tries to get a grip on the fish.

"Damn, those are ugly bastards," Wayne says.

"We'll dress him up in a little cornmeal, and he'll look real nice on a plate."

The fish is in a bucket of water, occasionally raising a quick, furious splash in the stern of the boat, and Wayne is working another chicken liver onto his hook. "You reel yours in, too, and let's have a look. Make sure one of the bastards didn't slip off with your bait."

Bad starts to reel up and the line suddenly snags. He gives a tug; it gives and tightens again. "Hot damn, hold the phone there, Wayne." He works it up slow, and when it breaks the surface, he lifts the rod with his arms and shoulders. Even in the moonlight, he can see the rod is bent nearly double. They are more efficient this time, trapping the fish between the seat and Bad's cast. This one must go a good six pounds.

"He's a nice one," Wayne says.

"Son-of-a-bitch was just going to stay down there with a hook in his jaw, hoping it would go away. No telling how long I had him on there."

"They'll do that every now and again," Wayne says. He

baits Bad's hook and sends it over the side again. Bad lets the line out until he feels it slack and then tightens it. He wedges the grip of the rod under his leg and digs out a cigarette. "Anything else you need?" Wayne asks.

"Hand me one more of those barley pops and I believe I'll be settled for a while." He opens the beer and takes a long swallow. He looks up to the stars. "I hate to admit this," he says, "but this was a damn good idea."

"Yeah, you can get awful damn peaceful on a lake at night."

For a while they just drift at anchor, not conscious of how their lines might be tangling with the boat, Bad drinking his beer and smoking, Wayne puffing on his pipe.

"Listen," Bad says, "you know anything about this guy Rounds who's running for Senate?"

"Congress. Running for Congress. Yeah, I know a little. Why?"

"What do you think of him?"

"Seems right to me. He don't like Communists, I don't like Communists. I guess I'll vote for him."

"What's he going to do about Communists?"

"Stop the little fuckers. I mean, they're breeding like fleas now. I mean, first it was China and Vietnam, now they're in South America. Like a swarm of fleas. Somebody's got to stop them. Hell, you want them living that close to you?"

"Well, no."

"There it is. Congress won't do squat to stop them. I think it's time for some new blood."

"Cuba's closer than South America, ain't it?"

"So?"

"That don't really bother me, that's all. I mean, the Communists in Cuba. I never think about it."

"Maybe you better. They're like fleas, tough to get rid of when they get a hold somewhere."

"So you think this Rounds guy is O.K.?"

"Yeah, I think so. Why?"

"Nothing. Just wondering."

They drift at anchor, sipping their drinks and smoking. From the shore, the sound of crickets and cicadas rises and falls.

"So," Wayne says at last, "you called your son."

"I called my son."

"And he said?"

"I told you. He didn't want to talk to me. And I can't blame him. He's right. I had no right to call him. I should have just left him alone. I was wrong."

"You were wrong twenty years ago. And you've been wrong since, because you didn't call him. But you weren't wrong when you did. He was wrong, not you."

"Wayne, I went twenty years without trying to find him. He's right. It's too little, too late. It's the same damn old story."

"But that's just it. It's not the same old story. The same old story is not calling. This time you did it. You were late, real late, but you did the right thing. What you're blaming yourself for is not calling him, but for all the years you didn't.

That's over now. You changed it. You called him. Don't give up now that you're on the right track. Keep after him."

"He doesn't want to talk to me."

"The way I figure it, you don't have a lot of rights here. You gave them up a long time ago. But you got the right to talk to him. Don't you be like that damn fish there, hanging in with a hook in its jaw, hoping it was going to go away."

"When he was just little, I was gone most of the time. I was on the road, or I was off on a tear. And when I'd come home, he was there, happy to see me. Marge might be cold enough to crack a tractor block, but Stevie was always happy to see me. He'd come running and give me a hug and want to know what I brought him. And I always brought him something. Even on those vicious benders. I might give away my car, but when I got sober, I got him something. I always had something for him."

"Sure you did."

"Hold it. Just shut up for a minute. The last time, the time I came home and they were gone, I'd stopped along the way, and I'd bought him this jeep. And I stood outside the house, just holding that jeep. I mean, it was big, big enough for him to ride in, and I just stood there trying to figure it all out, holding on to that jeep. I took it with me when I went to L.A., and when I came back to Nashville I brought it with me. And somewhere down the line, somewhere, I lost it. I lost the damn jeep. How could I lose the fucking jeep?"

"Stop kicking your own butt for what's past. You're doing the right thing now. Don't let what you can't help fuck it up."

He has the catfish filleted, breaded and in the frying pan along with a couple of hush puppies from the left-over breading, when the phone rings.

"Hi. You all right?" Jean asks.

"Yeah, I'm fine. How about you?"

"Oh, fine. I called you last night."

"I was fishing."

"Fishing?"

He holds the phone down near where the fish is popping and crackling in the skillet. "Six-pound catfish," he says.

"I was worried. You sounded so depressed the last time I talked to you."

"Well, I went fishing, and tonight I go back to work. I feel better now. How's Buddy?"

"He's still playing with the cars you sent. He's having a great time."

"Yeah, I know how to pick those toys. He's a real boy, and I know what real boys like."

"Real girls?"

"Sooner or later."

"You still want me to come to Houston?"

"Oh God. Yes, I want you to come to Houston."

"I've got a little time coming. I can take off at the end of the month. And, well, I'm kind of lonesome here. I'd like to come."

"What are the dates? I work Wednesday through Saturday night. Sunday through Tuesday I'm off."

"The twenty-eighth through the second. I already made the reservations. On Western. Oh, and I have to bring Buddy."

"Of course. Of course. I wouldn't have it any other way."

"Then it's all O.K.?"

"Goddamn. Goddamn right it's O.K. Hold it." He runs back to turn off the fish, which has begun to smoke. "Goddamn. You bet it's O.K. I'll be so damned glad to see you all."

"I am real glad to see you all here again," he tells the audience, most of them regulars, but mixed with a lot of new ones the radio ads have brought in. "Since the last time I saw you, I've been on the road. Came back with a broke ankle, a new bass player you all are going to really like, and a big case of homesickness I'm going to cure tonight with my band, and all my friends out there."

The stool he has to sit on limits what he can do in terms of stage movement, but it makes him more conscious of the guitar. He starts his own flat-picked bluegrass intro to "Wildwood Flower" and lets the band catch up to him. On the breaks, he feels both more deliberate with the melody and at the same time more free to improvise, holding the guitar up on his knee and closer than it is when it's strung across his neck.

At the first break between sets, he stays where he is and lets people come up to talk to him. The rest of the band goes out into the bar to talk with wives and friends, to sit and drink. Most of the people who come to talk with him are regulars, old friends who have been coming to the club over the five years he has been there. He gets requests, but not for the standards. Instead, these people want to hear the odd stuff he doesn't get to play very often. The regulars work at coming up with new requests, trying to catch him up on a song he doesn't know. Most of them he does.

It is a relief to get away from a play list. Even with the addition of Al, the band knows four or five times more numbers than they will be able to play tonight. He will keep bringing up new songs for Al during the Thursday rehearsals, and when Al has settled well, he won't hesitate to call songs that they haven't rehearsed together, knowing that the band will be tight and familiar enough to pull Al through any rough spots.

"What do you think of the new bass player?" he asks Tiny and a few of the other regulars. Everyone says the same thing. He is fine, though he doesn't have that thump Dave had. "It'll come," he tells them. "It'll come," he says, "it'll come."

By the last set, he is tired. On the road, he plays for two, sometimes three hours. At home, he plays five. Even with long breaks, going on thirty minutes, he is tired of sitting. The odd posture has thrown a strain on his back and shoulders, and his butt aches. He is sweating hard and running out of voice by the time they pack it up for last call. It takes a week or two to get back into shape after the road, though in the last couple of years it seems it takes a little longer each time.

"You pulled it off real well up there on that stool," Wayne says.

"How'd we do?"

"I can't tell until I close out the registers, but I ordered an extra twenty cases over the usual. We got maybe a half a dozen left. I'd say we had ourselves a real fine night. The band sounds as good as it ever did."

"If I didn't know you didn't have any kind of an ear at all, I'd take that as an insult, but it's coming together. It won't be too much longer until we're back where we should be."

"You want to take me to breakfast?" Kim asks.

"Not tonight, darlin'. I've had it for tonight."

"I'll take you to breakfast."

"No, really, darlin'. I'm tired. I'm sure someone else will be glad to go."

"You're really pissed, aren't you?"

"No. Sorry to tell you this, darlin', but I'm not pissed in the least."

He is onstage, the Ryman Auditorium, in the middle of a number. Tommy Sweet is behind him, Will Samuels is on drums. When he begins the chorus, Marge joins in on the harmony. But then it is Jean and then Marge again. When the chorus is over and they move into the bridge, he realizes he doesn't remember how to play this bridge, or any other one. He just looks at the guitar around his neck, and the singers and the band stop and wait.

Chapter Thirteen

The phone keeps ringing. He can't remember what day this is, or why he is getting up. When he finds the phone and answers it, he can't make out what the person is saying.

"Who is this?" he asks.

"Steven."

There is a pause while that registers and then jolts him wide awake. "Steven. How are you?"

"O.K. I've been thinking over what you said the other night. I guess maybe I do want to talk to you."

"Sure. Hell yes. When? Where?"

"Well, I don't have any vacation or sick leave coming. I could come to Houston next weekend, or you could come here."

"What the hell time is it?"

"Seven ours. I guess nine yours?"

"O.K. What are you doing this afternoon?"

"Watching football, I guess."

"I'll be there. I'll call you back in about an hour or so from the airport and tell you when to come to get me."

"This afternoon?"

"I don't have to be at work until Wednesday. I'm coming."

He parks in the private lot off I-45 and takes the shuttle into Intercontinental Airport. It is eleven forty-five. He has thirty minutes until the Continental twelve-thirty boards. He has a shoulder bag with two clean shirts, underwear, shaving kit, and an extra boot. Getting up the escalator on crutches is more difficult than he thought it would be. He can't seem to find the timing for the next step, and he knows if he misses it, he is going to fall when the step rises fully. "Aw, for crap sake," the guy behind him says, and puts his arm around Bad's back. Together, they step onto the escalator. "I'm afraid I'm going to have trouble getting off, too," Bad explains. "Shit," the guy says, "there are elevators here, you know." But at the top, he takes Bad's arm and guides him off.

The rest of it is easy. People make way as he crutches his way to the ticket window and an agent takes his Master-Card and gets his ticket while he sits down and smokes. His crutches set off the metal detector on the concourse, and he has to stand while they sweep him with a hand-held detector. But by the time he has called Steven in L.A., it is boarding time, and he gets to board with the kids and old people.

The flight takes off at twelve-thirty, and lands in Los Angeles at one-thirty. Flying time is three hours, but in clock time it is only one hour. The kid next to him, who looks about college age, in polo shirt and jeans, keeps fiddling with the switch on the music headset. "What's good?" Bad asks him.

"Nothing really," the kid says. "It's all about the same. The R and B on channel two is O.K. Four is just country crap."

Bad points up at his hat. "It's fine, I'm used to it." But when he switches to channel four, he gets Kenny Rogers, followed by the Gatlin Brothers. "Just country crap," he agrees.

He buys two little bottles of Jack Daniel's and a cup of ice for five dollars. He considers dumping both bottles in at once, while the ice is still hard, but figures that by doing that, the drink will go quicker and inflict even more time on him. He sips at his drink and looks out the window.

Steven is twenty-four, was twenty-four in April. The night he was born, in Vanderbilt University Hospital because Bad Blake, by God, could afford the very best, Bad was in Joplin, Missouri, playing with the boys. Word came while he was on-stage, a phone call from Marge's mother, who had been flown down from Lima, Ohio, to be with her. The message had been passed from stagehand to road manager to Will Samuels, who left his drum kit at the end of "Cheatin' Night Tonight," to announce that Bad was the father of an eight-pound-three-ounce boy. Two thousand people cheered in the auditorium; Bad Blake smiled, tipped his hat and went right into the introduction to "Lost Highway."

After the show, Bad called Marge and then took the band to dinner, stood them to rounds of drinks and bought cigars and passed them out to everyone in the restaurant, announcing, "Don't you all go home and put those away for a souve-

nir. When Bad Blake buys smokes, by God, they get smoked."
Later, in the hotel, he held a party in his room for the band,
and when that was done, feeling paternal and righteous, he
went to bed alone, the first time he had done that at a hotel
stop during the whole tour.

Steven was three weeks old the first time Bad saw him,
the smallest thing Bad had seen in his life, too small, it
seemed, to hold. Later that afternoon, he invited the press to
the house and posed out by the pool, holding Steven, who in
the most famous picture is holding the fringe at the yoke of
Bad's shirt in a tiny fist. The label wanted to use that picture
on the *Slow Boat* album, but Bad thought it was the wrong
image and went with the shot of him with his guitar on the
front fender of his black Cadillac.

He tries to remember the last time he saw Steven. He may
have been playing cars in the dirt or hiding in the bushes playing soldier, but Bad can't remember, though he has images of
both. Either would explain why he came home with a jeep.

Though he was the first one on the plane, he is the last one
off. The flight attendants will not even take his crutches from
aft storage until the rest of the passengers are off the plane.
An attendant escorts him off the plane and up the jet walk
to the terminal. He assumes that this is to protect the airline
against a lawsuit if he falls, but he is actually grateful for the
help. His hands are sweating so hard he is afraid they are
going to slip on the grips of the crutches.

When he is suddenly through the door and out in the terminal itself, he searches the faces, unsure who exactly he is looking for, but sure he will recognize him. He feels a touch at his sleeve and a voice says either "Bad" or "Dad," he is not sure which since it happens so fast. When he turns his head slightly left he is looking at the man who must be Steven.

He is as tall as Bad, taller than Bad hunched over his crutches. His hair is dark, nearly black, like Bad's at his age. He is thinner than Bad ever was and dressed in an open-collared striped shirt and khaki trousers. He smiles tentatively and offers his hand. "I recognized you from your pictures," he says.

"You don't look like any of the pictures I have of you," Bad says, "but I recognized you."

"Let me take your bag."

"It's O.K. I can manage."

"What happened to your leg?"

Bad waits outside the terminal, fighting off cabdrivers who want to take his bag and load him in. Steven has gone to get the car. Bad lights a cigarette and looks around. It has been nearly twenty years since he was in L.A. Even from the airport it looks too damned big, too much like what Houston is becoming. The crowding is intense. No one looks twice at a big old man in a cowboy hat and one white boot.

There is honking to his right, and Steven steps out of a little tan car. Bad moves toward him. "It might be a tight fit with the crutches," Steven apologizes.

As they drive out of the airport, Bad has his first chance to really look at him. If he took thirty years off himself, they would be close, but not quite a match. There is something of Marge in the eyes and the mouth. His hands, on the wheel, are large, but the fingers are not as long or as graceful as Bad's. "I hope this won't be too uncomfortable. We've got a way to go yet." Steven's voice is higher and softer than Bad's, probably close to what Bad's would be without the years of singing, whiskey and cigarettes.

"No," Bad lies, "this is just fine. Nice cozy little car. I like it." He can't get his left leg fully stretched and there is already painful pressure on his shin from the cast.

"You don't remember my cowskin Cadillac, do you?" Bad asks.

"No."

"You used to love to ride in that. You drove. I'd put you on the seat between my legs and you'd put your hands on the wheel and you'd steer as much as I'd let you, and you'd honk the horn. You'd make it moo."

"Moo?"

"Yeah. The damned thing had a horn that mooed like a cow. It had cowhide seat covers and silver dollars worked into the dashboard. It was a black fifty-nine Cadillac convertible."

"Black-and-white seat covers? With hair?"

"Yeah, sure as hell."

"God, I do remember the hairy seat covers."

"I'd say, 'You want to go for a ride, pard?' and no matter what you were doing, you'd put it down and take off for that car. Maybe it was more yours than mine. What else do you remember?"

"Not much, scattered things."

"Do you remember the house?"

"A little. I remember flowers, lots of those. And I remember the leg of something—a coffee table, maybe? It was curved and gold."

"Yeah, we had gold on all the furniture. There was a coffee table. Do you remember the sofa?"

"No."

"It was ten feet long, custom made in blue velvet. A real monster, but your mother liked it."

"You live in Houston."

"For the past twelve years."

"Why Houston, why not Nashville?"

"I was in Houston in the mid-fifties, before I met your mother. It was hotter than hell, but I liked it. I just sort of drifted back and stayed. It was nice when I got there, then it got big, something like this."

"I thought you'd live in Nashville."

"I could, I suppose. I've still got some friends there, and I go back now and again, but I couldn't live there. I could find a lot of work as a sideman, you know. But I'm not a sideman. I know some who have gone from front men to sidemen. It doesn't work. It drives them crazy. No. I've got my own band in Houston. They're good boys and a good band. We play in a club there, and we do all right. It's steady and we do what we want to."

"Does it bother you? I mean, that you're not as big as you once were?"

"I like what I'm doing. That's something. There's a world of people who don't like what they're doing and never have. Would I like to be back on top again? Hell yes, I would. It was good up there. I liked the money, I liked the fame. I liked it a lot. Too much, in fact. But I'd like to have another shot at it. I'd do it better this time. I've learned a few things over the years. And I guess one of the things I've learned is that I can live without all of that.

"And then, maybe I ain't done yet. I've been writing songs again. I'm doing another album with Tommy. You remember Tommy? You were probably too young, but he used to be at the house all the time. And then I have this deal cooking with a guy who's running for Congress. I'm going to campaign for him. Things may be coming around again. You never can tell."

"Good," Steven says. "It sounds good."

They have exited the San Diego Freeway and are on the Santa Monica, heading west. Bad looks out over the stretch of rooftops that gradually disappear in haze. "I remember this road. I remember it all purple from some kind of tree that bloomed along here."

"Jacarandas. They're still here. In spring and early summer they still bloom like crazy. Some days you can see them through the smog."

They ride on in silence, off the freeway at Lincoln and north, up a street for two blocks, then left for another to an apartment building behind locked wrought-iron gates. "This looks nice. Good and secure."

"I've lived here a couple of years. It's O.K. I like it all right."

"Close to the beach?"

"It's about a mile. I don't go very often."

"What do you do for fun?"

"The usual. There's a pool here, and a tennis court. I watch TV, go to the movies."

Bad struggles out of the car, working his crutches from the back-seat and through the door. "No girlfriends?"

"No. A wife."

"A wife? Jesus. It never occurred to me you might be married. How long? What's her name?"

"Judy. You'll meet her. We got married a year ago in July."

"My God. I had no idea. I guess congratulations are in order."

"Thanks. You'll like her." Then, "She convinced me to call you."

Steven helps him slowly up a winding wrought-iron stairway to a second-story apartment. Inside, it is sparsely furnished, mostly in white and chrome and glass. This is, Bad assumes, a sign of taste. It looks cold to him. Steven leads him to the white sofa and helps him down.

"Mr. Blake." A tall, thin blonde in T-shirt and shorts, barefoot, has come into the room. She reaches out her hand. "Don't get up. I'm Judy."

"Judy, I don't believe I could get up. I'm kind of scrunched down here. But I'm real happy to meet you. And call me Bad, please."

"Can I get you something to drink? A beer maybe? I know Steve will want a beer." Steve is across the room at the TV set.

"Would you have anything a little stronger?"

"I'm sorry. We have beer and wine. We really don't drink."

"Beer's fine. And do you mind if I smoke?"

"Go right ahead. We have an ashtray somewhere. I'll bring it with the beers."

"Who's playing?" Bad asks.

"Rams and Bengals. They're in Cincinnati."

"Who's going to win?" Bad really has no interest in the game, but he is grateful for a distraction.

But it is Judy who makes small talk, running for beers, getting a chair to rest Bad's ankle on. Steven watches the football game and makes noncommittal answers. From Judy he learns that Marge spent most of her life as a buyer for sportswear at The Broadway, never remarried, though she had a relationship with another buyer that lasted nearly ten years. She died of lymphoma after a year and a half of treatment. Steven adds a comment or clarification here and there.

And it is Judy who brings out the sweater box full of pictures. The pictures go all the way back to Marge as a girl. There are pictures of their wedding, pictures he has forgotten even existed. Bad in wide-lapeled western suits, always with a scarf knotted at the neck, Bad in shirts spangled with sequined wagon wheels and cactus. Marge in a dress that billows around her body and gathers in again at the knee. There is a picture of Bad playing guitar to Steven on the blue velvet sofa. The skinny kid, grinning, with a beer in his hand, is Tommy Sweet.

In the pictures, Steven grows up, from infant to man lounging by the pool, Judy at his side. In between are school pictures, vacation pictures, several including a man Bad does not recognize. Steven as cub scout and boy scout. Steven in football gear, and standing stiffly in suit and tie next to a girl in a formal dress. Steven's high school graduation picture could be a picture of a young Bad Blake in a green cap and gown.

Marge ages subtly, holding her looks through most of the pictures, until near the end, sick, she becomes a very old woman. Judy takes two pictures out and holds them together. They seem to be pictures of Marge taken ten years apart. "One year," Judy said. "It happened that fast and that hard."

Gradually, Steven is drawn in. "That was when I was seventeen," he says of one picture. "We were living in Culver City then." When Bad asks why she never married the thin, balding man who appears in many of the pictures, Steve answers. "She told me that once was enough. It changed things. So they just kept seeing each other."

"He ever move in?" Bad asks suddenly.

"No. He was around most of the time. I'm sure they talked about it, but they never did. He was really broken up when she died. He comes by every week or so. He's really sad."

Bad wants to say something about his own sorrow, but feels he is intruding on grief that he has no right to. Grief seems to belong to this man who watched while Bad's son grew up away from him. "What did she tell you about me?"

"Not much really. She never lied, and if I asked her something she would tell me, but she never volunteered much. I knew who you were. For a while, I must have been nine or ten, I told everybody I knew, everybody I met, that you were my father. No one ever believed me. I mean, we had different names, you weren't around. Finally, I just gave up, and after that I never told anyone."

"Steve and I had been going out for nearly a year before he told me he was your son."

"It never seemed to matter very much."

"She told you about the drinking?"

"Not at first. But later she did, yeah. Once, I was sixteen or seventeen, still in high school anyway, I came home one night really ripped. I thought she was going to kill me. She started hitting me. First she slapped me, and then it was like she couldn't stop. The next day she told me about you and what she went through."

"I won't lie to you, either. She went through hell. I made her life about as miserable as it's possible to make someone's. I was one mean son-of-a-bitch back then."

"Did you beat her?"

"Once. I hit her once. I used to bust up the furniture pretty regular. I liked to throw television sets out of windows. I'd always find the expensive stuff. If I couldn't throw it, I'd throw stuff at it. Anyway, one night I busted up most of the bedroom, and instead of running like she usually did, Marge tried to stop me. I just hauled off and backhanded her. She was such a little thing. I knocked her about halfway across the room. After that I sobered up for a while. I must have quit drinking for about six months, and then I just got started up again. It was about a year later that she left."

"You still drink."

"Yeah. I still drink. I guess I always will now. But I don't drink like that anymore. I don't go on benders, and I don't get drunk. It may not be right, but it's a hell of a lot better than it was."

"And women and drugs."

"That, too. I did all of that. I mean, part of that is road life. I mean, you can't know unless you've done it, what it's like to be on the road for a couple of months at a time, living in a touring bus with a hotel thrown in every once in a while for variety. You get bored, think you're going crazy. And there are always women and drugs and booze, and they pass the time for you. I'm not making excuses now. There are people who go on the road and they handle it. They have it all worked out, and they deal with it all. Part of my problem was that I didn't make it, really make it, big until I was in my thirties. And I had been doing it for fifteen years. By that time I figure I must have spent at least a damn five years of my life on a bus, mostly as someone's sideman.

"When it got to where it was finally my bus, my sidemen, my show and my songs, I just figured everything else was mine, too. I knew I had paid my dues, a hell of a lot of dues, more than a lot of people do, and I also knew that the world owed me. All that stuff was just interest on a great big debt that the world was going to have to start paying back to old Bad Blake. And I guess I figured that Marge was supposed to understand that, to understand that I was just collecting on my debt, just like a banker. What she understood that I didn't understand, didn't understand until years and years later, was that she and you were the payoff, principal and interest. It's the damn shame of the world, the way you don't figure things out until it's too goddamned late to do anything about it."

"Is that what this is?"

"What?"

"Trying to do something when it's too late."

"Steve. Bad," Judy says, "let me get you guys another beer."

"Maybe," Bad says, "maybe that's just what it is. It's too late to do anything about Marge, that's for sure."

"What were you going to do for her?"

"I don't know. Tell her I loved her, mostly. Tell her I never stopped loving her. You know, I had two more wives after her. I've had four altogether. But damn, I really loved her."

"And what do you want to do about me?"

Bad waits, then digs in his pocket. He pulls out a sheaf of bills in the gold money clip.

"I don't need money. I make good money, so does Judy."

"No. Not money. I bought this on your eighteenth birthday. I was going to send it to you, but I didn't know how. I've been carrying it ever since, just in case I ever found you. Here, it's yours." He hands Steven the money clip. "It's a little worn, but it's real."

Steven takes the money clip, holding it by its edges as if it were delicate or dangerous. It is battered and scratched. He keeps looking at it as if mystified. Then he tosses it back in Bad's lap. "Keep it," he says. "I don't want it. I don't want anything from you. I gave up wanting from you years and years ago."

Bad looks at the money clip in his lap. He picks it up and sets it on the coffee table. "Why the hell did you call me back?"

"I told you, Judy convinced me I should meet you."

"How. How did she convince you?"

"She said I needed to."

"Is this what you wanted to see, an old, fat singer, pretty close to broke down? The busted ankle is an extra, no charge. I don't know what the hell you want. I know what I want. I wanted to see my son, to know he's all right. I wanted to know that you grew up and you did all right. I've seen that. I guess I better go."

Bad gets his crutches and works his way up. "I'd appreciate it if you'd call me a cab."

"I'll drive you."

"No. Call a cab. I don't want to put either of us through any more of this. You think maybe you want an apology. All right. I apologize. I understand what I was, and I understand my fault in all of this. But if you're thinking that I was having a wonderful time during the last twenty years, let me explain a couple of things to you.

"There may have been a day or two in those twenty years that I didn't think about you. There may have been. But by God, I don't remember a single one. I've spent the last twenty years of my life wondering what happened to my wife and son, and at the same time, I knew that whatever happened was my damned fault and there was nothing I could do about it. Not a damned thing. I wondered what you were doing and what you were thinking, what you looked like and what you liked to do. I bought that damned money clip because I didn't know one goddamned thing about you. I didn't know if you were short or tall or skinny or fat, if you liked sports or cars or what. I went to get you a present for your eighteenth birthday, and all I could find was a goddamned money clip, and then I didn't know where to send the fucking thing."

"Crap."

"What?"

"I said 'crap.' That's all it is. You come here after twenty years and find me because you say we've got to talk. But you aren't talking to me, you're giving me a load of crap."

"Call me a goddamned cab."

"No. Sit down. You've had your say. I'm going to have mine. You didn't know anything about me. You didn't know where I lived. Well, I lived right here. Right in Los Angeles, where you found me when you tried to find me. As long as I can remember, Mom had her name in the L.A. directory. It would have cost you a dime to call information and find us anytime you wanted to. If you were so damned concerned about my birthdays, all you had to do was make two phone calls. I don't think you ever cared enough to even make a phone call to me. I don't think you cared twenty cents' worth."

Bad sinks back to the sofa. "That's not true. I cared. I always cared. I was scared, mostly. I came looking for you right away. The record company stopped me, afraid that between grief and booze I might finally snap. Later there were injunctions—court orders to keep me away. After that I was just afraid to face up to what I had done. I pretended it was all Marge's fault. The longer it went on, the worse it seemed. In nineteen sixty-nine I came to town for a show in Inglewood and I found your mother, but she was a step ahead of me and she had shipped you off somewhere. You were staying with one of her friends. I followed her for two days but she never got near wherever she had you stashed. And she called the cops because I was following her. I spent two hours in the North Hollywood police station, glad-handing cops and talking my way out. But mostly I was afraid. It all comes down to that. I was afraid of what I used to be. I didn't want to look at that again."

Steven walks over to the television set, adjusts the volume and then switches it off. "It doesn't matter. It doesn't matter how much you talk. You can't talk away twenty years. When I was a kid, I'd hear you singing 'Slow Boat' and I'd think about you coming back, and we'd all get on this boat and just sail off someplace together."

"Did your mother tell you I wrote that song for her?"

"No. And that's not the point anyway."

"I did. Right after we were married. I still sing it. God, do I still sing it. And I never sing it without thinking of her, and you. Everywhere I go, people want to hear 'Slow Boat,' and I keep doing it, and every time I do it, it hurts. It's like this little burr that keeps sticking me. Funny, isn't it? That's the one song everyone will remember me for."

"What are you telling me this for? What do you want from me?"

"My son back."

"You've come to the wrong place. I'm Marge's son."

"I guess I'll go, then. There doesn't seem to be any more to say."

"I guess there isn't."

"Well, you take care of yourself. Judy, it was real nice to meet you. Think it over. Call me if you want."

"I don't think so."

In his motel room, he wakes to a woman's voice. It is still dark and smoky in the room. "Bad," she says, "I'm sorry. I didn't know it would be like that. Forgive me." Gradually, he recognizes the voice and face as Judy's. She is sitting on the edge of the bed. She reaches out and touches his forehead. "I wanted to do the right thing," she says. Things just don't work out, Bad explains. No matter how much you want them to, they just don't work out. Her hand is soft and warm, stroking his face. She leans to him, as if comforting a child. He reaches his left arm around her shoulder and pulls, his right hand going naturally to her breast.

He sees the flash of light and his face goes cold. Steven is standing at the side of the bed, Judy at his side, the bloody razor in his hand. Bad holds the flap of skin to his cheek, trying to reattach it. Everything is slippery with blood, and the skin keeps sliding off his face. "Things just never work," Steven says as he and Judy walk out the door. Bad does not know how to hold the blood in.

"It is seven o'clock," the voice on the phone says. He is covered with sweat and the air conditioner works with a steady rush of cold air over him. He lies still, trying to orient himself. He is in California, but he is leaving.

He gets a standby seat on the noon flight. Buckling himself in, he calculates that it is a three-hour flight, but he will arrive in Houston at five o'clock tonight. Yesterday he gained two hours and walked into his past. This afternoon, he gives them back.

Chapter Fourteen

He has three days before Jean comes to town, two weeks before he gets the cast off. What he has to do is clean the house up before she gets in. When he looks, he sees dirt he hasn't seen before. The furniture is old, the pictures on the wall are crooked. There are records scattered over the floor. The walls need paint, the wood floors are scuffed and scratched. There is grease caked around the burners of the stove, the kitchen faucet leaks.

He could, he supposes, hire someone to come in and do this. He is, after all, a cripple. But he starts, first just straightening up, sweeping and vacuuming. Then he begins to wash the door and window frames. He moves to the kitchen and works on the stove, the refrigerator, the cabinets. This done, the floor looks even grimier than it had. He gets a bucket and a mop. He mops with one hand, balancing on his crutch.

He is on his hands and knees, trying to drag himself along the wooden floor in the living room, pulling his cast behind him, when the thought hits him. He is an old, fat man with a broken ankle, scrubbing and waxing his floor for a woman he has known only a month. Worse yet, he suspects he will try to paint the bedroom walls before he is done. He tries to make sense of the whole thing. He goes to the telephone.

"I know a bunch of the people who work on the newspapers here," he tells her. "You want me to get you some interviews?"

"I've been thinking about it. Maybe. Maybe it's time for me to make a move. Would you mind doing that for me?"

"No. No, that's fine. I'm glad to do it. You think you might want to marry me?"

"Jesus, you're serious."

"Well?"

"Oh God. Jesus, Bad, no. This is all too much. I've only known you a month. No, Bad, I can't marry you."

"But you think you might want to stick around for a while?"

"Look, Bad, this is all a little too much for me right now."

"O.K. Forget it. I'm sorry I said it. I'll see you in three days. I'll be at the airport to meet you. I'll be the big cripple with the cowboy hat. The one grinning like an idiot."

"Right. I'll see you then."

What is so bad about housework he really can't figure out. He knows everyone hates it, and he avoids it. But he is having a good time. He likes the way his house takes on a fresh look. The stove gleams as if it was fresh from the showroom, and like a television woman, he can see himself in his kitchen floor. Maybe what he has always done wrong is keep his women at home while he went to work. This time he could be the one to stay home while she went off to work. It is after midnight, he has Bob Wills on the stereo, and he feels like he could go on all night.

He is working in the bedroom, washing blinds and scrubbing sills, when the telephone rings.

"Bad, I'm sorry to bother you, but like things are getting really strange."

It takes him a second to place the voice, which is hushed and slurred.

"Kim?"

"Bad. Look, I hate to ask this, but can I come over? I mean, for the night?"

"How much you had to drink, Kim?"

"A lot. But there's this guy, Bad. I'm scared. I want to come over. I don't want to stay here."

"What the hell guy? What the hell you talking about?"

"There's this guy, Johnny. We've been going out for a while. We had a fight, Bad. I think he's going to hurt me."

"Is he there?"

"No, he left."

"Well, lock your doors, Kim. Don't let the bastard in."

"Bad, he's a big guy. I'm really scared. Can I come over? Can you come and get me?"

"Kim, it's one o'clock in the morning. You've been drinking, darlin', he's been drinking; he's somewhere sleeping it off. You better do the same."

"This guy's serious. He rides with this motorcycle gang. I'm scared."

"O.K. I don't think you better drive. I'll come and get you.

You stay in the house, don't let anybody in, except me. If anyone else comes to the door, call the police. Ol' Bad's on his way, darlin'."

"You'll come?"

"Lock the doors. Don't let anyone in. No one."

Outside, the night air is still and heavy. His foot, though, is cold where he has sloshed cleaning water onto the cast. He climbs into the truck and is putting the key in the ignition when the thought hits him. He is fifty-six years old, fat, going toward bloat, hobbled by a busted ankle, and he is scared. He pushes the key into the ignition, but he can't turn it.

What can he do if Kim's motorcycle boy comes back? In the house, he has a Ruger .38 caliber pistol that he has not fired in over twenty years. In the van are a tire iron and some chains. What good will any of this do him? He tries to turn the key, but his arm feels heavy and boneless. He goes back into the house.

The gun seems to be in good shape, though when he holds it up to the light, he can see dust and pits in the barrel. He cannot remember the last time he fired it or the last time he cleaned it. He can't figure out how it got so dusty sitting in a drawer wrapped in an old T-shirt. Probably it would fire, though the ammunition is also twenty years old. He slips the gun into the waistband of his jeans and starts back for the door.

He can't do this. He can't face the motorcycle guy with or without the gun. He worries that he couldn't pull the trigger if he had to, then that he could. He puts the gun on the end table and sits on the sofa. He picks up the phone.

"Are you O.K.?"

"Yeah, I guess so. I think I fell asleep."

"Look. I can't get my car started. I'm going to call the police."

"Don't call the cops. Johnny will kill me if you call the cops."

"I'm afraid he'll kill you if I don't. I can't get over there."

"I'll drive over myself."

"Kim, don't do that. You're drunk. Let me call the cops."

"No, no cops. In the morning, when he sobers up, Johnny will be O.K. I just don't want to stay alone tonight."

"I can't come and get you, and you can't drive."

"Oh hell, forget it, Bad, just forget it."

He holds the phone for a couple of seconds, listening to it buzz. He gets up, goes to the kitchen and fixes a long drink. He comes back, picks up the phone, deciding to call the police, then puts it back down. She is drunk. The motorcycle guy is drunk. Probably they just need to sleep it off.

In 1967, in Nashville, he drives for hours with a bottle of whiskey wedged between his legs and the .38 tucked into his belt. He has just finished cutting his album *Back in the Crying Place*. The title cut, the one cut he is sure of for a single, has been released two weeks earlier by Cal Farrell on Decca. It sits at thirty-two with a bullet.

This is the last album on his contract, and the next contract depends on how well it does. His own label has sold the rights to his song to Decca. He hasn't been told. He only finds out when he hears it on the radio. Its first week out, it hits *Billboard*'s Hot 100, and his album won't come out for three more weeks. He has no chance.

The deal was, Arthur Turock of J.M.I. tells him, that Cal Farrell's album wasn't supposed to be released until a month after his. Decca is in violation, and J.M.I. is going to sue. What the hell good does that do him? He wheels around the corner and takes another long pull at the bottle. It's clear to him. There was no deal. J.M.I. has sold the rights to his song clear and simple. They figure that Farrell can get a hit on it and he can't.

He guns the car and takes another long drink. When he pulls into the driveway at Arthur Turock's, he cuts the engine, recorks his bottle and tucks it under the seat. He gets out of the car and slides the gun around behind his back, where his coat covers it.

"Why, Bad Blake," Bonnie Turock says at the door. "We haven't seen you here in ever so long. You come in. Arthur and the children are in the den, watching *Bonanza*. You come in and join us."

"I'm obliged, Bonnie. You're looking real nice."

Bonnie Turock is a large, horse-faced woman in a floor-length print dress. She is from Macon, Georgia, and has never made the switch required of a record company executive's wife. At cocktail parties, she serves home-baked pie. Maybe

Arthur has hung on to her because she has the homey touch he doesn't. Around Bonnie, Arthur Turock could pass for a real human being.

Arthur Turock is sitting on the sofa in his stocking feet, wearing chinos and a blue knit shirt. Next to him, his daughter, nine or ten, four feet six, one hundred and forty pounds, stares up at Bad. Her thick-lensed glasses magnify her eyes and make her appear even more cross-eyed than she probably is. She has the look of a startled fish. His sixteen-year-old son has hair that damn near covers his eyes, and skinny zip-up boots.

When Bad comes into the room, Arthur jumps up, confused, regains his composure and comes forward to Bad, hand outstretched. "Bad, this is a surprise. I wish I'd known you were coming."

"Arthur. June, Teddy. I'm sorry to bother you all. I just had an idea, something we need to discuss. It won't take but a minute. I hate to break in on your television. Just one minute is all it will take."

"Why don't you fellows go into the dining room?" Bonnie says. "I'll fix you all some coffee or some ice tea, and bring you some pie."

"Don't trouble yourself, Bonnie. This will just be a minute and then I'll be gone. I didn't really mean to barge in. Maybe we can just go out to the back porch for a second."

"Hell, let me get my shoes," Arthur says.

"This will only take a second, Arthur. You like the Beatles, Teddy?"

"Yeah."

"Me, too."

"Sure."

Out on the back porch, Turock turns on him. "Look, I know why you're here. We've discussed this whole thing. Decca slipped one by us. Legal will screw them, screw them real good, but there's nothing we can do about the record, it's out. It's in stores all over the country."

"My record."

"Your song. Hell, you're going to make money off it anyway, and we can release 'Remember Us?' as the single. Hell, I think it's a better song. Six weeks from now, we'll have Decca tied into legal knots and you'll have 'Remember Us?' at the top of the charts and old Cal will be staring at your ass, wondering what the hell happened on the way to the top. Don't worry about it, Bad."

"There was no deal. You just outright, fucking sold my song. You just let him take it. You figure I can't take one up anymore. You're just going to let the album die, just to fulfill the contract. You're just going to let me die."

"No, Bad. It's like I explained it to you. We just slipped up and let them pull a fast one is all. Now, I think you better go home and sleep this off. You're going to see things a lot clearer in the morning."

"You are just letting me die." He slips the gun out of his pants and points it at Arthur. His hand shakes, and the barrel of the gun describes shaky eggs in the air.

"Oh Lord," Arthur says, "oh Lord, oh Lord, oh Lord."

"Shut up." He leans closer, so the gun is less than a foot from Arthur Turock's belly. "I'm Bad Blake. I made you a lot of money, I bought you this fucking house. And now you're going to let me die."

"'Remember Us?' Bad, it's going to do real well. We're getting it out on a priority. If it doesn't go, we'll get 'Staying Power' out right behind it. No one is fucking you, Bad. We're behind you, one hundred percent."

"The hell. I'm going to kill you."

"Oh Lord. What do you want me to do? I can't stop Decca. It's over, Bad. It's history. What do you want me to do?"

The gun is shaking harder now, and Bad's balance is getting shakier. He looks around. "There," he says, pointing to a ceramic pot of petunias. "There. That's what I want. I want you to get down on your knees and eat dirt. Like I'm eating dirt."

"You're crazy. You're drunk and you're crazy."

"That's right. I'm drunk, I'm crazy, and you're going to eat dirt." He pushes the gun into Turock's belly.

Slowly, Arthur Turock sinks to his knees, leans forward and puts his face into the petunias. His face is bloodless as Bad watches the muscles in his jaw work. Bad stands and watches, the gun slowly lowering by his side. "I am Bad Blake," he says. "Don't you understand that, you son-of-a-bitch? I am Bad Blake."

He turns and walks away, out the side gate and back to his car. He sits there for nearly half an hour, waiting for the police to come. When they don't, he starts the car and drives away.

Back in the Crying Place is released a month later. There is no single. The album sells five thousand copies without an ad campaign and is cut out less than a year later. There are no more solo albums.

In the morning, he calls Jack first.

"I've got everything straightened out with Wayne," Jack says, "so don't mess anything up. I squeezed the bastard for another three percent."

"Jack, you son-of-a-bitch, Wayne's my friend. Don't talk like that about him. That's not why I'm calling anyway."

"What's up now?"

"I got two new songs. I'm transcribing them now, and I'm going to send them to you. You send them on to Tommy, and you make sure he holds up his end of the bargain. I want three cents on the mechanicals and all other rights on line with that. You also make sure he agrees that both of these are singles, A sides. Don't let him fuck with you. Both of these are better than anything he's done in the past ten years. If he won't do them as singles, I want them back. Tell him the deal's off. He'll take them. Hell, I made Tommy Sweet a star, and I'm going to keep him a star."

"Bad, even without singles, you'll make a hell of a lot off two songs on a Tommy Sweet album. He's got to be good for at least a million copies."

"If they don't go single, I'm going to cut them myself. I'll find a label somewhere. No single, no deal. Got that?"

"I'll do what I can."

"You do what you can, you'll get it done."

"No promises."

"You have problems, call me. I'll talk to Tommy. And listen, I'm going to do these Sunday gigs for that politician guy."

"It's probably smart. His politics suck, but it'll probably work out for you in the long run."

"Wait, Jack, what's wrong with this guy? I need to figure this out."

"Hell, Bad, he's another one of those born-again right-wingers, that's what."

"Yeah, so?"

He spends the rest of the morning at the kitchen table with his guitar and a pack of staff-ruled paper. He works his way through the melodies slowly, picking out the notes, trying alternates, making sure the moves are the right ones. He transcribes the songs bar by bar. When he is done, he signs and dates the sheets, copyrighting them to himself—Bad News Music.

"You want to go to breakfast after we close up?" he asks Wayne.

"I doubt it, I'm beat to hell. I want to go home now."

"I've been writing all day. I need to unwind a couple dozen turns."

"You're just full of piss and vinegar because your lady friend is coming. You been jumpy as a wet cat all week."

"You're going to like her."

"I'm sure I will. Any woman who puts up with you has got to be a dandy."

Halfway through the second set, Ronnie Burke comes in and takes a seat near the front. He nods and raises a beer bottle to Bad, then sits back and smokes and watches. Bad hobbles over to his table at break. "It's good to see you again," he says.

"I was passing through town and thought I'd just stop in and have a listen and say howdy. You're sounding good."

"I feel pretty good. I hang in."

"I'll say you do. You got yourself a pretty good little band there, too."

"We're still breaking in the bass player, but the rest have been with me awhile. Terry on guitar has been with me for going on five years."

"He's good. I've been watching him. He's real good."

"I'll tell him. He'll be pleased."

"I'd rather tell him myself. That is, if it's O.K. by you."

"What's on your mind?"

"Well, I'll tell you, Bad. We're getting ready to release another record, and I'm going to be hitting the road for several months, maybe even over to Europe. I could use a picker who's also a good tenor."

"I don't think Terry's real anxious to go on the road."

"Terry isn't or you aren't?"

"He's my best man. Damn right I don't want to lose him."

"I don't like to mess with another man's living, Bad, but I'd like to talk to him."

"He's not available."

"Look, Bad, you can't keep him tucked away here in Houston. The kid's good. He deserves a chance to get out on the road and let people hear him. I realize I'm asking to take away a good musician for a while, but this may be a real good chance for him. Hell, someone gave us our starts, maybe this is his. The kid can't play a bar gig in Houston for the rest of his life."

"I can't stop you from talking to him. I don't own him. But he's the heart of this band, and I worked a long time getting him there. Do what you think is right."

"I appreciate that, Bad."

On the way back to the stage, he pulls Terry aside. "You see that skinny son-of-a-bitch in the black shirt over there, the one with all the gold chains and hair? That's Ronnie Burke."

"Yeah, I thought it was."

"Well, he wants to talk to you next break."

Bad stays away between the third and fourth sets, but while he stands talking at the bar, he watches Terry sitting at Ronnie Burke's table. His stomach is starting to churn and he is sweating hard.

"Well?" he asks after the last set.

"He wants me to go on the road with him."

"I know that. What are you going to do?"

"I don't know. I'm happy here. I mean, this is my home. And I really don't want to be on the road for six or eight months. And I don't want to leave you stranded while I'm gone. Still, it's a good deal and all. I mean, this is what it's all about, isn't it? And this isn't going to last forever, is it?"

"No, I guess it isn't."

"I don't know, Bad. What do you think I ought to do?"

"I can't give you any answers, son. You got to figure this one for yourself."

By the time he has packed up for the night, he has lost any desire to go to breakfast. When he climbs into the van, he feels too tired to turn the key. As he is heading out of the parking lot, Kim passes him, waving from the back of a loud, drawn-out motorcycle.

At home, Clint Eastwood is on the late movie, a Union soldier, wounded, tended by the teachers and students at a girls' school. Bad has seen this one three or four times now. At the end, the girls, mad with jealousy, will poison him with mushrooms. He watches it anyway, with the ads for discount furniture and apartment complexes where "you can find the lifestyle you have always dreamed of." Bad is into his fourth drink. Clint Eastwood has found the lifestyle he always dreamed of. Women and girls lie awake all night in the school building, waiting for him to drag his wounded leg to their beds. And what of it? In thirty minutes he will die, screaming and farting.

He is heading for the kitchen, ready for more ice, when the phone rings.

"God," he says, "I'm glad it's you, honey. It's been a hell of a night. It looks like I'm going to lose Terry. I just break in a new bass and I have to start looking for a new rhythm guitar. Sometimes this business is the shits. How are you?"

"I guess I'm all right. I'm sorry about your guitar player."

"Aw hell, that's all right. You can't throw a rock anymore without hitting one. Take it from one who is one, guitar players are cheap and available."

"I'm sorry anyway."

"It's O.K. Everything will be O.K. in a couple of days. I've been missing you real bad. I'm going around tomorrow to see about those interviews."

"Bad, I'm not sure."

"About what? What's the matter?"

"I just can't. This isn't right. I mean, it's not working out."

"You mean because I asked you to marry me? Hell, I just said that. I didn't mean it. I didn't mean to make you feel bad about it. Just forget it."

"You did mean it. And that's part of the problem. I'm not ready for this."

"You don't have to be ready for anything. Nothing's changed. It's not any different than it was last week."

"Yes. Yes, I think it is."

"Come on, darlin', I was feelin' out of sorts. I got all jumped thinking about you comin' here. I just blurted that out. It was liquor talkin', that's all, liquor and being happy. That's the only damned thing it was."

"Oh God, Bad. I don't know. I like you, I really do. But I don't want this to get out of hand."

"Nothing's out of hand. We have a good time, you and me and ol' Buddy. I'm just anxious to see you two. I've been looking forward to it like you don't know how. Me and Buddy're going to rip and snort. Me and you will figure something to do, too."

"Maybe I overreacted a little. I don't know. I guess I want to see you, too."

"There you go, darlin', there you go."

Along the concourse, he lurches like a truck on ice, trying to move faster than his crutches allow. Still, all around him, people are moving faster than he can, pushing past him, pulling up behind him, struggling into step behind him, then darting out and around him with sighs of exasperation. A man in a tan cotton suit rams him full from behind, sending him into the wall and almost knocking him down. "Come back here, you son-of-a-bitch," he yells. "I may look crippled, but I can still kick your ass down this hall, horseshit."

At gate twenty-three, there are no seats left. He stands away from the chairs, across the concourse against the wall, smoking cigarettes. The plane, due in ten minutes, is running twenty minutes late. He is able to brace himself against the wall, leaning on his crutches, his bad foot resting on the wall. He smokes and he tips his black hat to people who pass. Celebrity fades, but its obligations don't.

After ten minutes, the crutches have begun to dig into his armpits. He can't find a position that doesn't hurt. He moves across the concourse to the seating area. There still aren't any empty chairs. He finds a man in a blue seersucker suit, reading a newspaper. "Howdy," Bad says. The man looks up, blinks, and goes back to his newspaper, reading it like a child sounding out the words. Bad lights a Pall Mall and blows the smoke over the man's head. After several seconds of this, the man looks up again, blankly. "Ashtray's on the other side of you, old buddy." The man looks over at the ashtray, back to Bad and then to his paper. "I'm a cripple, for Christ sake," Bad barks. The man scowls and moves off. Bad slides gratefully into the seat, crushes out his cigarette, and realizes he wants a drink.

He keeps his seat for a good twenty minutes. He leans over and asks the woman next to him the time. The plane should be landing now. He heaves himself out of the low seat and to the window. Around the terminal, men are lounging in baggage carts. There are no screens that give arrival times, only departures. At the podium, one attendant is checking in passengers. "Darlin'," he asks, "where's the plane from New Mexico?" She stares at him blankly. "There is no plane from New Mexico."

A wave of fear passes through him. "What the hell?" he asks. Then he remembers the note in his shirt pocket. "Flight four twenty-one," he says.

"Denver," she says. "Flight four twenty-one is from Denver."

"But where the hell is it?"

She stares the same blank stare. "I don't know," she says. "It's running late."

How late? he begins to ask, and then gives up and starts back the concourse to the screens in the lobby, which give arrival times. The bastards have lost the fucking airplane.

The arrival time has been pushed back another half hour. He heads for the bar.

He leans against the bar, orders a double Jack Daniel's, and while he waits, the guy on the stool next to him gets up and offers it. Drinkers are the last decent people on earth. He gets another double before he has to work his way down the concourse again.

They are there waiting, looking for him. Jean is wearing a yellow dress he has never seen before. He has expected to see her in blue jeans and shirt and he is disappointed, though she looks good, younger and prettier than he remembers. Buddy is holding her hand, staring wide-eyed. Jean sees him and smiles and pokes Buddy, pointing to Bad as he swings toward them. Buddy grins hard, then goes serious.

The feel of her pressed against him is better than he remembers, better than his expectation. He doesn't want to let go. When he looks down, Buddy has retreated behind her, holding her skirt. "Hey," Bad says, "old Buddy." Buddy looks down and blushes.

"He's pretty excited," Jean says. "He hasn't talked about anything else for a week. We'll have to take it a little easy."

To get to the baggage claim they have to take the escalator. He still can't find the rhythm to match it with his crutches. Jean helps both of them onto the moving steps.

"I don't know why they make airports into goddamned obstacle courses," he complains. "These bastards don't give a damn about anything. Everything is a goddamned mess. They lost your damn plane."

"We had to wait out a storm in Denver."

"I don't know why the hell you went to Denver in the first place. Denver's way the hell north, Houston's south. Should have gone to Albuquerque or someplace. Why the hell can't they fly straight lines?"

"For God's sake," she says. "I wasn't flying the plane, you know."

He stops, looks at her, and then grabs and hugs her in the middle of the baggage claim, where people are jostling and rushing to get their bags. "I was just so anxious for you to get here," he says. He thinks he might cry.

On the way into town it hits him that the city is ugly and looks cheap. He wants something better. As they near the North Main exit, they can see the skyline jutting out of the late afternoon haze. "My Lord," Jean says.

"I'll show it to you at night. It's a lot prettier than this. It really is. It isn't like this at night. You've got to see it."

He wakes mired and struggling to get free. Fully awake, he finds Jean snuggled into his back, Buddy up from the sofa and curled on the bed against Bad's legs. Cramped and sweating, Bad cannot remember the last time he woke like this— completely happy.

. . .

"You like them rocket ships, ol' Buddy?" Bad asks. Platters of oysters and shrimp on ice keep appearing on the table. Bad can't convince Buddy that letting cold oysters slide down your throat is eating, but Buddy keeps eating shrimp, alternating them with pieces of fried chicken.

"I've never seen him eat like this," Jean says. "We have to slow him down before he makes himself sick."

"Let him go, hon. I've always believed folks could live a real good life with nothing but shrimp, bourbon and ice. The boy's learning stuff that can keep him happy the rest of his life. He'll always know that old Bad taught him the finer things."

"That building there, the one with the star on top. That's where Sam Houston and his boys beat Santa Anna and his Mexicans. Texas got its start right there. If it wasn't for that spot, we'd be speaking Mexican right now. You know any Mexican, Buddy?"

Buddy doesn't, but he wants to stop and see the battlefield, and Bad obliges, wheeling the van off the road. He is tired and aching from walking miles through the Johnson Space Center in the morning, twisting and turning to get his crippled bulk through the narrow passages of the space shuttle mockup, but he is catching Buddy's enthusiasm.

Where are the dead Mexicans? Buddy wants to know. Behind all of his enthusiasm is disappointment. The rockets at the space center did not move, and the battlefield is a green and grassy park which suggests picnics and Frisbees and not death and gunpowder. Maybe you just had to be there, Bad guesses.

"I know this fellow down at the *Post*. He's O.K. He does music, but he's been there forever, I reckon he knows everyone he'd need to know. I told him you were coming."

They are tired and happy from lovemaking, moving and talking slow. Jean raises up on an elbow, pulling a sweated lock of her hair that has stuck to Bad's chest. "I'm really not sure about this, Bad."

"Hell, it's career stuff. I know that. But you're good, hon. You got to work with that. You wrote better about me than anyone else ever has, even when you told the truth."

"Well, I guess I know you better than any other reporter, right?"

When he doesn't respond, she repeats the question, curling some of his chest hair around her finger and pulling gently but firmly. "Right?"

"Maybe," he says, "you know me better than it's good for you to know. But what I got to tell you is that this is career stuff. I understand. If you came here, that would be nice. We could have more times like this. You'd like that, wouldn't you? I sure as hell would. But there wouldn't be any hold on you. I ain't trying to trick you into something. You ain't got nothing to worry about as far as I'm concerned."

She moves up and closer, so her breath is warm and loud in his ear. "More times like this would be nice," she whispers.

I ain't so bad, he thinks. I'm going to make me some

money. I got steady work, I could cut back on the drinking. I could even quit if I really put myself to it. He goes to sleep thinking, I wouldn't be so bad, really.

"The *Post* wants you to come by around ten-thirty," he says, coming back to the breakfast table. Jean is dressed in a white blouse and beige skirt, a matching jacket over the back of her chair. She is reading the position papers Martin Wilks left. Buddy is in the chair next to hers. Bad, unsure what Buddy would eat for breakfast, has bought boxes of Froot Loops, Count Chocula, Smurfs and Captain Crunch. Buddy has opened all of them and is busy mixing them together in a bowl.

"You need some pickles to go with that, old Bud?"

"Jesus, Bad, tell me you aren't going to work for this guy."

"Hell, I don't know. It seems like a good deal. Lots of publicity. I like a lot of things the guy says."

"Of course," she says. "Because he only says things he thinks people want to hear. These aren't position papers, they're just a collection of the worst clichés of the Bible-Belt right."

"Well, he's a Christian. I respect that. I mean, I ain't done real well with it, but I was brought up to believe it."

"No, Bad, it's not even that. One sentence he's a right-wing Christian, the next he's a feminist, the next he's pro-labor. This doesn't even make sense; he's just thrown in a bunch of sappy things he thinks people want to hear. There's nothing in this."

Bad pauses and thinks. "Like the Baldwin Boys," he says. "He's doing politics the way the Baldwin Boys do music, is that what you're telling me?"

"What? What are you talking about?"

"The Balds. They don't do music, they do hooks. It's all a bunch of hooks. You throw out the hooks, you haven't got a mosquito fart left. It's empty. That's what you're telling me, isn't it?"

"God." She laughs. "I guess. Damned if I know."

"A fucking Baldwin Boy," he says. "Goddamn. The bastard shows up around here again, I'll kick his butt so hard it'll land across the street two minutes before the rest of him. I hate that shit."

She gets up from her chair and hugs him from behind, laughing. "I hope to God He didn't make more than one of you." Then, "And I'm glad I found the one He did."

"This is the way we'll work it," he tells her. "I drop you off at the *Post* at ten-thirty, and then you can take a cab downtown to the restaurant and I'll buy you a good Cajun lunch, then you can head over to the *Chronicle* after lunch."

"What about Buddy?" she asks. "What are you going to do?"

"I got that all figured. I'm going to take Buddy downtown and we're going to see the tunnels. Hey, Bud, you want to see a city underneath the city, with all kinds of tunnels right under the streets and buildings?"

"Tunnels?" Jean asks.

"Yeah, tunnels, all under the city. They're all air-conditioned, and they have shops and restaurants. Buddy will love it. He's never seen anything like it. You just go talk to the newspapers and Buddy and I'll have a good time. At noon, we'll just rise right up out of the ground and take you to lunch."

"Yeah," Buddy says, "right up out of the ground. Like that man on TV."

"What man?"

"On TV," Buddy insists.

When they get off the elevator in the parking garage, they are in the tunnel. It is lit with fluorescent light and there is gray carpet that rises halfway up the walls. "Let's stop and listen," Bad says. "People are walking right on top of our heads, maybe we can hear them."

When they have walked for half an hour, moving from the carpeted tunnel into the tiled tunnel, Bad is getting tired and sore. Worse, he is starting to sweat and shake. It is still half an hour until time to meet Jean up on the street. "Hey, sailor," he says, pulling Buddy up short. "What do you say we go into that place right there and wet our whistles?"

"Double J.D.," Bad says, "and a ginger ale—double." He looks down to Buddy. "I want mine rocks, Bud, how 'bout you?"

"Rocks."

"Kind of slow today," he says as the bartender brings their drinks.

"Another forty-five minutes, an hour, it'll pick up."

The bar is dark and paneled, full of small tables and up-holstered chairs on twisted brass legs. While the chairs look comfortable, the tables are small and crowded, designed to keep the clientele moving. It is no bar for relaxing over long drinks. Muzak fills the air. Bad looks around. There is no jukebox.

"That music drive you crazy?"

"Never hear it," the bartender says, "until I turn it off at night."

"Here," Buddy says. He holds a maraschino cherry in the palm of his hand.

"What am I supposed to do with it, Bud?"

"Eat it."

Bad pops it in his mouth, chews vigorously, then stops, holding his breath and widening his eyes as if it were hot coal in his mouth. Buddy watches in alarm until Bad smiles and pushes the still whole cherry between his lips. Buddy shrieks with laughter.

"He's a great kid," Bad tells the bartender.

"Yeah, kids are O.K."

"You got any?"

"No. Don't really plan to."

Buddy has found the garnishes at the barmaid's station. He brings Bad cherries, olives, lemon and lime slices. The lemon slices Bad bites with his front teeth, then curls back his lips to show the yellow smile. "Hit that again," he tells the bartender, pushing his glass forward.

"I had a kid once. I fucked that up. I really did. You ought to have one. He was the best thing in the world. You don't have a kid, you're going to regret it someday."

Buddy is back with pretzel sticks. Bad wedges them into his mouth like the bars of a jail, then breaks them with his tongue. Buddy screams and runs off to find something else.

"I'm serious about this," Bad says. "I've had just about everything a man could want in his life. Hell, I've had money, fame, houses, cars, women. Anything I damned wanted, I got. And I lost most of it, too. And if you're lucky, you realize when you lose the stuff that it didn't mean that much anyway. But my boy. My God. That means a whole hell of a lot. My boy won't even talk to me now. That's a hell of a thing," he says, paying for another drink.

"Well," the bartender says, "my wife's got a good career. She's with a Big Eight firm. I'm going to night school. It's hard to have two careers and kids, too. Maybe. Someday. But I don't think so."

"A woman can have a career. Hell, there's nothing wrong with that. That boy's momma is out interviewing at the *Post* right now, but she's one hell of a mom, too." He looks around for Buddy.

"Buddy, come on back. Finish your ginger ale. We've got to be going."

But Buddy doesn't come back or answer. Bad looks around the bar. It's empty. What the hell, he thinks. "Did you see the boy?" he asks.

"No, I wasn't watching. He might be in the bathroom, though."

"Sure," Bad says, "that's right. He went to the bathroom." He takes a long sip of his drink.

He waits a full minute, then two. "Hell," he says, finishing the drink, "I better go get him. His mom will have little fits if we're late for lunch."

The inside of the men's room echoes as the door crashes open. It is a tiny room—a sink of fake marble, brass fixtures and framed mirror, a single urinal and one stall. The walls are glaring orange tile. "Bud," he calls. "You O.K., Bud?" When there is no answer, he pushes open the stall. There isn't even graffiti on the walls.

"Did he come by here?" he asks the bartender.

"No, I haven't seen him."

"Where the hell?" Bad pants, feeling the panic rise in him.

"Jeez, I don't know. I thought you were watching him. Weren't you supposed to be watching him?"

"Goddamn motherfucking son-of-a-bitch. Where the hell is he?"

"Take it easy man, he's around. There's a drugstore right around the curve here. They have candy and stuff. I bet he's in there. That's where I would be if I were him."

"Which way?"

"Go right at the door. He'll be there. That's where he is."

But he isn't. Bad swings up and down the aisles, asking

the woman at the front counter, the pharmacist. No one has seen a little boy.

Back out in the tunnel, he looks both ways. Then he has to stop and lean back against the wall. How many drinks has he had? He really should have stopped and eaten something. He can feel the band of his hat growing slippery with sweat and sliding down toward his eyebrows. He wipes his forehead with his handkerchief, replaces his hat and starts down the tunnel away from the bar and drugstore.

He stops at a travel agency, where the man behind a computer and in front of a poster of a blond woman with "Cozumel" printed across her yellow bikini bottom recognizes him. "I used to see you at Larry's Torchroom in the fifties," he says. "You were great. I knew then you'd be a star someday. I'm awful glad to meet you after all this time."

"A little boy," Bad says. "He has brown hair. He's only about this tall. He just wandered away. Just a couple of minutes ago. Did he come by here?"

"I've been at the computer," the man says, looking over his half glasses. "Everybody's got new rates. It looks like another war is starting up."

"Just a little boy."

"No. I haven't seen anyone. Good luck, though. Awful nice to actually meet you."

The tunnels have become a series of intricate and complicated curves. The gentle turns on the way down have increased and sharpened. He is not sure whether he has come this way already or not. He keeps swinging his weight forward on the crutches. Traffic in the tunnel is starting to pick up. People pass him from both directions. "A little boy," he says to them, "I've lost my little boy."

He checks his watch. It is five minutes to twelve. Jean is surely already at the restaurant, waiting for them. He pushes forward. At an intersecting tunnel, he turns right, and runs into a blue-uniformed security man.

The security man, a heavy, sweating young man with a brown mustache and thin tendrils of hair oozing out from under his hat, listens dispassionately. "What was he wearing?" he asks at last.

When Bad pictures Buddy, he is dressed only in a pair of saggy briefs, holding a sloshing bowl of Cheerios and a paperback book. When he tries again, he gets a bewildering assortment of images of Buddy in different clothes. He can't remember which he was wearing today.

"Where did you last see him?"

"In the bar."

"Which one?"

"The bar. I don't know which the hell one. It was a little bar, dark, tables, Muzak. Some kid tending bar. His wife works."

"Which way?" the guard asks, sweating and efficient.

Bad points to his right, unsure, now, which way he has come.

"All stations," the guard says into his walkie-talkie. "We have a lost boy, four years old, brown hair, named Buddy. No other information at this time. Report back, please."

"Thanks," Bad says, starting back down the tunnel.

"Sir, sir. I think you better stay here with me."

"I have to find him," Bad explains. "He's lost. He's from New Mexico. His mother is waiting for us."

"We'll find him. Just stay here. There are eight guards down here, and they're all watching for him."

"I've got to go. His mother is waiting."

"Sir, I think you better stay with me. You'll be a lot more help with me. Come back to Control with me. We'll find him. You just sit and wait. How much you had to drink?"

"I had a drink. What the goddamned difference does that make?"

"You lost him, sir."

Bad pauses, rocking on the crutches that have slipped into his armpits. He is having trouble moving his arms and keeping balanced at the same time. "Yeah," he says. "I lost him. And I'm going to fucking find him."

If the tunnels were merely horizontal, it would be fairly easy to find one little boy. But the tunnels are also vertical. Elevators move up from the tunnels to the buildings above and back down. Buddy could have climbed into any one of them and ended up at street level and then back out on the street.

Bad stops to consider the possibilities. There is the steady flow of traffic—taxis, buses, hundreds of people moving down the sidewalks. And there are the winos, the hookers

and the junkies. People run out of alleys screaming obsceni-
ties and loving Jesus. Buddy is four years old and from Santa
Fe, New Mexico.

He leans up against the wall of the tunnel and tries to
figure whether he should go up or stay underground. There
are eight security guards underground, all looking for Buddy.
Above, no one is looking for him. The tunnels are crowding
up with noontime traffic. He has trouble pushing away from
the wall and cutting across to the other side to get into the
flow of the traffic.

Out of the elevator, he is in the lobby of the Hyatt Re-
gency, and it is also crowded. The bar is right off the lobby,
almost a part of it, and he swings through, thinking Buddy
may have gotten confused and is waiting here. A waitress in
a black skirt waves an exasperated hand. "Everybody and his
brother is here, but there aren't any little boys."

Outside, he tries to figure where he is. Louisiana Street,
as close as he can tell. It's still hot, well into the nineties, and
down here the air is dead, stopped by the concrete and re-
heated by the exhaust of cars and buses. People shove past
him or move in wide arcs to avoid him. He tries to look at this
from the view of a four-year-old, but it's no use. He starts off
to his right, turns and heads left.

In two blocks, he realizes his mistake. It is too big out
here. There are too many streets, too many people. Each block
has a half-dozen or more stores and restaurants. Some he
checks, some he passes by, with no real reason. He is hobbling

off in no particular direction, with no plan. He feels Buddy getting farther and farther from him.

He is tired and sore. He has started to let his weight shift and the crutches are digging under his arms, pressing the tendons. Back in the Hyatt, he looks around the lobby once more. The air-conditioning turns his shirt icy. His arms tremble from holding the crutches. A drink wouldn't hurt. Goddamn, he thinks. It's his only thought, just goddamn.

He sits in Control, lighting cigarettes off the butts of other ones, listening to the static-filled voices on the radio. He keeps hearing the phrase "lost boy." Security guards and men in cheap suits walk in, get coffee, joke with the dispatcher and leave. He's been waiting for nearly an hour. He tries not to think of stories about missing children.

Finally, he hears his name and looks up. "Where's Buddy?" Jean is white and shaking. "Bad, where's Buddy?"

"They're going to find him, hon. All these guys are looking for him. They're going to find him in just a couple of seconds here. You don't need to worry."

"How the hell did you lose him?" she keeps asking. "How the hell did you do it?"

"We just stopped for a second, to get a drink. I turned around and he was gone. He just disappeared."

"A drink? A goddamned drink. Bad, he's just a little boy. A baby. He's a baby. In this city. You know what kind of people they have here?"

"He had a ginger ale."

For the next thirty minutes, she does not talk to him or look at him. She keeps getting up and walking to the dispatcher, who speaks quietly and sympathetically. Then she sits down and looks away from Bad.

He keeps getting up, heading toward the dispatcher, then swinging around and coming back the other way. He is nearly out of cigarettes. He keeps pulling the same one from the pack and putting it back again, figuring he's going to need it later. He has had four cups of coffee and his bladder feels like a burning grapefruit under his belt. He sits again and this time lights the cigarette.

"Jean. Hon. They're going to find him. He couldn't get very far away. He's O.K. I know that. You know that. Come on now."

She turns to him and starts to cry. "He's just a little boy, Bad. He's so scared."

The pressure on his bladder is increasing. "He's O.K. Hell, he probably doesn't know he's even lost. He's found some guy painting a wall or fixing a light, and he's probably just having a ball. He has no idea we're looking for him."

"I'm so goddamned scared." She holds on to him, crying.

He can't sit still any longer. "Hon, I just got to find me a bathroom, and I'm out of smokes. I'll be right back. Just a second. Can I get you anything?"

She stops her crying and looks at him evenly, her jaw set. "No. Go, just go."

Being able to sit still does not make the waiting any easier. He keeps lighting cigarettes he doesn't want, until his throat is dry and itching. Jean keeps turning the pages of a magazine, looking up and sighing at each page. Bad watches her and tries not to look at the clock. When he does, he calculates how long Buddy has been gone. It is going on two and a half hours.

Ten minutes later, the dispatcher stands up. "Mrs. Craddock, hold on, I think we have something here. I didn't catch the end of that, fourteen, come back, please."

A woman in a blue dress comes in, holding Buddy by the hand. A security man is behind her, white-haired and smiling. Buddy's eyes are swollen and tearing. He takes one look at Jean and begins to scream.

While Jean holds Buddy and tries to quiet him, the woman talks to Bad. "He was just walking down the tunnel crying. He kept saying 'bad.'"

"I don't know," Bad says. "I was just talking and then I turned around and he was gone. I don't know what the hell happened. I just don't know. Buddy . . ." He starts toward them. The woman holds his arm.

"He's pretty scared," she says. "I think he just needs his momma right now. Just let them be. He'll be all right."

Jean has picked Buddy up from the floor. She holds him horizontally, rocking him back and forth. They are crying in counterpoint to each other, though Jean keeps trying to laugh and talk at the same time.

"I just needed a drink," Bad says. "Just a drink. Then he was gone. I mean, he wandered away from me."

The woman looks at him, long but not hard. "He'll be all

right. He's a pretty scared little guy, but he's got his momma now. He's right where he needs to be. I'd just leave the two of them be for right now." She writes her name on a slip of paper, and under it, her number. "If things get rough," she says, "call me."

Jean carries Buddy back to the van. Buddy is crying in a steady, unrelenting rhythm now. Bad tries to keep step with them, but he feels distant already, first ahead, then behind, as Jean walks steadily forward, stroking Buddy's hair and whispering in his ear.

"It's going to be all right, old Bud," Bad says, catching up to them. "We just got our wires crossed. Once, back in Indiana, I got lost out in the woods—"

"Shut up," Jean says. "Will you please just shut up?"

"This ain't solving a damned thing, you know that," Bad tells her.

"It's getting me out of Houston and back to Santa Fe, where I belong."

"Look, Buddy's scared, but he's going to be O.K. Hell, I'm scared. But putting him back on a plane, that's just going to scare him more. Stay a little while, he'll be all right. Everything is going to be O.K."

"Everything is not going to be O.K. He's scared half to death. He's never been away from home before, and you take him into some tunnels under downtown Houston and lose him."

"Aw, hon, I love Buddy. I wouldn't do anything to hurt him. It was an accident. I just feel like a dog about this. You've got to believe that."

"Oh, I believe you feel bad. I believe that. I might even believe you love him, but I know you love your damned bottle more. You had to stop for a drink. Don't you see? You had to stop. You didn't think about him. You had to have that damned drink, or three drinks or four drinks, however many it was. It's not your fault. I know that. It's my fault. You can't help it. I'm a goddamned idiot."

He tries dragging the suitcases out the door, but the cabbie is there. "If you've got to go, I can drive you. Let me do that at least."

"No," Jean says, motioning with her hands as if pushing something gently but firmly down. "No." Then, "Goodbye, Bad." As they are getting into the cab, Buddy waves and says, "Bye." He is crying again.

Back in the house, Bad falls into the sofa and sits, trying to think. Then he gets up and goes to the kitchen for a glass and ice. He goes back to the sofa and pours a full glass. "Fuck," he says aloud. Then, louder, "Jesus, fucking, Christ."

He's still on the sofa when the phone rings.

"Hey there, old-timer."

"Wayne? Look, I don't feel like talking just now."

"Wayne? Who the hell is Wayne? This is Tommy."

"Tommy?"

"Tommy. Listen, I just got the songs. My guys are going to

get in touch with your guys for the details, but it's like I said. The songs are good, Bad. Real good. And I'm real glad you sent them. This is going to be good for both of us."

"Yeah. Yeah, well . . ."

"'Is This Going to Hurt Again?' Bad. It's the best song I've heard in years. This is a goddamned monster, Bad. And you're going to like what I do with it. It's your song, and I'm going to do it nice and straight. You're going to like it. I've been thinking, maybe just a couple of acoustics, a little flat-picking in the bridge. You're going to like this, Bad."

"Tommy, Tommy, you do what you want. Right now, I just don't give a shit."

Chapter Fifteen

He sleeps without dreams, but he wakes hung over. He gets up and has a beer to settle his stomach. On television there is college football. He tries to watch. Football interests him less than baseball, but he likes the NFL. College football is too full of pom-poms, streamers and fresh-faced rich kids between every play. Around him, the house is clean, his laundry is back from the cleaners. There are dishes in the sink. He leaves them. Michigan scores and he decides he will be for the other team, which also seems to be Michigan. In the middle of the third quarter he turns it off.

The bar is so dark he is sun-blind when he walks in. A jukebox is blasting out old Rolling Stones. In the middle of the bar, a stage is lit with red light. An Oriental girl is dancing behind a column at the edge of the stage, peek-a-booing her little breasts from either side of the column. He takes a table near the stage.

"Hi," a black waitress in a sheer white dressing gown says. "What can I get for you?"

"Bourbon rocks, beer back."

"No bourbon. Beer and setups."

"Beer. Bud."

"There's a package store around the corner. I can bring you a setup if you want to walk over. Tell them you're here and they'll give you ten percent off."

When he comes back with a six-dollar pint, she brings him a can of Bud and a glass and ice. He pays her with a twenty and she gives him his change in singles. He hands one back.

The rest go to a progression of women who come up, asking to be tipped for their next dance, or for jukebox money. He gets two more glasses of ice, at two bucks a shot. Onstage, three girls alternate dances—the Oriental, his black waitress, and a blonde with hollow cheeks and eyes thickly lined in blue. Each one dances to three songs from the jukebox, taking off all but G-strings and bras in the first, shucking their bras in the second, and then dancing braless in the third, bending over and sliding around on the stage. None of them pays much attention to the beat of the music playing behind them. He sits through the entire rotation twice. Naked deaf girls. He goes through thirty bucks.

At six, he starts for home, but ends up at Denny's instead. It is as bright as the bar was dark and the noise of conversation and plates and silverware is nearly as loud as the jukebox. He eats a plate of road food and drinks coffee until eight. He goes home and watches TV.

Sunday there is nothing to do. He watches the Oilers lose and then the Cowboys, too. He has forgotten to buy bourbon, and there are no package stores open. He buys a case of beer at noon and drinks them steadily through the games.

At five he calls Wayne but gets no answer.

At seven he is out of beer and sick of television. He remembers the woman in the blue dress. He fishes through the pockets of his shirts and jeans until he finds the slip of paper with her phone number.

"Bad Blake?" she says. Her voice is soft and lyrical, a fairly pure alto.

"From the tunnels," he says. "You found the little boy."

"Bad Blake," she says. "I know that name. You're a musician, aren't you?"

"Country. I sing country."

"Yes. Yes. I'm sorry. I don't really listen to country music much. I guess I should have recognized you."

"You said we could talk."

"Of course. When you lost the little boy, I felt so sorry. I could see how bad you felt about it. Is he all right?"

"I guess," he says. "He's gone. Him and his mother went back to New Mexico. Things got pretty messed up."

"I know about that. I know all about it. You see, Bad, I'm an alcoholic. I understand just how messed up things can get. I'd like to help if I can."

"They've gone back to New Mexico. There isn't anyone around to talk to."

"You can talk to me. I listen real well."

She greets him at the door dressed in blouse and pleated

skirt, ready for dinner and an evening out. She is older than Jean, taller and thinner, maybe even bony. Her blond hair is carefully arranged and her makeup is skillful. And there is a slight gleam in her eye that he likes a lot. Her apartment is neat and nondescript except for large arrangements of red and yellow paper flowers on the coffee table and in the corners of the room.

"Would you like coffee or a soft drink?" she asks.

"Maybe we just better go."

"Don't be in such a rush. How about some tea? I have iced tea."

They drink iced tea from tall glasses with multicolored bands. The air-conditioning is going hard, and still the glasses sweat so much Bad's coaster keeps sticking to the glass and then falling into his lap. Between cigarettes, he fingers the paper flowers at the end of the sofa.

"Mexico," she says. "I got those in Mexico a couple of years ago, when I was still drinking. I was down there for a whole week, and I don't remember a damned thing about it, except that I got those flowers. I don't even remember who I was with. Those flowers were the only things I came back with."

"You're lucky if flowers are the only things you bring back from Mexico."

"Nothing else. Not even the '*turistas*.' Never touched a drop of water the whole time I was there," she says, laughing.

"Years ago," he says, "I used to come home from benders with nothing, not even the car I left in. I gave 'em away. I must have had two dozen Cadillacs in my life, and I bet I gave nearly half of them away."

"I used to pawn my engagement ring, until I lost the pawn ticket and couldn't remember where I'd pawned it, but I never had a Cadillac to lose."

"If you'd known me back then, you probably would have had one."

At the restaurant, she is calming and comforting. He chain-smokes Pall Malls and taps his fork on the table to a tune that keeps going through his head. Halfway through the meal, he realizes that he is playing his own arrangement of "Is This Going to Hurt Again?" over and over.

"Don't worry," she tells him. "You don't have to do anything that you don't want to do. This is an open meeting. You can just sit and listen. No one is going to pick on you or embarrass you. You do what you want to do. That's the whole point. This is what you want to do. Nobody can make you do it. You do it yourself. There are some nice people who will help you, but you'll do it all yourself."

Early on, he stands and introduces himself—Bad Blake, a guest of Linda's. "Hi, Bad," reply twelve people sitting in the living room of a small house in Spring Branch. He is surprised at the casualness of all this, of these people sitting in a living room, drinking coffee and talking.

He is more surprised when he finds himself standing and

announcing, "I am an alcoholic. A couple of days ago, I lost a little boy. I was drunk. I've been drunk most of my life. I've lost a hell of a lot."

Later, in the kitchen, he and a small, red-haired man named Pat lean against the counter, drinking coffee and smoking. "I'm glad you came tonight, Bad," Pat says. "It's a hard step. We all know how hard it is."

"Linda wanted me to come."

"I know. Linda's a gem. Listen, can I ask you something? Is that your real name—Bad?"

"It's my legal name."

"But not your Christian name, not the one you were born with?"

"No."

"It's your drinking name, right? I mean, from what you said out there, you've been drinking ever since you started in the business. What's your given name?"

Bad laughs. "Otis."

"Think about this. Think about being Otis again. Let go of the things that are a part of the life you want to get away from."

"I can't do that. I'm a musician. I have a career. That's my name. I've worked my whole life for that name. You can't give up your name. It's the way the business is."

"Well, you could work under that name, but learn to think of yourself offstage as Otis. Leave the other up on the stage, don't keep living with it. Think of it as a microphone or a light or something, something you can leave up there when you're not working. Let your friends call you Otis, call yourself Otis."

"Besides that, I hate that name." He is staring at the Mr. Coffee. The base of it is thick with dried coffee.

"I think you could learn to love it, Otis. We all have to learn to change the way we think about ourselves. That's a big step to getting free. We're all actors, Otis. But sometimes we have to rethink our roles. If you have a role you have to play when you're up on stage, it doesn't mean you have to play it all the time. Those roles keep us from ever finding out who we really are, and that's no good. You've got to know yourself before you can learn to like yourself."

"I really feel good," he tells her, back at her apartment. "Damn, I really feel good."

She smiles. "I know. But it doesn't last. Pretty soon you're going to feel real bad. It's going to get rough. I can help you with that. I want to help you."

"You have, darlin'. You have."

"We help each other. That's how it works. The whole group of us together. The strength of the group gives each of us strength. You took a big step tonight, but it's only a step. You keep taking steps, and we'll be with you. I'll be with you."

He pulls her to him. "Thank you, darlin', thank you."

Her hand pushes hard against his chest. "No," she says. "Wait, you have to understand something here." She settles back, straightening her blouse and patting at her hair. "When I was drinking, sex was a big part of it. When I got started I could always find a man. And it was a way of always having a bottle and someone to drink it with. That's why I keep those flowers. One day after I sobered up, I took the flowers to the kitchen sink, and I was all ready to put the match to them when I stopped myself. 'Linda,' I said, 'you can't ever let yourself forget.'"

Bad leans back heavily on the sofa and lights another Pall Mall. He lets the smoke out with a long sigh.

"What you have to understand is that sex isn't a means to anything. It can't ever be selfish or insignificant. It's a gift from God. It's a great and wonderful gift." She leans forward and kisses him on the forehead. "I'm here to talk, I'm here to help. I'm here to be your friend. And I'm going to be here for you all the way, Otis."

The phone wakes him. He has no idea how long it has been ringing or, for a minute, where he is.

"Mr. Blake," Brenda says, "Mr. Greene would like to talk to you."

There is a long pause. "Bad," Jack says, "how are you this morning?"

"I'm not dead. Other than that, it ain't too bad, I guess."

"Well, you're going to feel a lot better in just a minute. I just got off the phone with Tommy's people. You got yourself a deal. Both songs, the first two singles off the album."

"That's fine, Jack."

"You bet that's fine. To tell you the truth, I didn't think he'd go for it, but he took the whole damned package."

"Yeah, great. Listen, there's something else I want to talk to you about."

"Sure. What's up?"

"Does my insurance cover sobering up?"

"What?"

"I want to sober up, Jack. Does the insurance cover that?"

"Probably. I'll have Brenda check. No, hell, go ahead; we'll get it covered."

He is two days out of detox. He is sober and they have cut the cast off his ankle. He has the feeling that he is floating free, that he might float away. He takes slow, careful walks. He takes Antabuse and cleans the house. Linda has come over while he was in the hospital, and there is no booze in the house. There isn't even a shot glass, though he never used the ones he had. He is trying to get organized, trying to change as much as he can. He has signed himself out of the hospital, Otis Blake, Jr.

He makes lists. Change of name. Laundry on Mondays, housecleaning on Tuesdays. Tuesday afternoons, rehearsal, followed by A A. Wednesdays, work on songs until time for work. Remember the Antabuse. Exercise. Get oil change and lube for van. Call Jean. And under that, he writes, sorry, sober, money from new songs, sorry (underlined twice). Call Steven.

Linda comes over a couple of times a week. "Take it easy," she tells him. This is hard enough, don't try to take on too much at once. "Remember," she says, "one step at a time, one day at a time." He still has two days before he has to go to work. He is doing great, he tells himself. One day at a time.

What do you think? he asks Terry after the last set. It has felt like something other than working, but it has felt like music. He has done a whole show sober.

"It was O.K., Bad. You did it. You did a good job."

"It was stiff."

"A little. But that'll work itself out. That will come. It was a good show. The way I figure, it's like breaking in a new guitar. It just feels strange for a little while. Pretty soon, it's better than it ever was. Pretty soon, you'll be able to stand for a full set, too. That'll help."

As they are packing up, Terry tells Bad that they need to talk. Bad lights a cigarette, takes a deep drag and says, "Right. Let me get a drink."

He comes back from behind the bar with a glass of club soda.

"I talked to Ronnie today," Terry says.

Bad holds up his hand to silence him, and lights a cigarette off the butt of the old one. "I figured."

"Bad, I just can't pass this up. I don't want you to get mad or feel like I'm cutting out on you. This is something I've just got to do."

"When you going?"

"I go to Nashville at the end of next month for rehearsals, two weeks later the tour starts in New York. I got to learn a whole show of new material in two weeks."

"You'll do it. It's full-time work. You won't have any problem."

"It won't actually be that long. It's only for three months unless this Europe thing comes through. Then I'll be back."

"No. Then it's studio work while you wait for someone else to go out with. Trying to hustle a record here and there."

"I got a wife and family here, Bad. I'll be back for them."

"When do you want out of here?"

"Not until you find somebody else. I'll play here the night before I leave if that's what it takes. I won't leave you stranded."

"Damn, you're going to do it, buddy. You're going to make it," Wayne says, coming up to the table and resting his hands on Bad's shoulders.

"Yeah," Bad says, "I'm going to make it."

"Well, you know you can call me. Day or night. You just call me. I'll be right with you. And you sounded real good up there."

Bad shakes his head. "Wayne, sometimes I think you'd say a fart sounded good."

"I guess that depends on who's doing it, now, don't it?"

"Road work," Bad says to Terry, "you're either going to love it or hate it. Either way, you're fucked."

"Billy Paulsen's band just broke up. He'd probably fill in for me while I'm gone. He's good. Real nice voice."

"The road," Bad says. "That's when you find out. That's what it's all about. There's nothing in the world like the road. Everything changes out there."

"I can call him if you want."

"I found you. I'll find someone else. Say hey to Sandra for me."

He walks three blocks, still careful, watching for holes and sticks that could throw his weight and snap the ankle again, but three good blocks without much of a limp. He is tired and a little sore when he gets in, but he is determined. He has worked it out in his head while he walked.

He has planned it all out, but he is still stunned by Jean's voice when she picks up the phone.

"Just listen to me," he says. "Just listen. I'm sorry about what happened. It was all my fault."

There is only silence on the other end.

"The thing is, it hit me finally. I figured it out. I'm sober. I did it. Detox, Antabuse, AA—the whole bit. It woke me up, Jean."

There is another pause, then, "That's good, Bad. That's good. I'm glad."

"No, not Bad. Otis. I'm going back to Otis. I'm changing things. I really am. But that's only half of it. I heard from Tommy. He's going to do my songs. It means some pretty good money for me."

"That's good, too."

Then he doesn't know what to say. "Yeah, things are all right. How about Buddy, is he O.K.?"

"Yeah, Buddy's O.K."

"That's great. That's what I wanted to hear. I'm really happy about that. Listen, can you ever forgive me?"

She sighs. "Yeah, I guess. I guess I can. But that's not really the point, is it?"

"Sure it is. What do you mean, 'that's not the point'?"

"I mean it was all a mistake, my coming there. I knew it before I came. And I'm sorry about all of it."

"No, no. I made the mistake, but I figured that out. It's O.K. now, I'm sober. I've been in the hospital. I'm O.K. now."

"That's good. That's real good."

"Jean, listen. I want to come out there for a couple of days. I want to see you, talk to you, show you how it's changed."

"No, Bad. No, please no."

"It's O.K., you'll see. It's all different now. I'm different. I need to make some things up to you and Buddy. I got a whole lot to make up for, to a whole lot of people. But especially to you and to Steven."

"No. You aren't coming here. I'm not coming there. And I don't want you to call anymore."

"Jean, you've got to understand. . . ."

"Goodbye, Bad."

He listens to the steady tone in D flat until the recorded voice comes on. "If you would like to make a call," it says, "hang up and dial the number. If you need help, hang up and dial the operator." Later, it begins to beep until he finally hangs it up.

He works the childproof cap of the Antabuse bottle, takes out a pill and lays it on the kitchen counter. He stares at it for a while. The problem, he figures, is that the little fucker doesn't give you any choice. He pours a cup of coffee and tries not to look at the Antabuse. He wants a drink, he reasons, but he doesn't need one. He can live without one. He picks up the phone and dials Linda's number. After it rings three times, he hangs up. He puts the pill back in the bottle and starts gathering up his laundry.

"You have to turn to God," Linda says when he finally gets hold of her. "He didn't make you an alcoholic, you did that yourself. But He can get you free."

Bad has the Antabuse out again, pushing it across the kitchen counter with his finger while he talks. He has gone over thirty-six hours without it.

"It's when we think we can control everything. That's when the trouble starts. We pride ourselves and blame ourselves. We've got to stop and understand, there's Someone more powerful than we are. You ask Him for help, and He will."

"I've done what I've done. I guess I can keep on."

"It doesn't work that way, Otis. It's time to turn to Someone stronger."

He pushes the white tablet into the corner of the counter and crushes it with his fingertip.

Chapter Sixteen

"As long as you're not a truck driver, I don't care what you do," she says.

Bad lights another Pall Mall and studies her. Her age is a tough one. Her skin is a little loose around the eyes and jaw, but her face is thin. Her makeup is pretty thick and a little sloppy around the edges of her mouth. She holds her cigarette at the side of her face, wrist cocked. He tries to place the gesture—Bette Davis, maybe. Her tongue works the edges of her front teeth.

"My last old man, he was a truck driver, the worthless son-of-a-bitch. They're worse than sailors—the whole miserable lot of them. Think they're cowboys. God's gift to women."

"Really," Bad says, "I'm a singer. Bad Blake. 'Slow Boat.'"

"The hell. He's dead."

"Not yet I ain't, darlin'."

"Donna. That's O.K., honey. Buy me another?"

Bad signals toward the bar, holding up two fingers. The bartender brings two more and sets them on the table. Bad hands him a twenty. "Just hold on to that. Start a tab."

She picks up her glass and raises it to him. "Bad Blake, no damned truck driver."

"No damned truck driver."

"So, Mr. Bad Blake, you rich?"

"Used to be. Now I'm poor as a damned nigger again."

"Money doesn't mean anything. This world is full of rich bastards who aren't worth the water it'd take to flush them down. I never met anyone rich I liked."

"Me, either. That includes me when I was."

"I'll drink to that. Money brings out the worst in people. Take the money away from those bastards, they might find out they're like the rest of us. Do them a world of good. They could give it to me. I'd be doing them a damn favor."

"What would you do with it?"

She lights a cigarette. Bad reaches out and holds her wrist to steady it. "I'd buy me another drink."

Bad signals and leans back, lighting a cigarette of his own. "'Smoke, smoke, smoke that cigarette'—you remember that one?"

"You do that?"

"I used to sing it, but I didn't record it. Tex Williams did, Merle Travis, too. They wrote it. It was a little before my time. That must have been nineteen forty-six, forty-seven, somewhere in there. Old Travis—God, could he play."

"You know who I like?"

"Who?"

"Glen Campbell. God, he is so damned good-looking."

"He can play."

"I felt real bad when he and Tanya broke up. It was in all the papers. I bet she's sorry now."

"Most of us are."

"Drink to that," she says.

"I spent most of nineteen sixty-one on the road," he says. "God, it was a great year. I had this Silver Eagle bus. We rigged it out for about ten thousand dollars. A hell of a lot of money then. We'd leave a show about three o'clock in the morning and hit the highway. Everybody in the back of the bus, drinking and playing cards—Will, Tommy, Bob. We'd drive all night and then the next afternoon we'd wake up in some other town, some other state, and it would be showtime again. Jesus, I loved that bus. We did the whole damned country that year."

"I drove from Atlanta to Barstow, California, one summer. It was so goddamned hot. The car broke down in Arizona. I thought I was going to die. I wanted to die."

"Sometimes I'd just go up to the front of the bus with the driver and let the rest of them sleep. It was so damned quiet. And all around, you'd see the lights of towns, and up ahead, there was a city where they were waiting for Bad Blake."

"Gila Bend. Goddamned Gila Bend," Donna says. "We broke down right out of Gila Bend. I was so hot I got a rash on my arms."

Bad keeps ordering drinks.

"So what do you want to do, Bad Blake? You want to go back on the road?"

"Yeah. I want to go back. I'm booked here for another six months."

"Let's go. You and me. Let's go out on the road. You show me what's so great. What do you and those cowboy truck drivers like so much about the road? Show me."

Because it is after nine, they cannot buy a bottle. He drives to the club. Ernie is tending bar. "Wayne here?" Bad asks.

"Took the night off. Just me and Larry."

"Look," Bad says, "I'm taking a bottle. Let Wayne know. I'll make it good."

"Right," Ernie says. "You have a good time. See you Wednesday."

He keeps heading up 59, north, through Cleveland, Livingston, Lufkin, Nacogdoches. The night is cool and he's not sweating. Donna doesn't say much. He passes the bottle over and takes it back.

In 1961, driving through Nebraska, he sits up all night with a bottle and his guitar, showing Tommy delicate runs, trying to explain the importance of a hesitation or a pull. Tommy is quick and sure, running the board as fast as Bad can, but missing the intonations. Bad shows him again and takes another pull from the bottle and pushes it over to Tommy. The kid is good, if he can only learn to slow down and listen to what he is doing.

The horizon is lightening when Bad heads back for his bunk. Tommy is on his knees in front of the chemical toilet, heaving. Bad stops, goes in and holds his head. "It's all right, son. You're good. But it's going to be a while before you're another Bad Blake."

He awakens to the steady pulse of the red light on the dashboard. "Oil," it flashes, "Oil." It is raining and the wipers are going, though he does not remember turning them on. The van is full of the sharp smell of hot oil. As he is wheeling it off the road, he can hear the shrill whine of the bearings.

Donna wakes up. "Where are we?" she asks.

"I don't know, maybe Arkansas."

"Where are we going, Bad?"

He tries the key. The starter grinds once before it jams. "Nowhere. The engine's seized up."

He gets out of the van. He has no idea where they are, or where the highway is. The road is dirt, softening into deep mud in the rain. The way to go back is the way they came, he figures. He goes back to the van.

She is asleep again. He takes the bottle and a flashlight. He nudges her awake. "I'm going to walk for help. If someone comes along, I'm going that way. You going to remember that?"

"You going for help, Bad?"

He can barely walk. He is drunk, his ankle is tender, and the road is inches deep in mud. Twice he falls and pulls himself, crawling and stumbling, to his feet. To either side are trees, and he can see nothing but the few feet of road ahead of him.

His heart is pounding. He can't gauge how far he has come, but he can still see, faintly, the taillights of the van behind him.

The third time he falls, he can't get his feet back under him. He crawls to the side of the road, hoping for something dry where his feet can find purchase. His hand slips through a rill of wet mud and the rest of his body follows down the ditchbank. He lands in cold water and rights himself. It is less than knee-deep, but the bank is slick with mud and he can't pull himself up.

He lies with his back against the ditchbank, resting and trying to get his heart to slow to a quick shuffle. He has lost the flashlight, but he still has the bottle. He lays his head back on the ditchbank and takes a long pull, then lets the rain wash over his face. "Otis," he says, "goddamn."

About the Author

THOMAS COBB was born in Chicago, Illinois, and grew up in Tucson, Arizona. He is the author of novels *Shavetail, With Blood in Their Eyes,* and *Darkness the Color of Snow* as well as the short story collection *Acts of Contrition. Crazy Heart* was adapted into a major motion picture. He lives in Rhode Island with his wife.

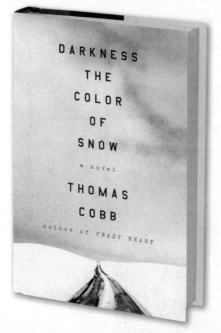

COOL PAPERBACKS, COOL PRICE

Tales of the City — Armistead Maupin

Beautiful Ruins — Jess Walter

Alas, Babylon — Pat Frank

The Bridge of San Luis Rey — Thornton Wilder

OLIVE EDITIONS for $10 EACH

Available for a Limited Time Only

Black Boy — Richard Wright

Lit — Mary Karr

The Dispossessed — Ursula K. Le Guin

Crazy Heart — Thomas Cobb

Available for a limited time wherever books are sold, or call 1-800-331-3761 to order.